PRAISE FOR

The Light Through the Branches

"This deeply absorbing and beautifully written novel explores the difficult relationship between Kate and her mother, Elizabeth, whose heartbreaking betrayal of her young daughter haunts the rest of their lives together. Anne Matlack Evans illuminates the complex emotional ecosystem at the heart of this story with piercing insight and courage. Kate's journey—through vivid landscapes of time and memory—will strike a chord with anyone who has ever yearned for some kind of accounting from the universe and one's own family. Throughout, the novel shines with beautifully articulated notes of grace and forgiveness that fall across these wounds like gentle shafts of slanted light."

—Andrea Bewick, runner-up Nelson Algren Short Fiction

"*The Light Through the Branches* is the filtered light of time, with which Anne Matlack Evans gracefully illuminates Kate, her siblings, and the complicated, fallible, resilient love of families. One of the great pleasures of this novel is the way it deftly braids its strands of story, making us feel how the past lives in the present—and how the present may transform the past, not by undoing it, but by bringing its perspective on the forces that have shaped our lives. The result is a quietly stunning novel, brilliantly evocative of its California settings of the last six decades, yet broadly eloquent about the way that memory is like the 'interlacing branches, leaves, and light . . . always shifting, making, and remaking.'"

—Nan Cohen, author of the poetry collections *Unfinished City* and *Rope Bridge*

"[Evans's] deftly crafted tale of Kate Laidlaw's trauma, nostalgia, and longing lulls readers with her vivid experiences of growing up in the '60s and '70s, grips us with memories of her stepfather's mendacity, and challenges us to move beyond resentment to access the better angels of our nature. Adolescent naivete, unbreakable family bonds, coming of age late in life, and being asked to care for those whom we might initially rebuff—Kate's quest for insight gifts us profound inspiration."

—Debbie Danielpour, Pushcart Prize nominee in short fiction

"Through the eyes of a character as memorable as the title of this singular work, Anne Matlack Evans has balanced the deep impact of childhood trauma with the desire to understand the mother who allowed it to happen. *The Light Through the Branches* takes uncomfortable turns, but it never surrenders its humanity. In fact, that is its distinctive strength. Her characters are eminently human, complex, flawed, and resilient, and we see pieces of ourselves within them. With clear, lyrical writing and a firm grasp on what it means to transcend the sins of the past, Evans has created a work that merits multiple reads."

—Greg Fields, author of *Through the Waters and the Wild*

"In *The Light Through the Branches,* Evans makes her way through the brambles and thickets of a woman's relationship with her aging mother, navigating complexities of the past and the role reversals of the present. A thoughtful, radiant novel about the said and unsaid, the unforgiven, the unforgotten, and the love that yet abides."

—Sherri Hallgren, book reviewer, San Francisco *Chronicle*, Pittsburgh *Post-Gazette*

"*The Light Through the Branches* is at once a sweeping family drama and an intimately detailed portrait of one woman's life, as she untangles a thread of meaning from a painful knot of secrets and betrayals. Probing the depths of the mother–daughter bond and the limits of forgiveness, Anne Evans's brave and tenderhearted novel wraps its arms around the reader and doesn't let go."

—Christine Henneberg, author of the forthcoming novel *I Trust Her Completely*

"Elegantly written and compulsively readable, *The Light Through the Branches* bravely plumbs a difficult mother–daughter relationship with honesty, insight, and grace. Kate's lifelong desire to have a loving relationship with her mother—and a frank reckoning of their past—speaks to a particular and beautiful form of human folly: never giving up on connection, on love."

—Michelle Huneven, author of *Search*

"This beautiful debut novel from Anne Matlack Evans deftly peels away the layers of a mother and daughter's complex and emotionally charged relationship to reveal the beating heart of that bond, how we are haunted by both pain and love, and the final path to grace."

—Tara Ison, author of *At the Hour Between Dog and Wolf*

"At the core of this deeply affecting novel is the troubled relationship between intelligent, artistic Kate and her emotionally detached mother, Elizabeth. As Kate attends to Elizabeth's dementia-fraught last days, the book weaves together two compelling timelines, one that follows a challenging mother–daughter road trip and one that takes us further into the past, where we bear witness to an abusive family history Elizabeth would sooner ignore. With lucid, precise language, Evans draws us into Kate's journey from a proscriptive 1950s childhood through the radical changes of the next decades. As she explores the far-reaching legacy of sexual abuse and stunning parental betrayal, she suggests a daughter's hard-won insight—into the frustrations that made Elizabeth such a complicated influence and the unexpected resources of love."

—Angela Pneuman, author of *Lay It on My Heart*

The Light Through the Branches
by Anne Matlack Evans

© Copyright 2024 Anne Matlack Evans

979-8-88824-554-5

All rights reserved. No part of this publication may be reproduced, stored in a retrieval system, or transmitted in any form or by any means—electronic, mechanical, photocopy, recording, or any other—except for brief quotations in printed reviews, without the prior written permission of the author.

This is a work of fiction. All the characters in this book are fictitious, and any resemblance to actual persons, living or dead, is purely coincidental. The names, incidents, dialogue, and opinions expressed are products of the author's imagination and are not to be construed as real.

Lyrics from "26 Miles (Catalina)" by Bruce Belland and Glen A. Larson, and "Greenfields," by Terry Gilkyson, Richard Dehr, and Frank Miller, reprinted with permission from Hal Leonard LLC.

Published by

köehlerbooks™

3705 Shore Drive
Virginia Beach, VA 23455
800-435-4811
www.koehlerbooks.com

The Light Through the Branches

ANNE MATLACK EVANS

VIRGINIA BEACH
CAPE CHARLES

For Greg

Prologue

OUR FAMILIES GATHER for the photo under a one-hundred-year-old oak tree. Its trunk is deeply ridged, lit by green moss, with limbs arching over us. It is the winter solstice, my wedding day, and the sun has already dropped behind the coastal mountains.

We've chosen to marry at the home of Richard's parents. "Their house is so pretty at Christmas," I tell my mother, to save her from hurt. The real reason is more complicated.

The photographer, an old friend, has trouble wrangling the familes. I coax Richard's nieces—six and eight years old, each carrying a bouquet I made today—into the front row. The girls and grown women wear long, colorful dresses, the men jackets and wide ties. My mother beckons her husband—her third—to her side. My father looks rumpled and bewildered. His wife holds a toddler. My older brother Peter proffers a giant toadstool.

I stand close to Richard wearing a full-skirted, high-necked dress that shimmers silver in the fading light. I squeeze his arm, taking in his warmth and solidity. He grins broadly, his dimples showing. My sister, matron of honor, laughs next to me.

The group is finally in place and still. From under a black cover, the photographer snaps his shots.

We troop back into the warm house. Friends arrive, along with the minister and his wife. From the landing on the stairs, I look down to make sure that the candles have been lit. My younger brother,

Michael, begins a minuet by Bach on the piano. The crowd quiets. Richard and I descend the stairs, arm in arm. Nothing against my father, but I don't want to be given away. The two of us have created this union, we ourselves, alone. Our marriage will be different—nothing to do with the marriages and divorces that came before us.

"Let us not to the marriage of true minds admit impediment," I read. Richard takes the next line. Hearing the tremor in his voice, I hand my bouquet to my sister and fold his hands in mine.

After the ceremony, everyone rushes forward to hug us, sparkling wine is poured, and toasts are given. A family friend finishes his with a flourish. "I just hope she can *handle* him!"

"And I hope he can handle *her*," my mother-in-law says quietly.

"A union of the best and the brightest," quips my dissertation adviser.

More champagne and wine are poured and the noise level rises. Our guests descend on the buffet of poached salmon, salads, and breads made by family and friends. We eat standing and sitting in the living room, the hall, and the sunporch. "Eat, eat!" my friends tell me. I've lost weight, but not on purpose.

I sink into the sofa, wishing someone else would take over the spotlight.

We dance on the living room carpet to Bob Dylan's "Forever Young." Then Michael plays jazz until someone starts a clamor for Christmas carols, and I sit down to play. The candles burn low.

"When are you going to throw the bouquet?" my sister, Megan, asks me. "People are starting to leave."

She and I round up the unmarried women—my college roommates, other old friends, my sister-in-law, and stepsister. I wave the bouquet, which I made—pink roses and babies' breath stuck into a paper doily. "Pretty lame, isn't it?" Little nieces Carrie and Beth join the group at the foot of the stairs. I climb to the landing and toss. My friends look at each other and laugh. Carrie leaps and catches it.

"You didn't even try!" I say, coming back down the stairs. "Come on!" I repeat the throw. Carrie catches it again.

"You're not any *fun*," I say. "One more time." Before I climb the stairs again, my mother bears down on me, wearing her stern, schoolteacher face. She snatches the bouquet from me. "Carrie has caught the bouquet fair and square, and she shall have it." She hands it to the stunned girl.

My sister and friends rush off to find their coats. Voices ring out from the foyer and the front porch. "Goodbye, good night!" I lean against the newel post, feeling deflated, angry, and ashamed.

Richard and I make love that night, knowing we should. The next day we go home to the farm where we live, where he raises chickens, and I study. In the short, gray days leading up to Christmas, the feeling I had after the wedding stays with me. A tiny voice, hardly a whisper, sounds in the back of my mind. *You don't deserve this. You don't deserve happiness.*

Chapter 1

I pull into the parking lot of Brookvale, my mother's care home, maneuvering around a Sysco truck at the entrance. The building is so aggressively cheerful it makes me think of Disneyland. Covered in yellow siding, with gables and a turret, it looks like an oversized Midwestern farmhouse. White Victorian fretwork decorates the front porch. Everything is clean and spanking new.

On my way in, I say hello to the driver unloading cartons of canned green beans and beets onto a dolly. The concierge greets me by name, smiling broadly, and I do the same, acting the part of the good daughter. She buzzes me into the memory care unit. "Yakety Yak" plays on the sound system, part of an endless loop of '50s and '60s hits.

My mother is sitting in the hall beside a younger woman in a blue smock who's tapping away on a laptop.

I bend over to kiss her. "Hello dear," she says, looking up at me and smiling. She looks tiny in her pink flannel shirt and pants that are three sizes too big. Her hair, cut short, is still more brown than gray. With dementia, her face has relaxed.

"You're the daughter!" says the physical therapist. "Now we can start!"

Kendall, the therapist, asks me to sit next to Mom and do the exercises with her. "Raise the toes of your *right* foot!" she commands. "One, two, three, four, five. Now the left foot. Good job."

I touch Mom's knees to remind her of right and left.

"Now your heels!" Kendall calls out." One, two, three, four, five!"

"Now your whole foot. We're marching! Heigh ho, heigh ho, it's off to work we go!"

Up until a year ago, Mom walked two miles a day up and down the hills of her Berkeley neighborhood, to and from the drugstore. Five years ago, she hiked in the Sierras with my sister and me. A photo of the three us against a granite boulder is posted on the door to her room.

Kendall sets the walker in front of Mom. "Time to stand up!" Mom struggles to rise and topples backward. She laughs.

"Nose over toes!" Kendall shouts; Mom tries again.

"Concentrate now. Small steps forward. First the right foot."

We inch along the corridor. The walls are decorated with ladies' hats trimmed in flowers, men's bowlers and caps, and wooden tabletop radios.

Mom veers to the left. "Straight ahead," Kendall cries. "Look where you're going!"

While Mom rests, Kendall instructs me. "You'll need to repeat these exercises with her once a day."

No, no! I scream inwardly.

"In the morning," she reminds me. "That's her good time."

My good time, too! I think. The first two and a half hours of each day when I write. And fail, mostly. Especially since I've become her caretaker.

"But you're coming back Thursday," I say, pointedly.

"My colleague. I do the initial visit."

No matter how much practice and repetition of "nose over toes" Mom gets, I don't think she can learn. Every day it will be as if she's starting over again. That's what she told the gerontologist over a year ago when she explained how it felt when *she* sat down at her computer to write.

Jean-Pierre, the home's director, swoops down on us, a handsome man in a suit, exuding enough *bonhomie* for two care homes. "Kate and Elizabeth!" he calls. "So glad to see you looking well, Elizabeth!"

She smiles up at him like a schoolgirl. "I feel quite well."

He beckons me to the side. "Your mother is settling well into Life's Neighborhood, don't you think?"

Life's Neighborhood is Brookvale's name for memory care, a concoction that strikes me as absurd. Mom was transferred out of independent living two weeks ago after being found naked in the hall in the middle of the night. The image of her pale, ninety-five-pound body with the little protruding belly still burns inside my head.

"I guess so," I tell Jean-Pierre. "Can she spend more time in her room?"

"Ah, no, it is a pity. But safety, you know."

I push Mom into the common room where her fellows sit in wheelchairs or recliners, covered in afghans or blankets printed with cartoon figures; she faces Hanne, the activities director. On a whiteboard, Hanne has written the date and the weather forecast. She beckons Mom to the first row of the circle, her usual place.

"Today's word is *botany*. Can anyone define botany or use it in a sentence?"

Mom's hand shoots up. "Botany is the science of plants."

I bend to kiss my mother goodbye, grateful that she has Hanne's company.

On my way back down the hall, I go into Mom's room where the blind is lowered, and I raise it, letting the meager light in. Only a few pieces of her furniture and belongings accompanied her on this move: her bed with the lone star quilt I made forty years ago; the small maple desk she's had for as long as I remember; the dresser topped with a woven green scarf and a wooden jewelry box; the bookcase holding her favorite authors—Brontë, Stegner, A. E. Housman, Wordsworth; and framed photographs of her late husband, Karl, her fourth, her four children, Peter, Megan, Michael and me, and her three grandchildren, Julia, Lily, and Sam.

I check the laundry basket to make sure an aide hasn't thrown a wool sweater in again. One came back last week, child size.

On my way out, an aide rushes to me. "Your mother is almost out of Depends. Can you get some? And bodywash."

Bodywash? Don't they have soap? It's almost eleven when I pull out of the parking lot. My husband, Richard, is shopping near Walgreens. Easier for him to stop there than me. But he's been irritable lately; the adult continence aisle would be his undoing.

At home, Richard unloads groceries. Six or seven bags clutter the counter, a frightening quantity. *New paper bags,* I note. He never remembers to take reusable ones. The sight of all these bags makes me crazy. I can't stand waste.

I tell him about the annoying physical therapist. "She expects me to practice with Mom every day!"

He mumbles a reply, still focused on his food. Twisting the tops off carrots, loading them into the produce drawer.

"What about you?" I ask. "What have you been up to?"

"I had my PT appointment," he says curtly.

He's hurt because I should have remembered. He had rotator cuff surgery in August, two months ago, and has been slowly recovering.

"Of course. What did they say?"

He carries on, dipping into the bags, pivoting from counter to frig. He moves with the grace and balance of an athlete. Broad-shouldered and muscular, Richard is still handsome. He has blue eyes behind glasses, fair skin, and wavey, silver hair encircling a bald dome that his dermatologist watches closely.

"The PT said the pain along my arm may persist for a few months. It's normal nerve damage. She said I can start putting."

"Great," I say, breathing out. He'll be happier when he's back on the golf course. And so will I.

I help put things away—crackers into the bread drawer, cereal on a high shelf, dog food in the laundry room, on top of the cans we already have. Irritation, static along the nerves, mounts inside me. Richard never checks the frig or shelves before he goes out. He never thinks about where we'll put it all.

"Did you do something about your mother's couch?" he asks, pineapple in hand.

He means the chintz loveseat now crowding our storage room. "I thought I should offer it to Julia and Dareh before I do anything else," I say. "Or the ladies." Julia is our daughter, Dareh, her boyfriend, and the ladies our cleaners. "We already have a pineapple."

He ignores me. "Have you called them?"

"No." My voice rises. How could I? My desk is cluttered with files, one for each of the twenty financial institutions I need to contact as my mother's trustee. Karl died a year ago leaving enough money for Brookvale and Life's Neighborhood, but a mess for me.

I begin pulling containers out of the refrigerator—leftover spaghetti sauce, chicken soup, pickles—to make room, to reorganize. *We'll never fit all this in.* The vegetable drawer is so crammed, the parsley on the bottom is getting crushed. Scallions rot. He never cleans out, just puts in. Richard senses my rising anger, I can tell, and is readying his defense. We've had this argument a million times. *Be nice,* I tell myself.

He hefts a half gallon of milk out of the bag.

"We already have one!" I cry.

"So? We'll drink it."

I hold up two packages, wrapped in white butcher paper. "Why two meats?"

"They were on sale."

"Why do you always buy so much! We waste it!"

He hurls a bag of muesli onto the counter where it skids onto the floor. "Do your own shopping!" He storms out of the kitchen.

Bitter regret floods my chest. I run down the hall. "Please," I say. "I'm sorry. I've had a hard morning."

"And I haven't."

"I'm sorry," I repeat.

"You're always sorry."

By the end of the day, I get him to talk. I sit on the couch in the TV room with our dog, Zorro, between us. He turns off the TV. *Go slowly,* I tell myself. *Don't expect much. Don't touch him.*

"This is too awful," I say. Neither of us has the slightest cushion, the least bit of forbearance. "I can't bear it."

"I can't either."

"You're under a lot of stress," Greta, our couples' therapist, says, after we tell her why we're here. We've driven an hour from Napa to Berkeley, referred by Sharon, a local therapist I sometimes see. Greta's face is strong boned, reminding me of the women Picasso painted in his neoclassical period. Thick brown hair coiled at her neck.

Richard and I sit on a sofa, propped up by pillows covered in rosy Kilim fabrics. Behind us, large-leaf plants fill a greenhouse window.

Greta crosses her legs and leans forward, training her deep, brown eyes on us. "If we don't break into your toughest issues right away, we'll just waste a lot of time. Okay?"

Richard sits forward, meeting Greta's gaze. He likes her.

"Tell me about a serious fight," Greta urges.

Richard looks at me. "New York?"

My breath catches. It is so hard to tell. I begin. "I'd just moved my mother into assisted living, and I felt guilty for leaving her. We were in a nice restaurant, a place we'd been before. We were all dressed up." We tell Greta how it started, how it exposed the resentments of years, how we said terrible things. How it lasted for days.

Tell them, tell them, a voice inside my head sings. "When we have a bad fight," I say, "I fall so fast. Into darkness. It's very hard to say this. Sometimes, I think about killing myself. I did that night."

"Oh, dear," Greta murmurs.

Richard reaches for my hand.

"Have you told Sharon?" Greta asks.

I shake my head. "I haven't told anyone," I say.

"You must see someone about this," Greta says firmly. "On your own. You both must take this seriously. I'll find someone for you."

Chapter 2

Frances' office is a small, cozily furnished room, autumnal in color and filled with objects that look like they have meaning—a small, tightly woven basket, a dish holding feathers, a framed photograph. She sits in one corner under a small, shaded lamp, I in another.

Her waiting room, on the other hand, is not cozy. It looks like it was furnished decades ago with castoffs from her parents. It's all brown leather, scuffed, heavy wood, brown carpet, and gray Venetian blinds.

"Your waiting room," I tell Frances, "reminds me of a brown study."

"A brown study?" she says, studying me closely.

"In nineteenth century books, like *Little Women*, if a character is in a *brown study*, they're depressed."

"Hmm." Frances raises her eyebrows. "You seem to take the décor personally."

"Considering that people come here when they're depressed, it might matter!"

Frances is a psychoanalyst, the first I've ever tried. Once you confess to having thought about suicide you get passed to the head of the line. Her fee is shockingly high. Is it part of the treatment? A steep investment so you'll commit? I don't know yet. I remind myself that Richard spends as much in membership dues at his golf club, that we spend as much sometimes on dinner and a bottle of wine.

"It's nice in here, though," I add. Frances and I sit on low, Danish-modern armchairs, a pair of French doors centered on the wall between us. A studio couch with a gold cover occupies the interior wall. I wondered on my first visit whether I'd be expected to lie down. Frances is barricaded by a bookcase and an array of tote bags at her feet.

"I'm feeling quite a bit of resistance from you today," she says. "Is it because of what I asked you to think about last time? About why Greta referred you to me?"

I don't yet know how to describe Frances. She's always sitting when I come in, enthroned, so I don't know how tall she is. She has wavy brown hair, graying naturally, either pulled back or framing her face. Her voice is decisive, self-assured, and she speaks with a New York accent.

"You and Greta think it's remarkable that I didn't tell anyone before."

"Why do you think you didn't tell your Napa therapist?"

"I didn't see her much. Just off and on."

"She allowed that?"

I nod, not understanding. "She was a nice woman. She went to the same Pilates teacher as me, and maybe I didn't want to shock her. She'd be a fine therapist for most people."

"But not you . . . because?"

I wonder. *Who was I? What part of me did I suppress with Sharon? The darker, complicated part.* I look out onto the small patio beyond French doors where two redwood trees stand. The wind stirs their branches. "She asked me what I wanted most. 'To do a good job of taking care of my mother,' I told her. I wanted to look normal, like a good daughter."

"Even though your mother harmed you."

I feel as if I'm talking to the voice of the Oracle.

"For you, not telling is an old habit."

"I guess."

"You told me last time about breaking your collarbone when you were six and not telling anyone you hurt. Most children would say,

'Ow! I hurt!'"

My eyes smart with tears, and I warm to Frances. "I didn't want to be any trouble. There was a baby in the family, my sister. My mom was sick and pregnant again."

"And yet now you're caring for her. You're having to sleep with your cellphone next to your bed. You're worrying about leaving her to take a vacation with your husband. You've interrupted your writing schedule to visit her and to meet with physical therapists."

Frances flings these duties and worries at me. They pile up like dirty laundry overflowing the basket. Anger builds in me. "Every time I go to see her, an aide tells me she needs something, body wash or Depends. There's always pressure to get the item right away."

"You could get the Depends delivered."

"That would be better than going to Walgreens. That aisle is awful—a staggering array of pink and green packages." I feel a sharp pang. "When I'm there, I can't help thinking about when I started my period. At eleven. And she didn't remember to buy me napkins."

"She knew you needed them?"

"Yes!"

Frances shakes her head angrily. "Was this around the time your stepfather—"

"Yes," I say.

"Did you ask her for some?"

"I was too ashamed. Once I took one of hers, but I felt like I was stealing."

"Have you talked about this with a therapist?"

"Maybe not. Not at this level of detail."

She raises her eyebrows and lets a pause settle. I take this to mean that she is different. I've never put myself under the lens of her microscope, never been stretched over the rack of psychoanalysis.

"Tell me about your other therapists."

Outside, a branch of the redwood tree bobs up and down. "In my early twenties, when I lived in Boston, a friend took me to an encounter group run by a psychologist. Pretty soon I was seeing him privately. We sat on pillows on the floor and smoked." I remember hurrying from the T-stop to his office building on Beacon Street. No question but that I had a crush on him. "He was a Maslovian therapist, you know, all about self-actualization." I look at Frances to see if I've impressed her, but her expression stays the same.

I tell her about the next therapist, whom I saw in my late thirties when, driving home from a ski trip with Richard and my daughter, I started crying for no reason. Richard was caught up in his career, and I felt lonely and lost. "She was all about codependency," I tell Frances now. I don't want to be boring.

"Then, many years later, in my fifties, Julia had to drop out of college because *she* was so depressed. I felt as broken as I'd ever felt in my life. I found a new therapist, who I loved. She taught me mindfulness."

Frances nods. "How is your daughter now?"

"Fine. She's married." A stronger gust of wind shakes the branches outside. It's November, getting to be winter but still dry in Northern California. I wonder how much time I have left. The clock is on the wall behind me.

"And you've told these therapists the full extent of your childhood story."

"Yes."

"When you talk to me about it, I feel as if you're speaking at a remove. I don't know if it's because you're a writer or you've already gone through this with other therapists. It's like you're giving a report. I'm not getting your feelings."

Her words smart. I feel as if I've been scolded. "You're not a very touchy-feely person."

"If I were a touchy-feely person, you'd run a hundred miles away."

"My husband thinks I'm emotional."

She shrugs. "Did your previous therapists urge you to talk to your mother?"

I laugh. "Oh yes. The Maslovian doctor had Mom come in for a session. He set up actual chairs for her. And later the codependency therapist made me ask my mother why she was hospitalized when I was little. She got panicky and started hyperventilating. 'Don't you remember? I was abusing you children. I slapped Megan and knocked her highchair over.' Megan is my younger sister. I wanted to get in my car and drive straight back to my therapist's office."

"You experienced the feelings you repressed as a child. The terrible fear of your mother being out of control."

I nod and wait until my heart slows. Frances waits with me. "Another time, she reminded me that the last time I brought up the subject, she almost jumped out a window. Her husband at the time had to hold her back."

Frances shakes her head rapidly. "In other words, 'You are killing me.'" She resettles herself in the armchair. "When was the last time you talked with her about this?"

"A long time ago." I look back, past Mom's ninetieth birthday when we gathered in San Diego at Megan's house; past the visit to the gerontologist where she was diagnosed with dementia. I'm looking for the mother, the woman, when she was still competent. I see her striding across a hotel lobby, wearing baggy striped summer pants and a worn yellow T-shirt. I smile. "It was ten years ago," I tell Frances. "We went on a trip together, to Omaha, where she grew up."

Frances glances at the clock. "We'll talk about Omaha next time. We've covered a lot today." She folds her hands in her lap. "You don't have to do all the work, you know."

"What do you mean?"

"I know you think and write a lot between sessions. But the most important work is in here, between us. You don't have to carry all the weight."

I pick up my jacket and purse, still trying to get my mind around her words. I let myself out by the French doors, onto the small patio, where the redwood branches are still tossing in the wind. Patients don't leave through the brown waiting room—for confidentiality, Frances says. I open a gate in the redwood fence, feeling lighter than when I went in.

Chapter 3

Mom and I begin the trip in high spirits, meeting in the lobby of Americas Best Value, a second-rate hotel next to a freeway interchange in Omaha. She strides quickly over to meet me, a trim, 85-year-old in striped summer trousers and a worn yellow T-shirt. Uncharacteristically, she throws her arms around me.

In the elevator, we laugh over the lack of an apostrophe in Americas Best—we're both English teachers—and I hold my tongue about my disappointment in the hotel. It's miles from the river and city center, and a sign at the entrance warns that it's locked after 10 pm. It pains me to see my mother settle for such a depressing place. But this is her trip, I tell myself, and I'll go along. We've booked separate rooms.

"I almost went to Boise!" I say, once we're in my room. "In Salt Lake City, I got on the wrong plane!"

She laughs, enjoying this demonstration of my incompetence. I'm known in the family as the absent-minded child, washing my doll's clothes after a trip instead of my own. Singing and vacuuming when the officer arrived with a court order.

I put my toiletries in the bathroom. The shower curtain is torn and yellowed, the only amenity at the sink a tiny rectangle of soap.

She tells me about her day, spent at city hall in the records room. "I knew Daddy had separated from his first wife, but I didn't know when. Today in the census book of 1910, I found him listed alone, giving his address as the Magnolia Hotel, 1615 Howard Street."

While I unpack, she recites more dates and addresses from the 1890s to the 1920s, signposts in the lives of her parents. She's writing a book about them. Her notes and photocopies will go home to Berkeley, to the house she shares with her fourth husband, Karl. She works in an upstairs office, the sunniest and most lived-in room of the house, lined with bookcases and old family photos. Typing away at a small maple desk she's had since I was a child, making draft after draft. Essays, stories, a children's book once, a dissertation, and now these memoirs.

"The Magnolia Hotel is still there," she says. "I thought we could try it for dinner."

Daddy? I think, after she leaves. I've never heard her call her father Daddy before. He was an old father, thirty years older than her mother. I know him mainly from two photographs. In the first, he is portly and proud, very much the prominent physician, waistcoat and jacket, gold pocket watch and chain. Elizabeth, aged four, sits in his lap, her blond hair cut in a Dutch bob. She wears little black boots that button. In the second photograph, she stands over him, a well-grown girl of ten or so, wearing a proud smile and a ribbon in her smooth, brown hair. He's still well dressed but shrunken and bent. They look at the camera with the same almond-shaped eyes—his full of experience, hers bright with hope.

The Magnolia Hotel stands elegant and imposing in the late afternoon light, four stories decorated with pilasters and cornices. On the inside, signs of the past have been erased. The lobby is all beige carpet, chrome and glass, and a crowd of noisy office workers celebrating Friday spills out from the bar. We look at each other, make the same face, and retreat.

Farther down the street, we stop at Luigi's, a small place with red-checked half curtains at the windows. We're seated at a table bearing a candle in a straw-covered bottle. We both order spaghetti Bolognese. "A good bet," I say.

The waitress, a middle-aged woman in a white, ruffled blouse, nods approvingly. I ask for a glass of pinot noir and Mom orders a decaf coffee.

"My father's first marriage was never very happy," she tells me. "He proposed to the woman, and she turned him down. He left Omaha to go to Vienna, to study, and when he came back several years later, she let it be known she'd changed her mind. He didn't want to marry her anymore."

"But he had to," I say. "Grandma told me. It was the Victorian code."

Mom smiles knowingly, and a warm current flows between us. She looks pretty in her pink floral shirt, pearl studs on her ears. I want to keep talking about Grandma, who knits us together, whom we both love.

The waitress serves Mom's coffee and my wine. "Did your father know Grandma when he left his wife?" I'm teasing her; I know the answer.

"Oh, no! They met, when she was in nurses' training. I have a very fine photo of her, taken in 1915, in her student nursing uniform."

"That uniform! She loved to talk about her apron. How it had five yards of fabric in it, and when she looked out the window one day and saw a tornado approaching the hospital, she loaded three babies into it!" We both laugh.

Mom sips her coffee. "There was her other tornado story, too. About her sister seeing a telephone operator running down the street with her headset still on."

"And a man coming toward her saying, 'Hello, central!'"

We laugh again. Then Mom's face grows serious. "Grandma was quite the storyteller."

The waitress arrives with steaming mounds of spaghetti topped with a meaty red sauce.

"Is Julia enjoying her teaching?" Mom asks, after a few minutes.

Now we're on rocky ground. My daughter is one month into her first teaching assignment—summer session at an inner-city high school. The last time I saw her, she looked thin and complained about her workload and the kids' behavior. "It's like they all have ADHD!" she wailed. When I asked if she was taking her antidepressants, she shot me a dark look. "Mom!" she said warningly.

"It's her first job, so it's not easy," I say, avoiding Mom's eyes. If I tell her the truth, it will distress her. Five years ago, when I told her Julia had dropped out of college, she burst into tears. "I've been so worried about that child!" Mom cried. Worse, it will open me up to my own doubts and uncertainties as to how I've raised my daughter.

"I remember my first teaching job," she says. "First grade at Main Street School. The other first-grade teacher, Mrs. McClain, took me under her wing, and soon I was fine."

She smiles, proud of her teaching career. It's up to me to remember that Main Street wasn't her first school, that her first was in Torrance where we moved after she left my father. She enrolled me in first grade, and she taught second grade. One day I was taken to her classroom because I was sick, and I watched from my seat in back as the kids misbehaved and she was helpless to control them. She left that job after Christmas, and we moved to Grandma's.

The waitress appears and offers homemade *spumoni*.

"Oh, goodie," Mom says. In the spirit of happy beginnings, I ask for some, too, though I don't like *spumoni*.

The sky is still light when we come out of the restaurant, but a softer blue. "Can we go see the river?" I ask. We drive east, passing a Marriott Hotel with a brightly lit entrance. "That hotel looks nice," I say.

Mom doesn't answer. We park near the river, get out and walk along a promenade, bordered by native grasses and wildflowers. Mom points to a spot upriver, on the Iowa side. "That's where raw sewage used to enter, contaminating the drinking water. It was the cause of the typhoid epidemic of 1909. My father wrote an article about it that I'm hoping to find tomorrow at the historical library."

"But you promised me we could visit the houses you lived in, and the schools!" I protest.

"That's right. The next day then."

The sky bathes the river in pink and blue. I ask Mom to stand by the wall so I can take her picture. She looks young, her hair and face warmed by the rosy light.

———

That night, under a blanket made of foam rubber, I struggle to fall asleep. The window air conditioner whirs and whines. I miss Richard. I sit up and turn on the light. It's only 8:30 California time.

"I miss you!" I say.

"I miss you, too." I hear the clatter of dishes and the running of water. He's had dinner.

"How is Zorro?"

"He's fine. I took him for a walk. How's everything there?"

I tell him about dinner and the walk along the river. "The hotel is awful, though. It's in a bad neighborhood . . . bars on the windows."

He sounds worried. "That figures. Is it safe?"

"Probably."

"What's the matter with her? She can afford better."

"I'll see if I can get her to move."

"Good. You've got five more days with her. You'd better have your comforts."

Richard has known Mom for almost forty years, and he tolerates her. But he has a strong sense of justice.

Chapter 4

I wake up late and scramble out of bed, wash my face with the tiny square of soap which smells of childhood, Cashmere Bouquet, and dry it with a rough towel. A feeling of dread creeps over me.

I'm thinking of Torrance again, of the house we moved to after we left Dad. The bathroom was cold, the linoleum torn, and we didn't have much furniture. Mom was gone sometimes, leaving my older brother Peter to take care of us. I was sick to my stomach a lot, and I remember lying in bed there, in the gray light, feeling alone.

I hang up my towel.

I find Mom in a low-ceilinged breakfast room. A wall-mounted TV blares, flashing neon bright images. The buffet offers the standard industrial fare—orange juice sloshing in a plastic vat, coffee dispensed from another, frozen bagels, Sugar Pops, Corn Flakes, little tubs of yogurt, and a bowl of tired apples.

"Can we maybe eat somewhere else?" I plead.

"Breakfast is included, dear," Mom says. "I think we should take advantage."

The room is occupied mostly by families, and the children run back and forth from their table to the cereal boxes. *Get off your high horse,* I tell myself.

Mom struggles to cut her waffle with a plastic fork and knife.

"Did you notice the bars on the windows?" I nod toward them.

She doesn't answer. "I looked up the hotel we passed on Dodge

Street, the Marriott. It's only a hundred and fifty dollars a night."

Now she looks up, lips pursed. "I can see you don't approve of this hotel."

"It's not very convenient, is it? We have to drive miles to get anywhere. We could share a room at the Marriott."

"I get up and down at night."

She hasn't said no. I'll try later.

———

In the car, Mom directs me north on 30th Street toward her first home on Titus Street.

"This is the house from the photo album, right? 'The Country Home of Doctor and Mrs. D.A. Foote,'" I recite playfully.

As a child, visiting Grandma, I loved pulling out the heavy album with its gold embossed cover, settling down on the floor, and turning the stiff pages. It was like entering one of my story books. The first pages showed an old-fashioned house on a hill, with an orchard in back and a view. Next came shots of a garden with a fishpond where Grandma cut flowers, wearing a long, loose dress. Inside everything was spacious and elegant—fringed lamps, a colored glass lamp over the dining table, Grandma reclining on a fainting couch.

"Turn right here," Mom says. "Then right again."

Even before I park, disappointment comes over me. The hill is hardly noticeable, and the orchard is gone, along with the view.

"It looks different," I say, not trying to hide my feelings.

"Well, the city has grown up around it."

The stone retaining wall looks the same as from the photograph, so I ask Mom to stand next to it for a photo. She wears the same worn yellow T-shirt and striped pants as yesterday.

She raises her hand. "Don't take any more pictures. We should leave."

"You don't want to walk around?"

"No. People will see us."

"What are you worried about?" We're fastening our seatbelts.

She doesn't answer, just directs me back to 30th Street, a busy four-lane road leading south toward the center.

"This is where Daddy was driving when he had his stroke. They were on their way to the theater downtown, and Mother felt the car slow down. He had collapsed over the wheel, and she grabbed it and pulled the car to the curb. We had to move."

It was a disabling stroke, I knew, and my grandfather couldn't practice any more. For a second, I see the child with the Dutch bob, the apple of her father's eye, but no longer the center of attention. She probably felt she had to be good all the time. Mary, the hired helper, would have dressed her and cared for her.

"We moved to a large house in Central Omaha where Mother could take in boarders."

It's been demolished." She clears her throat. "Mother gave the upper rooms to boarders, and we lived in the basement."

Again, I picture the child losing her father, really, taken away from the house with the fishpond and the colored glass lamp.

"We lived together, in one room," Mom goes on, her voice strained now and hard to hear over the sounds of the road. "I had to watch my mother dress my father and put a truss on him." She shudders. "I didn't like that."

I have to think for a second. *What's a truss?* Then I understand. Mom had to look at her father's ruined body, his genitals even. All her life she's had an aversion to illness, and I wonder if it began there.

"Do you remember anything else?"

She's quiet for a few seconds. "I missed my mother's attention," she finally says.

I know all about Grandma's attention. She was slow and deliberate, but agile enough; her voice low and steady, never raised. She wore glasses that magnified her eyes, which were deep brown so that whenever she was near me, I felt her gaze. When I was six, we moved from Torrance to her house in Santa Barbara. My brother, sister, and

I were in Dad's car driving back to Grandma's on Highway 1, when we had an accident, a pileup, in the fog. I sat in the front seat and was thrown forward. When we got to Grandma's, she put me in her bed and sat beside me. "Do you hurt anywhere, dearie?" I pointed to my shoulder. Gently, she raised and lowered my left arm. "Does this hurt?" I nodded yes, telling her what I'd told no one else.

In the car now, I run my finger along my left shoulder and feel the bump where the bone mended.

Dundee is our next destination, a pleasant, leafy neighborhood where Mom and her family moved after Grandma got them back on their feet. I park at the intersection of 51st and Davenport, under a maple tree.

"First we lived on this corner," Mom says, as we stand before a comfortable looking gray bungalow with a half story above. "Through my grammar school years."

Over the wide front porch, upstairs, stretches a row of windows where the main bedroom must be. "Is this where your father died?"

"No. I believe he died in the hospital."

"But Grandma told me—" I look back at the upstairs windows, feeling uneasy about contradicting her. "Grandma told me she was sleeping next to him and heard him moan in the middle of the night. She woke up in the morning to find him gone."

Mom studies the maple tree, and I wonder how she'll respond. She might say, "That's true, I forgot, or "Are you sure?" or "When did she tell you that?"

She looks away from the tree, then steps off the curb. "From here, we moved across the street! My cousin Bill came over to help us, and I remember laughing as we went back and forth across the street, with a table or an armchair between us. We're having dinner with Bill and his wife tonight."

I follow her. Now we face a large, white, three-storied house, somewhat lopsided. "Mother bought it as a house and turned it into apartments. We lived on the third floor."

"In the turret?"

"That was my bedroom.,"

Her school, Dundee Elementary, is only two blocks away and we walk there. It's a handsome, two-storied brick building, built in 1920, according to the cornerstone. I take a photo of her under the entrance arch.

Down the street, we find a café with tables outside under a tree. "This looks good," I say, after we're seated. "Chickpea salad, Israeli couscous, roasted vegetables! After the breakfast we had—"

Mom looks up at me sharply.

After we order, a young woman at the next table says hello. She has long brown hair and wears a paisley skirt and sandals.

"Where are you from?" she asks pleasantly. "How are you finding Omaha?"

We make small talk for a few minutes. Then she tells us she just attended her grandfather's funeral. "This morning?" I ask. Her eyes widen and fill with tears. She tells us about him, clearly looking to us, two older women, for comfort. While I nod and murmur encouragement, Mom goes quiet. Frowning, head down, she straightens her knife and fork.

On the way back to the car, I speak up. "You seemed bothered by the young woman."

"Her conversation was too personal. She doesn't know us, and we don't know her."

"I see." Without comment, we pass the big white house at the corner of 51st and Davenport, then the smaller gray house across the street. A distance settles between us, a familiar one, partly generational, partly something darker. As we buckle our seatbelts, I remember Mom's shudder when she spoke of her father being helped into a truss. My hands tighten around the steering wheel.

Our last stop, Central High School, occupies a commanding position atop a hill—a citadel, of granite. When we get out of the car, the sun blazes down on us, and I hurry across a playing field to get out of the heat. She leads me inside the building, and we walk the U-shaped halls, empty and echoing. We pass glass-fronted displays filled with trophies and tributes to former students, the most impressive, Henry Fonda. Mom doesn't talk and I keep myself from prompting her. When we come out on the far side of the building, which is the main entrance, a panoramic view of downtown Omaha and the river extends before us, shimmering in the heat. I stare at it for a long time, and Mom has to remind me to take her picture.

At 5:30 that evening, dressed for dinner, we wait outside Anthony's Steak House. A life-sized brown-and-white cow or steer sits atop the entrance portico.

"Shouldn't we go inside?" I ask. "It's time."

"No, no. We'll wait here."

I move out from under the porch and take a photo of the cow or steer, then return to Mom's side. She glances around nervously, scanning the rows of parked cars. Two couples pass us, and when they open the door, a wave of sound and energy comes out—music, voices, dishes, and laughter.

"I think we should go inside. That's what people do," I say meekly.

"No, people wait outside."

After another five minutes, a tall man with a florid face bursts out. "*Here* you are!"

Cousin Bill is large and extraverted and his wife small and very kind. They smile at my mother and exclaim in pleasure then turn the same smiles and excited greetings to me. Mom is all smiles, too. Her face and voice light up.

Bill insists on ordering for us, and we tuck into the kind of dinner that's frowned upon in Northern California—heavy dollops of Roquefort dressing on the salad, giant portions of steak, and baked potatoes with sour cream.

"Where are you staying?" Bill asks.

"At Americas Best," Mom says.

"Next to the freeway? You're kidding! You can do better than that, Lizzie."

"I suggested we moved closer to downtown," I add. "Mom likes the river so much."

"Absolutely!" Bill crows. He wins Mom over. We decide to move to the Marriott tomorrow.

Chapter 5

At breakfast in the solarium of the downtown Marriott, sunlight pours onto an acre of mauve carpet, towering rubber tree plants, and white tablecloths. I duck into the gift store to buy the *New York Times*, the first I've gotten my hands on in three days. The paper holds the possibility of a few minutes' relief from relating to Mom.

Our plan today is to drive to Fort Omaha, to the Nebraska State Historical Society, where Mom will do research and I'll visit some old houses. The sky is cloudless, the napkins in our laps spotless, their neat folds guaranteeing what? A respite from care, a relaxed meal. So do the voices and manners of the couple at the next table, my age, early sixties; she is in aqua knit, he in madras.

Has Mom noticed the improvement in our accommodations?

"I don't often make oatmeal for myself," she says, glancing up from the menu. "Maybe I'll have that."

"You used to make us oatmeal a lot. With raisins," I say.

The woman in aqua looks over at me and smiles. Maybe she's lost her mother and wishes she were having breakfast with her. I'll try to be nice.

Mom sets down her menu. "Before we go to Fort Omaha, I want to stop by Americas Best Value to ask if they've found my yellow T-shirt."

"But you called them."

"I don't think they looked very hard. If I go there in person, I'll have a better result."

This is the yellow T-shirt she wore on her first days in Omaha, a worn, stretched-out garment, ready to be turned into a dust cloth. If one of the maids at Americas Best Value snatched it, so much the better.

"Are you sure it's worth it?" I ask. The trip will take us miles out of our way.

"I know right where I left it."

I tap my finger against my cheek. "I've never had any luck getting things back from hotels. Maids take things, you know."

She sniffs. In the Midwest, maids are Black, so I stand accused of being racist. "I don't mind taking the time," Mom says.

What about *my* time? I want to say, but I pick up the newspaper and give it a shake. "I wonder what Obama is up to." The waitress appears, and Mom orders eggs.

"With bacon and whole wheat toast. No butter."

"Would you like a section?" I ask after the waitress leaves, holding tight to the front section and extending the others.

"*I* always read the front section first," she says smugly.

I slam the paper down so hard so hard that my silverware jumps. The woman at the next table stares. "What's the matter?" my mother whimpers.

"*I* bought the newspaper, *I* said I wanted to read about Obama. Do you always have to have everything your way!"

She shrinks into her chair. "I didn't mean anything by it. I only said that's what I usually do."

"And you want me to drive all the way over to fucking Americas Best Value to look for a T-shirt that isn't worth a dime and that's probably *gone*! I'm the driver, yet you never even *asked* if I was willing to go there."

She dabs at her eyes with her napkins. "You don't have to take me," she whimpers. "We won't go. Of course we won't go. I didn't mean to anger you."

The woman in aqua is sneaking glances at us. I'm a monster, yelling at this tiny old lady, my mother!

"Do you ever put yourself in my shoes?" I say, struggling to lower my voice. In a minute, I'll be crying. We'll both be crying.

"I've been worried about you too," my mother says. "You seem overwrought. You talk so much in the car."

I sigh. "But that's what people do! People converse!"

"I'll try to be more considerate, Kate," my mother says. She shakes her head back and forth, as if beating sense into herself. "We won't go to the motel."

The waitress delivers our eggs, lovely bright orbs of gold next to a bed of hashed browns, a slice of orange on the side.

"No, no," I sigh. "We'll go."

At Americas Best, Rajiv, the desk clerk, shrugs, implying that time has moved on and the universe has forgotten us and our T-shirt. At Fort Omaha we park on a tree-lined street opposite a row of restored, nineteenth century houses. The Nebraska State Historical Society occupies a smaller house on our side. I linger inside long enough to pick up a leaflet and to see Mom settled at an oak table with a massive volume in front of her. It holds copies of the *Omaha Herald* from 1915 to 1920. She is looking for the article her father wrote on the typhoid epidemic.

My plan was to visit the General Crook House, but I don't feel like it. Don't want to tiptoe around a hushed, velvet upholstered interior where the shades are drawn. My mind is in turmoil, my heart crowded with feeling. A few steps from the library, I find a path leading to a huge, open field, the Parade Ground, according to my leaflet, formerly used for military exercises when the US Army ruled the state from this place.

I pass between towering elms, their leaves a soft, tender green that I hardly see. Eyes down, heart bursting, I barely notice the sun filtering through the branches. In the middle of the field, I sit on rough grass. I'm exhausted already, wishing my sister was on this trip. Megan would have given Mom the front section, sighing while she handed it over but telling herself it was only a few days. Mom doesn't seem to compete with Megan—just me, her first daughter.

I stretch out on my back and cradle my head in my hands. Billowing white clouds mass against the sky, making pillars and domes. A gust shakes the tops of the elms. The air is heavy with moisture. My body feels different in this climate—heavier, slower, yet excited, alert. The wind could pick up, the clouds darken and grow bigger and bigger until they burst.

When we were growing up, my mother was always talking about the Midwest, enough to make us think it was a superior country. The wonder of the changing seasons. The thunderstorms in summer. The big trees. The nice old houses. She loved the weather, the lush green of summer, and thunderstorms. She hated the dryness of central California, where we lived, the brown hills, and blank blue skies.

The insects are noisy here. *What is that clickety-clacking in the grass around me, cicadas?* I look back at the officers' houses, which look like my mother—resolute but blinkered.

She was always judging and ranking; the Midwest was better than California; old houses and hardwood floors were good; new houses and carpeting bad. People who belonged to the country club were inferior to us, they were Philistines. The city leaders were provincial. Teachers were better than insurance salesman. Ballet and piano lessons were good; Brownies and Boy Scouts were common. We couldn't be common.

The cicadas or locusts speed up their noisemaking, the air warms. Why did I get so angry this morning? What did I look like to the woman in aqua? What if she knew about our past?

A silence, which the cicadas fill. I sit up and look at the clouds, billowing high in the warming atmosphere making towers and domes.

Talking to my mother about the past does no good. She'll have a panic attack or make excuses that only make me madder.

It's too hot in the sun and I get to my feet and move toward the elms, where I sit at the base of the nearest one and lean back against the trunk.

Above me, a pattern of interlacing branches, leaves, and light—negative space, I remember the term—always shifting, making, and remaking. "Rockabye baby on the treetop . . . " I sang it to my little brother Mikey so he wouldn't cry, as our family drove the high, twisty curves of Highway 1, on our way to Big Sur. It was summer, 1959, just before everything happened. My stepfather, Ray, drove and Mom sat next to him in the front, her face pale, her body tense. When Mikey cried, she stiffened. I knew what she felt; she was afraid the car would plunge over the guardrail and into the ocean. So, I sang to baby Mikey, over and over, to calm my mother.

Chapter 6

Frances wears jeans and a sweater, and her hair is damp, as if she's just come from tennis or a walk. I'm curious about her age. Last week, I made a reference, from the fifties perhaps, and asked if she knew what I meant. "I don't know how old you are," I said.

"The same as you," she answered, with a wave of the hand I took to mean "or thereabouts."

Today I begin where we left off—with the trip to Omaha. "A few days after we got home, I got a letter from her. My sister got it, too. One and a half typed pages, no cross-outs or typos. She'd labored over it," I say, sighing.

"What did she say?"

"She said that staying with Ray was the greatest sin of her life. She begged me to forgive her."

"Do you forgive her?"

My body prickles with irritation, and I wriggle in my chair. I hate the word sin. "I don't know what to do about the sin part. I don't *believe* in sin or God's forgiveness. Can we talk about God in here?"

"Of course."

She asks if I was raised in the church, and I tell her yes, the Presbyterian Church. "We started going there when we were new to Santa Maria, Mom and the three of us. I loved Sunday school, sitting in a circle, being shown pretty picture books by a nice lady. When it was our birthday, we dropped pennies into a cardboard cake, one for each year. When my birthday came around, I forgot my pennies and the teacher gave me some from her purse. After Sunday school, we went to social hour, where we could run around and eat all the cookies we wanted. They were all different colors—pink, green, white. Letters and words appeared in my mind in color then. *A* for red, *C* white, *E* and *L* green. *S* for blue."

"Interesting. Did you stay in the church?"

"When I was in eighth grade I took communicants class and joined the church so I could take communion." I remember the sanctuary, with its dark oak pews and wainscoting, its steep, ribbed ceiling and faded, green blue stained glass. "One Sunday," I tell Frances, "the minister, Reverend Stephens, asked us to imagine the church turned over, so that it looked like an ark. The church was a sturdy vessel, he said, that would carry us through storms."

"This was after—"

I nod. "I loved the benediction. Reverend Stephens would raise his arms so they looked like big black wings. 'May the Lord bless you and keep you and make his face to shine upon you.' Or maybe his countenance."

Frances nods, a sober expression on her face.

"Once Mom started crying during the service. It was evening service, Maundy Thursday, and she was singing in the choir. This was during my religious phase. Before the service, she and Ray had a terrible fight, yelling and screaming at each other. She told him to get out. I'm not sure what the fight was about. In church, Reverend Stephens was praying, our heads were bowed, and a loud sobbing broke out from the choir loft. It was Mom, in the front row."

"How did you feel?"

"Ashamed, terribly ashamed. Everyone knew us. I was sure they could see the ugliness in our house. The sin."

"Maybe she was crying because of it."

My throat tightens. "She told us not to let anyone know, and I obeyed! Yet here she was letting it all hang out!"

"She lost control for a moment. To go back to her letter," Frances says, "it seems she believed in sin, and she wanted you to forgive her."

A fierceness rises in me, and I start forward in my chair. "It's still all about her! How much she suffered! How guilty she feels!" I press my fists into my thighs.

"What do you want?"

"I want a tribunal. A three-judge truth and reconciliation thing. I want her to answer for everything. Our Reverence Stephens could be the judge. Or you."

"Or you." Frances's alto tone soothes me. "And what would you accuse her of?"

"Oh, *lots* of things. The testimony would take weeks. We'd go back to my sixth-grade classroom and to each room of our house on Pony Street. Then Verbena Street. And the house I lived in in Berkeley. I'd produce house plans and street maps, calendars, and real estate documents. I'd call witnesses. I'd insist on exactness." I hope I'm being ironic, funny.

"Good."

"Of course, it's too late."

Frances smiles. "Not for you."

Chapter 7

On a sidewalk shaded by gray green pepper trees, I run. I am eleven, or about to turn eleven. On my feet, saddle shoes, white and brown. With each step, pink and white peppercorns burst under my feet, releasing their smell. A current of electricity runs from my toes up my legs and torso, all the way to my scalp. My blue dance case bangs against my thigh.

I've left one of my places, school, and fly toward another, Miss Sylvia's School of Dance, downtown. My town is small enough that I have the run of it.

Last year, Miss Sylvia promoted me to advanced intermediates. "Your feet and legs are strong, but you need to work on your arms," she said. Today's class is special, a master class taught by Monsieur Lembert, formerly of the Ballet Russe de Monte Carlo.

At Main Street, the wind blowing from the ocean and over fields hits me full in the body. The February sun slants strongly from the west. It will be dark by the time class ends, and Mom will pick me up.

Main to Broadway, Broadway to Church, and ten more running steps to the glass doors and a single flight of stairs. The studio is over a Chevrolet dealership. I enter a high-ceilinged room lit by industrial-style windows. On the far side of the studio stands Miss Sylvia, next to a slim man wearing a scarf. Miss Sylvia, also very slim and pale, wears a lavender leotard and a matching chiffon skirt. Her bright red hair is arranged like a flower on top of her head.

I'm first into the dressing room, but soon others join me. We take off our school clothes, talking and laughing. The sun filters through dust motes, lighting ponytails and cheeks.

The other girls wear bras, soft white training bras, but my chest is bare; I turn away, embarrassed by the swollen nubs that show beneath my leotard. I wriggle into my pink tights, soiled at the feet, never clean enough. There's a mark on each calf where my toe brushes my leg in *passé*. I pull on my beloved leotard, copen blue, a fancy word for sky blue, my dad's favorite color. At the armpits, there's a slight sour smell, my smell, from the effort of last Tuesday's class.

Next come my *pointe* shoes. From my case, I take the wad of yellow lambswool and wrap it around my toes. Other girls have crocheted toe covers, made by their mothers. I tie the pink satin ribbons across my instep, then twice across the ankle.

The advanced students claim the main *barre*, along the mirrored wall. Their grown-up figures, black and pink, multiply in the glass. We younger ones crowd along the shorter *barre*, under the windows. "Single or double?" my friend Linda whispers as class begins. We can't understand Monsieur Lembert! Miss Sylvia sends an older girl to help us.

Monsieur Lembert moves us to the middle of the room for the *adagio* combination. *Port de bras* but without the *barre*. "Let your arms be as soft as willow branches," he says. "Your fingers are leaves."

One leg lifts into *arabesque* and I wobble, catching Monsieur Lembert's eye. A few minutes later I see him watching me again as we do *tour jetés*—turning and leaping—in a circle. Legs and arms slash the air like windmills.

"From the corner!" Monsieur Lembert calls finally. "*Grand jeté* combination and *révérence!*"

"It's Kate's birthday tomorrow," Miss Sylvia says. "Let her go first."

The big girls push me to the head of the line. Shaking with nerves and pleasure, I let one measure of Tchaikovsky's waltz go by, then begin. *Soubresaut, soubresaut,* run, run, run, leap! I curtsy deeply to my teachers, and Miss Sylvia kisses me on the cheek.

In the dressing room, I am teased and hugged. Sweaty and giddy, still ringing with the music, I pull on my skirt and sweater. I pack my ballet things in the blue case.

Outside in the studio, I look for my mother along the row of chairs, near the entrance. She isn't there. My stepfather, Ray, leans against the doorway, wearing work clothes—overalls and a denim jacket—and chatting to the mothers. My heart falls, disappointment and embarrassment combined. I race ahead of him down the stairs.

"Not so fast, girlie," he calls after me.

"Where's the car?" I ask.

"We're not going to the car." He puts a hand on my shoulder and steers me past the lighted windows of the Chevrolet dealership. I grow nervous; his voice sounds different than usual. He's trying to be nice, to make me like him. "Maybe I have a surprise for you."

I relax. Maybe Mom has ordered the Ship 'n Shore blouse I want or new patent leather shoes, and she's asked Ray to pick them up. After all, it's my birthday! He pushes me around the corner onto Broadway, past two more shops until we stand in front of Colliers Apparel, the best women's store in town.

Mrs. Rheinhardt, from the church choir, stands behind the counter, tall, silver-haired, dressed in tailored navy blue. She greets us by name. "What can I do for you?" she asks.

"We're here to buy this young lady a brassiere," Ray says. "Her first."

My heart seizes, the blood rushes to my face. I want to disappear.

Mrs. Rheinhardt tells Ray to sit and me to follow her to the back of the shop, into a small, curtained dressing room, no more than a corner, with a mirror and a single chair.

"Your mother should do this for you," she says, her hands on my shoulders, her eyes finding mine in the mirror.

I redden and make excuses for Mom. "She's very busy, with teaching and little Mikey."

"Take off your blouse, dear, so I can measure you." Mrs. Rheinhardt pulls the red curtain closed.

Mom doesn't approve of me growing up too soon. This isn't her idea. If Ray is buying me a bra, that means he's been looking at me; he has noticed the buds forming on my chest. I hang my blouse on a hook.

Mrs. Rheinhardt returns and stretches the yellow tape around my chest. "Twenty-eight," she says. "Just as I thought." From a cardboard box she pulls a soft white garment which she helps me into, fastening the back, tightening the straps. She turns me toward the mirror and settles her hands on my shoulders. "Perfect."

I've wanted a bra just like this one, a training bra. Like the girls in my class at school and ballet have. But not like this, not from him.

Back at the cash register, Ray is talking to Mrs. Rheinbardt in his familiar way, not noticing her silences.

"Don't you want two? So one can be laundered?" she asks.

"Just the one."

I murmur goodbye and step out before him. The shops are closed, the sidewalks dark by the time we get into Ray's Pontiac. We take the same route home that I ran that afternoon, under the pepper trees. At Main Street and Broadway, we wait for what feels like forever for the light to change. I wanted the bra, and Ray guessed it—that's the terrible part. He'll expect something in return—gratitude, obedience. I hug my ballet case to my chest.

Tomorrow, I'll tell my best friend, Debbie, but not *how* I got the bra.

We turn from Main Street to Thornhill. Ray's shoulders are hunched over the wheel, and he smells of machine oil and pipe tobacco. He's a mechanic at the oil refinery plant, and he's worked the day shift. My real father lives in Santa Monica and works at a desk, solving hard mathematical problems. I'm proud of him; he's gentle, handsome, and smart. Yesterday I received a birthday present from him—a ballerina doll with a comical face and yellow yarn for hair. Her skirt is white tulle and her slippers satin. I need to name her.

Mathilda, I say to myself. *Mathilda,* I say again, closing my eyes. She's in a curtsy, the same as we just did in class. I cling to the thought of her now, at home on my whatnot shelf. *Mathilda.*

"Cat got your tongue?" Ray asks, his voice more like his normal one. Gruff.

I don't answer. As we enter our street, he looks at me, his eyes small and mean. "Aren't you going to thank me?"

I mutter the words under my breath.

Chapter 8

The next day, I tell Debbie about my bra. We're walking home from school, on an asphalt path that leads from the playground to our neighborhood. To our left, the winter fields open up, dirt and stubble now.

Debbie cheers. Wiry and quick, with big gray eyes and masses of curly brown hair gathered in a ponytail, she is half a head shorter than I am. When I came to our school two years ago, she—who knew everyone and was the best at hopscotch—made friends with me. Instantly, it seemed, we became best friends, walking to and from school together, playing at each other's houses, staying overnight, too. Today she wears a soft yellow sweater over a white blouse.

"Guess what?" she says. "A boy asked Cheryl to go steady." Cheryl is Debbie's older sister.

I feel a pang; her news outdoes mine. "Did your mother say it was okay?"

"Sure. It's no big deal."

We're in our housing tract now—pastel stucco houses, some with peaked roofs, some flat, all dotted with TV antennas. Bicycles and tricycles lie scattered on the lawns.

"My mother says girls shouldn't go steady until they're sixteen."

Debbie shifts her binder. "Larry and I went steady in fourth grade!"

I've met Larry, though he moved away before my family moved in. I met him last year when he came over to see Debbie. We played touch football, and I noticed how the other kids looked up to him. He was short and wore glasses, but he made them laugh. At Halloween, he came to our school carnival where I sat in a booth, dressed like a gypsy, in my mother's scarves and necklaces. I read his palm, feeling nervous because he was Debbie's boyfriend, and I wanted him to like me.

"I had a boyfriend then, too," I say. "But that was different." Cheryl has breasts and wears lipstick and shaves her legs.

We've walked as far as my street, Pony, which ends on our left in a low barricade and a row of poplars. Beyond it, the fields begin again. In spring, Debbie and I play there, trampling the grass into rooms and houses we imagine living in. Farther on is the truck in the driveway next to our house. They have a wooden plaque over the front door, made in shop by their eighth grader with their name burned in cursive. *The McDermott's* it reads. The apostrophe error drives my mom crazy.

"Cheryl says boys kiss with their *tongues*," Debbie says.

I'm half laughing, half squealing when we come through the front door. Ray is reading on the couch, and I worry he'll scold us. He gets up all smiles and comes forward to greet us. He points to a spot on Debbie's blouse. "What you got there?" When she looks down, he tweaks her nose. "Gotcha!"

She turns red.

He points to another spot right on the thin Dacron of her blouse, where her bra starts. "What you got *there*?"

I pull on her arm and drag her into my room.

A week later after school and Debbie's house, I find Mom in the kitchen. She's changed out of her school clothes and is folding laundry on the kitchen table.

"Something really bad happened," I say, panting. "On the way home, another girl called Debbie a Jesus hater," I say.

"That's terrible," Mom says. "What did Debbie do? What did you do?"

I tell her that Debbie screamed and told the other girl she never wanted to see her again. Then ran home with me chasing as fast as I could. At her house, Mrs. Levin was polishing the dining table. Debbie threw herself against her. Her mother shook her head knowingly and stroked Debbie's hair.

My mother gives such a shake to Mikey's overalls that they snap. "That's a very bigoted thing to say. Not all Lutherans are like that."

"The Levins are the only Jewish people I know."

"No. We had Jewish friends in Southern California. The Kaufmans. Grandma's friend Lenore is Jewish."

Debbie stopped crying when her mother told her they were having fried chicken for dinner. There is always plenty of food at their house. When I'm invited for dinner, we sit at the table in the dining room, and Mrs. Levin urges me to eat more. "Don't just take the wing, Kate. Take another piece."

Now Mikey makes crowing noises from his playpen, and I go into our dining area and swoop him up. Mom says it's a poor excuse for a dining room. The table is folded and pushed against the wall, a print of Van Gogh's *Sunflowers* hanging over it. We never eat there. The Levins' house smells different than ours, too. The windows, even the French doors, are draped in silky fabric; the carpet is thick and silky, the colors muted grays and mauves. A silver tea set glimmers on a breakfront.

I put Mikey down on the floor. "Ring around the roses," I chant. Around and around we go, him laughing, looking to the backyard, the hall, the front door, and the kitchen.

"Ashes, ashes, we all—"

"Fall down!" Mikey shouts. We land on the gold shag carpet, and I butt my head into his stomach, making him laugh harder. The carpet is worn everywhere, especially here, where everyone walks.

This is the heart of the house.

The pressure cooker is ticking loudly. "What are we having for dinner?" I ask.

"Stew."

Dear Dad,

Thank you very much for the ballerina doll. I've named her Mathilda. Do you think that fits her? In school we've been learning about number sets—pretty fancy, huh?

Miss Jensen is the best teacher I've ever had. She's an artist and we do all kinds of projects. We also have plays. She's young and pretty and funny.

If I were a better artist, I'd draw Miss Jensen for Dad. She's tall and full-figured, and she wears white blouses with the collar turned up and full skirts cinched by a belt. Her dark hair is cut in a pixie. Under her spell, we sixth graders behave. Her full name is Evelyn Jensen—a green and purple name. *E*s are green and *J*s purple.

One day in March, the principal takes the boys out and Miss Jensen shows the girls a film, *Growing up and Liking It*. She threads the projector and turns out the lights. "I'm here to tell you about your changing body," a smiling nurse tells us. We see a pretty girl brushing her blond hair and tying it with a pink ribbon. Now we see a diagram of the girl.

A light blinks on her forehead. "This is the pituitary gland. At just the right moment, it sends a message to other parts of your body." Two spots blink on her chest, then another two lower down. These are the ovaries, the size of walnuts. A new shape grows. "The uterus, shaped like a pear." Now all the points blink and buzz. The light on the forehead tells the walnuts to act and the pear to thicken, and now an egg is on the way. Two weeks later, the egg and everything is flushed out. "You can bathe when you have your period. And enjoy all your normal activities." At the end, the blonde girl rides her bicycle, pink ribbons sailing behind her.

Miss Jensen turns on the lights, she beckons us close to her desk. "Do you have any questions?"

"What does it feel like?" Linda asks Pammy. We all know who has started her period.

Pammy blushes. "You can't feel anything."

Debbie raises her hand. "The boys are going to tease us when they get back!"

"They will, won't they?" Miss Jensen says. "Let me handle them." She must, because when they file back in, they don't try to catch our eye or tease.

Walking home with Debbie, I tell her about our housekeeper's granddaughter. I was with my mother when we went to Mrs. Nowak's house to drop off her check. "Her granddaughter was there," I tell Debbie. "Her belly was so big she could hardly get out of her chair. Mrs. Nowak introduced her as Mrs. So-and-So, but later, Mom told me she wasn't married. She was only seventeen."

Debbie stops and stares at me.

"She's an unwed mother," I whisper.

"Oh God! My sister heard about a girl who was sent away."

We agree it's the worst thing that can happen to a girl.

———

A few weeks later, Steve Williams, the most popular boy in our class, asks Debbie to go steady. Walking home that day, she wears a chain with the ring hanging from it.

"But your mother!" I say. I feel panicky, as if the ground is shifting.

"I'll hide it before I get home."

The next day we play soccer, and I score two goals. Debbie is not impressed. I'm hot and sweaty as we walk home. Debbie grabs my arm. "Steve says Johnny wants to go steady with you. You have to say yes."

Johnny is Steve's best friend. His main interest is tetherball, which I hate, and we never talk. This is Steve and Debbie's idea. I stop. "I don't want to go steady with Johnny."

"Why?"

"I don't like him. And I'd have to lie to my mother!" I don't tell Debbie that I'm afraid. That going steady will make me a bad girl. That it will ask things of me that I don't want to do—like kissing.

Steve comes up behind us on his bike. "You have to say yes. He'll feel bad if you don't!" Steve's body gives off the heat and the smell of a boy.

Debbie trains her powerful stare on me. "Steve is right. You have to say yes."

A gust of wind blows dust into our faces.

The next morning, Steve tells me to meet Johnny in the kindergarten playground. When I do, Johnny opens his hand—dark and calloused from tetherball—without saying anything. The ring isn't shiny gold like Debbie's but plain gray. I let him put the chain and ring around my neck. When the bell rings, I walk back into the classroom, head down, afraid that Miss Jensen and everyone else will see. My chest tightens, my throat thickens. I put my head down on my desk.

"How many cloud types can you name?" Miss Jensen asks the class.

"Stratus!"

"Cirrus!"

"Cumulous!"

"Cocoa puffs!" Fred says. Everyone laughs, but I'm crying.

I feel a hand on my shoulder, the brush of Miss Jensen's skirt against my knee. "What's the matter, Kate?" she whispers. She asks Steve to take over the class and leads me into the supply room.

I show her the ring and tell her Johnny asked me to go steady. "Oh no," she says and pulls me close; she puts her arms around me.

"No wonder." Her shoulders and arms hold me, her breasts are soft, and she smells of Cashmere Bouquet. I want to stay here forever.

She lets go and holds me at arm's length. "Can you give the ring back to Johnny? At lunch?"

I nod.

"You'll figure out something to say. Thanks, but no thanks." She lifts the chain and ring from around my neck and hands them to me, then looks deep into my eyes. "You must never do anything you don't want to do."

I hold my breath, trying to take in her words. I think she's talking about boys, that I must never let *a boy* do something I don't want him to do. I nod, caught in her gaze.

At lunch recess, I follow Johnny to the tetherball court where he grabs hold of the ball, making the chain clank loudly.

I tap him on the shoulder and, without looking him in the eye, say the words I rehearsed. "I can't go steady, Johnny. I'm sorry. My mother won't let me." I hold out my open hand and he takes the ring and chain from me.

"Oh," he says, shrugging. Still holding the ball, he pushes the ring and chain into his jeans pocket, then slams the ball hard, and I dart out of the way.

Telling Debbie is harder. "Why not? Why not?" she cries out, shaking me.

"I don't like him that way. And my mother. I told you!"

"Chicken!"

In two days, we make up.

At the beginning of April, Miss Jensen takes the class out into the field to sketch. We make nests in the tall grass, dotted with purple lupine and orange poppy. We take out our sketch pads. The wind is blowing from the ocean, twenty miles to the west, the way it does in spring. I try to draw the clouds amassed overhead—cumulous clouds.

At the end of the hour, on our way back, Miss Jensen takes me aside. "I want to show you something," she says. She opens her sketchbook and shows me a finished drawing, every detail perfect, every corner filled in. The sketch is of me, my face half turned, hair across my cheek, wearing my red sailor blouse, the tips of the collar lifted by the wind. My face is tilted upward toward the sky, and I'm smiling.

Chapter 9

My sister and I sit across from Grandma Stuart in the kitchen of her house in Santa Barbara. It's the Memorial Day weekend. We look out to the sidewalk where people pass and sometimes wave, and to the park, an expanse of grass and trees. We're eating grapefruit, sprinkled with brown sugar, with special spoons.

"If I'd known there would be swear words, I wouldn't have taken you!" Grandma says, chuckling. Last night she took us to *Kiss Me Kate*.

"Darned isn't a bad word, is it?" I ask, thinking about the song, *"It's too darned hot."*

"No. You can say that." Grandma wears a lime green coat dress with snaps, and her silver hair is loose down her back. Our *practical grandma*, she calls herself. Our other grandma fusses over us, spoiling us.

I tell this grandma about my reading triumphs, how I read through all the colors in the SRA kit, short for Scientific Reading Associates. I don't mention Johnny and the ring.

Megan asks Grandma to tell us about taking the train to San Francisco when she was a young nurse. In my mind, I supply details, things an author would include—thick, black smoke coming out of the engine; the cold wind sweeping the platform; the leather valise in Grandma's hand. Once arrived, she stayed at the Chancellor Hotel, she tells us.

"You were trying to forget Grandpa," I prompt.

"Yes," she says coyly. She brushes imaginary crumbs off the red-

and-white checked tablecloth. "We cared very much for each other, but I knew he was too old for me."

Someday, I think, this will happen to me. I will love someone deeply.

Now she's telling us about being a nurse on the prairie, taking care of people through the flu epidemic of 1919, and never getting sick herself. She helped deliver babies, too.

"One time I was on a farm. After the woman delivered, I handed the placenta to the husband and told him to bury it somewhere."

"What's a placenta?" I ask.

She pauses. "It carries food to the baby in the womb, and it's delivered after the baby. Later, when the mother and baby were resting, I went out to the front porch to rest. Next thing I knew the dog was there, next to me, and he dropped something." Grandma thumps her forehead, laughing. "The placenta!"

Her story is a little disgusting, but exciting, too.

"Can we look at the album later?" I ask. I mean the heavy book in Grandma's bookcase, inscribed with gold letters, *The Country Home of Dr. and Mrs. D. A. Stuart.*

"Yes, after you wash up and get dressed. Wash your hands and your faces. With a washcloth."

I cling greedily to Grandma's love story, proof that love and lasting marriage are possible. My mother and father's love failed. Mom's marriage to Ray doesn't count. Who'd want to be married to him?

After I get dressed, I go out onto the front porch. I know every inch of this house, from the Fiesta dishes in the kitchen to the starched nurse's cap on Grandma's dresser. Across the street, two sandstone pillars, topped with a ball, guard the entrance to the park. I used to try to balance on the ball. A diagonal path cuts across the lawn meeting another in the middle. A playground sits there, shaded by a huge magnolia tree dropping leaves in the sand.

We have lunch downtown at the Copper Coffee Pot, where Grandma insists we have the chicken pot pie, and we eat too much. Afterward, she lies down in her room, and Megan and I play anagrams on the living room rug, an oriental carpet given to Grandma by a rich friend. I stroke its surface—ruby red and amethyst purple.

Megan takes her time with her first word. She doesn't remember that we lived here, twice. The first time Dad brought our swing set from Pacific Palisades and set it up on the lawn. The second time I broke my collarbone and wore a metal brace.

Megan makes *deer* and I decide not to steal it. I make *shape*.

The phone on Grandma's desk rings. She comes in looking worried. For her the phone is for serious business only. She says hello in a low voice. A man says hello back.

"Oh, hello, Dr. Murdoch," she says, sounding surprised. She sits in the desk chair.

I stop thinking about stealing Megan's word. *Who is Dr. Murdoch?*

He talks for a minute or two. When she answers, her tone is guarded. "She's doing well," she says. "She's living in Santa Maria with the children. She has remarried."

My confusion begins to clear. Grandma hasn't talked to this doctor in a long time; he knew Mom when we lived here.

I strain to catch the meaning of their words and find that I can attach them to scenes and events. Memories and feelings I'd didn't know I had. Mom screaming in the kitchen. Mom silent and not seeing me. A babysitter combing my hair and putting the barrettes in. Feelings of fear, even when I was playing with Peter. Mom going to a hospital and not talking when she came back.

Is Dr. Murdoch a friend of Grandma's? A doctor for crazy people?

"No," Grandma tells the doctor. "No trouble of that kind."

She wants to assure herself, too, I can tell. Her mouth is a straight line.

Grandma says goodbye to the doctor and puts the phone back on its base. We go back to our game.

That night, Megan and I lie on clean sheets on twin maple beds in Grandma's guest room. The beds are covered with white chenille spreads decorated with tufted flowers. Tall sash windows look out on the back patio and an orange tree. Once, when we were little, I woke up to a loud shaking of the house, a rattling of windows and furniture. Megan's crib rolled into my bed. Grandma came in.

"Don't worry. It's just a little storm."

"It's not a storm," Peter said. "It's an earthquake."

I knelt next to Megan's crib and stroked her back, saying, "Don't cry, baby."

"Let's pretend we're actresses," I say now.

"In *Guys and Dolls*," she answers.

"Tomorrow, because we're in the troupe, we're going to take the train to another city," I say.

"To San Francisco!"

"We'll stay at the Chancellor Hotel."

"We'll ride on the cable cars. With our boyfriends."

"And go shopping. I want to buy a dress in a department store."

"With matching shoes and a hat."

Our exchanges slow.

After a few minutes, Megan turns over. "Who was that man on the phone?" she asks.

I don't answer right away. Does Megan remember anything about that time? She was so young, the baby.

"I think he was a doctor Grandma knows."

"Why were they talking about Mom?"

I hear the wakefulness in her voice and her need for me to explain. "Do you remember anything about living here, before we moved to Santa Maria?"

"I remember the swing set on the lawn. I remember playing on the seesaw and the slide in the park."

"Mom was messed up then."

"What do you mean?"

"She had to go to a hospital, a mental hospital, Peter said. You were too little to remember."

"How was she sick?"

I can't tell her it was like Mom wasn't there—or she would scream. I whisper, "She had a nervous breakdown." I know the word from television shows and the *Ladies Home Journal*.

"Maybe the man who called was a head shrinker." We've heard this term on TV. I decide she needs to hear more. "We lived here again, when Mom was sick. She was pregnant."

"With Mikey?"

"No. This was before we moved to Santa Maria. I saw her in the bathtub here. Her belly looked so big and white."

The window is open, the leaves of the orange tree rustle, carrying the smell of blossoms. "I guess it wasn't Dad's baby. No one talked about it." I'm only figuring this out now. If it had been Dad's baby, they would have gotten back together.

"What happened to the baby?" Megan asks.

"Grandma told me she lost it."

"Was it a boy or girl?"

"A boy, I think."

Megan is so quiet I'm afraid I've hurt her. I summon a cheerful tone. "Dr. Murdoch wanted to know how Mom is now. And she is all right."

"Um huh," Megan murmurs.

I tell myself the same thing. Though sometimes, if Mom hurts herself or the pot boils over, she screams in the old way, so loudly and suddenly, I'm scared.

Chapter 10

It's weeks since Memorial Day. School is out, and I've said goodbye to Miss Jensen. I'm sitting on the floor of the living room, a volume of the *Junior Encyclopedia* open in front of me. Outside the screen door, a cloudless sky arcs over the neighborhood, and a sprinkler turns, with its regular click-click sound. I'm babysitting my brother Mikey while Mom does errands.

From Volume M, I read:

Menstruation, also known as a period or monthly, is the regular discharge of blood and mucosal tissue (known as menses) from the inner lining of the uterus through the vagina.

There's that word I don't like. "I've seen discharge on your underpants," Mom said the other day when she bought Kotex for me. I put the pink box in my underwear drawer, along with an elastic belt in its wrapper. Debbie and I took a napkin out to feel it.

What do mucosal tissues look like? Like jellyfish maybe, slippery and transparent. Soon this will happen to me. I hope I get my period before Debbie.

I put the volume back and get up, wishing Debbie were here and we could play badminton. She's not allowed to come over when I'm babysitting.

The house is quiet, Mikey asleep in his crib at the end of the hall. I tiptoe into my mother's room. The windows are open, the bed covered neatly in a quilt. On her desk, a calendar, a dictionary, and a tray for bills.

In her closet, larger and neater than mine, I find the box holding her new shoes and unwrap the tissue paper from around them. *Pumps,* they're called, covered in moss green suede, pleated across the toe. I slip my feet into them and practice walking. I pose in front of the full-length mirror, one right foot ahead of the other, like the models do in advertisements. I put the shoes back in the tissue paper and close the box.

On top of her dresser a small wooden jewelry case sits on a green scarf. I try on her gold clip-on earrings, spray a little Yardley's English Lavender on my neck, then put the earrings back where I found them.

In the top drawer, I run my hand over her silky underpants, ignoring the baggy nursing bras. I hold up her nylon stockings, her garter belts with their fasteners that dangle like feet. I spot a tube, the size of a toothpaste tube but smelling differently; part perfume part medicine. Next to it, a plastic case holding a strange object, round and yellow white, with a springy rim. It's the shape of a breast, but there's only one of them. I unbutton my blouse and place it over my breast, feeling a tingle. This has something to do with sex, with the scary noises I hear my mother making in the night, noises I can put no picture to but that I know Ray is causing.

I hear Mom's car pull up and put the rubber thing back and slam the drawer shut. I run down to meet her and help with the groceries.

The next day Mom calls me in from the backyard. She's been canning the apricots we picked from our tree this morning. She asks me to sit at the gray Formica table. My heart grabs; she's noticed I was in her drawer yesterday.

She sits, looking serious but not mad. "I need to talk to you about your ballet lessons," she begins. "You know I've decided to teach part-time next year. I want to stay home more to take care of Michael. I'm afraid we can't afford your ballet lessons anymore."

The breath goes out of me, the same as when a kickball smacked me in the stomach at school.

"You mean I have to stop?"

She nods. "I'm afraid so."

I'd rather be in trouble. I'd rather be punished for going into her drawer.

She straightens the salt-and-pepper shaker in the middle of the table. "It isn't just the lessons, but the ballet shoes and dance wear, the costumes for recitals. I stayed home to take care of you other children, and I don't want to do less for Mikey." She speaks evenly, soberly. "You have other abilities and interests."

My eyes sting. *Wrong, wrong, wrong!* Nothing else matters! Ballet is everything. It *is* me. I start crying.

"Ballet costs eight dollars a week!"

Money is the final argument, the rock buried in the sand that you stub your toe on. Checks and bills and house payments and the cost of a babysitter. I'm one of four children, and not the most important.

"But I *love* ballet!" I cry.

"It's important to think of others, not to be selfish."

In my room, I throw myself on my bed and sob, unchecked, until there are no tears left. The word *selfish* stings. I hug Mathilda to my chest, stroke the soft tulle of her skirt. I want to be a ballerina. I want to go to Sadler's Wells, like Margot Fonteyn.

I pray for a miracle. I pray that Mom will change her mind, or that Dad or Grandma will rescue me, or that Miss Sylvia will give me free lessons.

In a week, I'll go to Santa Monica to visit Dad. He'll understand; he'll save me.

Chapter 11

I sit next to Megan on the right side of the bus—the ocean side—my body tense with excitement. Across the aisle, Peter reads *MAD* magazine. This is the happy direction, south, toward Santa Monica and Dad. He and Grandma Laidlaw, our silly, impractical grandma, live together in a nice flat on Second Street.

At night, we'll listen to records in Dad's big room, hung with stellations, the colorful many sided objects he makes that look like stars. He makes them at night at his desk, cutting, painting, gluing. No one else is as smart or has such deft fingers. We'll have pastrami sandwiches and milkshakes at Zucky's Delicatessen. In Santa Monica, it's okay to want things.

I catch myself. "Dad doesn't live on Second Street anymore," I tell my sister.

"I know," she says. "He lives with Sally now."

They got married at Easter, in Carmel. On their way back they stopped in Santa Maria to see us, and we went to the beach. On the way home in the car, he told us. He was nervous, I could tell, so I started a cheer, Megan and Peter joining in.

Sally is tall and red-headed, fond of long swirling skirts and big hats. When I walk with her, she squeezes my hand three times, meaning, "I love you." She has two boys—Donny, who's eight, and Hal, who's my age.

"Where will we sleep?" Megan asks.

"At their house, I guess. They'll make room."

The bus winds through a canyon lined with boulders and comes out into a grove of sycamores. I grab Megan's arm. "The ocean!" A sparkling, dancing July ocean, Dad's favorite color. I picture him meeting us, outside the bus station. He's never failed us.

In Santa Barbara, the bus stops and we buy candy bars. "Don't get chocolate on your dress!" I tell Megan. I got a smear of Hershey's once on my skirt. We have to be perfect; everything has to be perfect when we go to Dad's.

Megan dozes, but I can't. When the cliffs of Santa Monica come into view, I poke her. "We're almost here!"

We pass Will Rogers State Park and the Sorrento Grill, and our beach, which we walk to from Second Street. My heart races as the bus climbs the steep slope and I spot the palm trees in the park, then the faces of Manny, Moe, and Jack, on the side of a building. Megan's face is pressed to the glass. Peter puts away his magazine.

Dad parks on a wide avenue in front of a pale green apartment block. We've driven east a long way, past billboards and parking lots.

I turn to get my suitcase, but Dad stops me. "Just Peter's. You and Megan will sleep at Grandma's."

"Really?"

"There just isn't room here. I'm sorry, honey."

He leads us up a stairway with open risers.

"They're here, they're here!" Sally calls out from an open door. She meets us on the landing, barefoot, in black capris and a white gypsy blouse. Harry Belafonte plays on the stereo, singing about daylight coming.

"I'm so glad to see you!" She hugs me, squeezing tight.

My eyes dart around the room, which strikes me as small. Dad's desk is in the corner, covered with drawings and ink bottles. Hanging over it, the Van Gogh print of the man in a yellow jacket. But where are his stellations?

Donny runs in and throws himself against us. Hal is next—grown tall—smiling and nodding. "Is that your lunch?" he asks, pointing at my purse, a basket shape with a shiny clasp. It's my first purse, and I blush.

"Come see the rest of the place!" Sally shows us the dining area and a back door leading to an outside staircase. A counter divides the table from the kitchen. "We're going to Gammy's tonight," she says. "I've been making potato salad."

Who's Gammy? What about Grandma Laidlaw?

A short hall leads to a bathroom and two small bedrooms. In Sally and Dad's room, bead necklaces hang from a mirror. The boys have bunk beds. An eightball sits on the toilet in the bathroom, and I gush over it to cover up my disappointment.

Along with no balcony, there's no sunporch, or dormer windows, or palm trees waving out the window. The apartment speaks of crowding and tight budgets, the same as in Santa Maria. My heart sinks; I can't ask Dad to pay for my ballet lessons.

In the hall, Sally says, "Your father gave me the Belafonte record for my birthday even though he doesn't like him. Wasn't that nice?" *Where is Dad?* I look around anxiously. He's letting Sally take over.

At nine that night, Dad parks on Second Street and together, we climb the walkway toward his old house. The dry fronds of the palm tree rattle in the night breeze, and I smell jasmine and maybe the ocean. Dad crosses the rush matting on the front porch. I wish he still lived here.

Grandma Lily waits at the top of the stairs, tiny, with narrow hips and a plump bosom. She wears her good blue dress, heels, and earrings even though it's late. "Phil, you promised sooner. I was worried." She hugs Peter, then leans away from him, smiling. "Let me have a look at you, you're so handsome. Kate, your petticoat is showing."

Inside, her parlor is the same—dark mahogany, pink satin stretched over a horsehair sofa, all lit by small lamps.

Dad takes our suitcases to his old room, with its sloping ceilings and dormers. "My old bed is still here for you," he says. The white wooden bed sits in the corner, against walls covered in pale green wallpaper with white morning glories. The brick fireplace is the same, too. But the air in the room is stale and warm.

"I left the stellations for you," he says.

I look up, feeling a rush of happiness. But too much is missing—the desk where he makes them, the print of the man with the beard and a yellow jacket.

"In the morning I'll pick the girls up to take them to the theater," he tells Grandma. "They're going to help." The play is a musical; he's the producer and Sally, the costume designer.

"But I promised the Braithwaites!" Grandma cries. "They so want to see the children!"

Dad's brow pinches. "We've already talked about this, Lily. I'm expected at the theater. You said you would tell them."

Lying in bed against the wall, I touch the paper, tracing its pattern. Tomorrow I'll go to rehearsal. Maybe a dancer will fall and I'll be asked to join the cast. That happens in books. Grandma pads in wearing her nightgown and opens the window. "This will feel good." A cool stream of air comes in, along with sound of a television.

She sits next to Megan and strokes her hair. "You two are the darlingest girls in the world. I've missed you so." She grasps my shoulder with small, bony fingers, then kisses my cheek. Kisses me too many times.

"I'm a little put out with your father. We were invited to see your cousins, but he says he doesn't want to drive all the way to Sherman Oaks tomorrow. He has his theater instead."

She smells of wine, heavy and sweet, and I wish I could wipe her kisses off. I wiggle deeper into the sheets. "That's too bad, Grandma. Maybe we could go another time." I have trouble remembering my cousins—three boys who played with cap guns the last I saw them.

I hear Grandma bump into a rocking chair on her way back through the living room. Then the sensations and images of the day tumble through my mind and body—the shaking of the bus, the diesel smell, the apartment building on Barrington, Grandma's smell. The apartment without Dad feels empty and lopsided, like a ship tilted.

"I need to talk to you a minute, Kate," Dad tells me, after we park under eucalyptus near the theater.

I stop, frightened. *Have I done something wrong?*

Dad pauses and scratches his head. "Grandma has been feeling low and sometimes she gets carried away. She's very upset about not going to the Braithwaites."

"I know. She told me last night."

"That's the problem." Now he sounds annoyed. "I thought it was settled, and then this morning she brought it up *again*. She says *you* want to see your cousins."

"I didn't really want to go!" I burst out.

"You didn't know but you stirred things up. Shelly and Roy are Catholic, you see, and they disapprove of divorce. They won't see Sally."

Tears sting my eyes. I watch Sally unlock the door to the barn; the costume shop is upstairs.

"You didn't know," Dad says, his voice gentle, "but please be more careful next time."

I look away and wipe my eyes.

I follow Sally to the costume shop. Santa Monica—the whole idea of Santa Monica—has changed. Dad is married and we can't stay with him; Grandma is unhappy; and he doesn't even live in Santa Monica anymore! Barrington Avenue is in Los Angeles! We won't go to Zucky's. It would cost too much.

Later, from the upstairs window, I watch Dad, Peter, and Mel, the director, move sawhorses out onto the asphalt. Peter says something and the men laugh.

"We need this kid," Mel says. "Can he stay for the run?"

Peter looks longingly at Dad. "Can I, Dad?"

Dad smiles sadly. "I wish you could."

My chest tightens and I slam the iron onto the board. I can hold a piece of plywood as well as Peter.

I must sigh loudly because Sally speaks up. "Did we tell you Jeanne and Walt are having us over for a pool party next Saturday? You can show off that new bathing suit you told me about."

Jeanne and Walt's pool is a dazzling turquoise rectangle taking up half the backyard. Their house, low and modern with white rocks covering the roof, sits on a hilltop in Redondo Beach overlooking the ocean. My suit is navy blue with a red-and-white band at the neckline, a junior size seven, ordered from the Sears catalog.

The men go in the water but just for a dip. A few women follow, wearing fancy bathing caps. Then Walt says the bar is open. The adults settle on redwood lounges and deck chairs, and we kids take over the pool.

We play Marco Polo and tease Donny, who cries easily. From the edge of the pool, I eye the women's smooth, tanned legs, and the drapes and tucks of their bathing suits. Arlene, full busted, in pink, has detached her straps. Sally wears black-and-white gingham. She has small breasts but shapely hips.

Later, the sun drops toward the ocean and we kids climb out of the pool. We swarm around the snack trays of potato chips and dip. Megan shivers and Sally wraps her in a towel. The men have changed out of their suits and hang them on a clothesline.

"Didn't know you were such a showoff, Phil," says Cap, Arlene's husband.

Dad looks at Cap, puzzled.

"Your jock strap on the line. You've let it hang out for all to see. Inviting comparisons?"

The adults laugh, Peter with them. Dad looks embarrassed. *Why? A jock strap is just underwear.*

"You should talk," says Walt. Cap wears a tiny suit that shows a lot of hair at the top of his thighs. And funny bulges.

"Have some more clam dip," Jeanne calls out.

The whole pool is in shadow now, its surface still. Peter sits next to Dad, and Sally is hugging Megan. I put my bathing cap back on and slip over to the diving board. I take three long steps, spring up into a pike—hands touching my pointed toes—and then cut the surface of the water like a knife. *Jackknife.* I hear shouts and clapping as soon as I surface.

"Encore!" Arlene calls.

"I'll get the camera," Dad says.

Peter jumps onto the board and tries a jackknife. Then a cannonball. Hal does a drunk man stumbling along the board and falling.

"You don't have your sister's grace," Jeanne tells Peter.

"She's a dancer," Sally tells everyone. "She takes ballet."

Dad returns with his camera and asks me to do the dive again. I mount the board but feel a stab, just as I spring up, as Sally's words penetrate.

———

The next day I ask Peter about the jock strap joke. We're alone at the Barrington apartment, he's reading on the couch, and I'm on the rug.

"Men like to brag about the size of their penises," he says, pretending to be casual. "You do know what a boner is, don't you?"

I shake my head.

"Your pecker gets stiff. I get them all the time. An erection." He takes a book from the shelf behind me. "Take a look. I found this yesterday."

The Ideal Marriage, it's called. *Male Anatomy and Physiology*, it says in the table of contents. *Female Anatomy and Physiology*. I flip through pages of dense text until I come to a full-page diagram showing the inside and outside of a man's body. I slam the book shut.

"Put it back," I say. "We shouldn't."

"Dad doesn't care. Here's another really dirty one." He hands me one called *Lady Chatterley's Lover*.

"Peanut butter and jelly for you. Cheese on rye for your dad." Grandma hands me the lunch bag. On our last day, it's just the four of us. The sky is still gray and foggy, but the glowing orb overhead tells us the sun is gaining and the fog won't last long.

We cross Ocean Avenue and the park that runs along the cliff. Climb over the barricade that says *Danger. Path Closed*. The dirt is powdery under our feet, brownish gold, the same color as the pinnacles around us. I keep up with Dad's bouncy walk. At the first turn, we look at the ruined castle that was once a casino; swallows fly in and out. We enter a tunnel where water drips from the ceiling. Down we go, now along steps shored up by railroad ties.

I hold Dad's hand and tell him about sixth grade, about Miss Jensen taking us out in the fields and drawing a picture of me.

"Just you?"

"Yes," I say proudly.

At the bottom, the traffic whizzes by on Highway 1, and we wait a long time for the light to change. Tomorrow we'll take the 9 am Greyhound, on this same route, going north. Away from Dad.

The sun has come out by the time we cross the parking lot behind the Sorrento Grill. We plod across the sand toward Lifeguard Station

37. On the last rise of dry sand, we lay our towels down.

Megan and I draw a circle just above the water line. We make a wall, then drip wet sand onto it, making turrets. We use shells and bits of seaweed for people and horses. After a wave slaps her on the bottom and levels our palace, I stand and rinse my hands.

"I'm going in," I tell Dad. "Does anyone want to come?"

"Later," Peter says. He's reading a new copy of *MAD*.

"Be careful," Dad says, looking out. "It's rough today."

I wade into the water, trailing my fingers, trying out names for the colors I see, from the crayon box—jade, azure, sapphire. It's so hard to name the color of water. I'm caught by a breaking wave, feel it knock me sideways. I'm ready for the next one, and dive under it. Out and out I go, swimming the breaststroke, my best stroke. I've been in lifesaving class this summer and can swim twenty-five laps. I know how to jump in the water and save someone. I'm past the breaking waves now, past being able to touch the bottom. I float on my back and daydream. *When I grow up, I'll live near the ocean, I'll live in Santa Monica and be a dancer or an actress.*

A gull shrieks near my ear and I right myself. I look around. The lifeguard station isn't in front of me where it should be, but over to the left. It looks small. *How did that happen?* I start swimming back toward it, but my strokes don't take me anywhere. I try to push off the bottom, forgetting I can't touch. My heart freezes. *I must be in a riptide.* From lifesaving I remember the rule; swim on a diagonal not against the current. *But diagonal to what?*

A lifeguard swims by carrying a white float. "Are you all right?" he shouts.

"Yes," I say. I've taken lifesaving, I can't ask for help. Other people need him more. He moves away.

Swim on a diagonal. I struggle. I see Dad on the shore, hand over his eyes looking for me. I swim harder, doing the crawl now, counting my strokes to concentrate. I must be making progress because the waves lift me up and break in front of me now. One pulls me up, very high, then hurls me down, tumbling me over and over, scraping my body against the gravelly bottom. The water churns over me, filling my nose and mouth. When I'm able to get up, I'm gasping and water streams out of my nose.

Dad is there. He gestures at my suit, which has come untied. My breasts are showing. I pull it up, too shaken to feel embarrassed. He puts his arm around me and guides me up the sand.

"Why didn't you let the lifeguard help you?" he asks.

"I don't know." I start crying.

I follow him back to the towels, and drop onto the sand, my body still tumbling, my head ringing. I'm shivering and my nose and ears run.

"It happened so fast!" I tell Dad. "By the time I felt the riptide it was too late!"

He nods. "The lifeguards have put up the red flag. I told Peter not to go in."

I burrow my cheek into the warm sand. The worst part was the end. It hadn't mattered that I could swim a mile or do a jackknife. The ocean did what it wanted with me.

Chapter 12

The visit to Dad's is behind me, my tan has faded, and Debbie is on vacation. I'm home babysitting again. I feel bored and restless. Once again, I wander over to the encyclopedia set next to the front door and pull out Volume M. No one will see if I look something up. *Male Reproductive System.*

The phone rings. I hurry to the kitchen before it wakes Mikey.

"Is this Kate? This is Mrs. Childers from Miss Sylvia's. I'm calling to sign you up for fall."

My stomach drops. For starters, I don't like Mrs. Childers. She's crabby and has beady eyes. At our recital last June, she plucked at the ruffle of my costume. "I told your mother how to sew this and she did it wrong," she said.

"Advanced intermediates will be on the same schedule as last year," Mrs. Childers is saying. "Tuesdays and Thursdays at 4 pm."

On the small chalk board in front of me, in my mother's perfect hand is written:

Milk

Eggs

Bread

Detergent

She is at the grocery store now, buying those things. Why isn't she here to answer Mrs. Childers? I don't want to be the one to say!

"My mother says I have to quit," I tell her.

I hang up before hearing Mrs. Childers' response. Forgetting the open encyclopedia, I run into my room and fling myself down on my bed, crying. This time I don't pick up Mathilda. I am lost, forever.

I imagine Mrs. Childers telling the other mothers, "*Kate's parents can't afford lessons anymore. They're poor. They have too many children.*" I imagine Miss Sylvia thinking I don't *want* to dance anymore! No, I want to tell her, I want to dance more than anything!

Thinking about class starting without me in September, the girls dressing and lining up at the *barre*, I feel a great gaping emptiness. I sob loudly into my pillow.

I don't hear the sound of the door opening and someone entering. Someone touches my shoulder, and I lift my head. Ray has come in. I'd forgotten he was home, sleeping in his room after working the nightshift.

"Whatcha crying about, little girl?" He pulls me upright and takes my chin in his hand.

I've been wrong about Ray, I think. He's nice, not mean. "Mom made me quit ballet," I say.

"*Ah,*" he croons and hugs me, then wipes my tears. My body relaxes.

"I don't like to see you so sad, smiley one." One hand moves from my shoulder to the top button of my blouse. His eyes dart down, eyes and hands quick and certain—the same as when he played the game with Debbie. His voice carries the same thickness, the same heat as when he took me to Colliers Apparel.

He undoes one button, then another, until my bra is uncovered. *He should not be doing this!* His breathing quickens and he pulls the straps off my shoulders. "How are these developing?"

He fingers my nipples, which I have barely looked at myself, let alone touched. He takes them in his hands, which are rough and creepy. A strange tingly sensation goes down my spine.

I have no voice to cry with, no arms to push against him, no legs to carry me away.

A car pulls into the driveway, and Ray lets go of me and backs out of my room.

———

A week later, after I get out of bed, I feel a warm, sticky wetness in my shorty pajama bottoms. I pull them off; they look as if they've been dipped in blood. A scarlet flood has come out of me.

"What happened?" my sister says, looking scared. "You're all bloody."

"My period, I guess." I put on a show of confidence and open the drawer holding the box of Kotex and the belt. In the bathroom I lock the door and fool with the belt until the clips are straight. The pad feels thick and strange between my legs. I won't be able to go to swim practice today. I don't feel proud or confident like the girl in the film. The blood has come out of me because of Ray.

After breakfast, I find Mom in the family room sorting dirty laundry. A few months ago, she and Ray converted the garage into a room, adding a round table where we eat and Mom sews, and an old green sofa given to us by friends. I stand beside her as the machine fills, gathering courage.

"Mom," I say. I hold up the shorty pajama bottoms in front of her. The water whooshes noisily into the machine.

Her face freezes. "What happened? Did you hurt yourself?"

Doesn't she remember getting me the Kotex and belt? "It's my period, I guess."

"Oh. Let me have them. I'll soak them."

When I ask about swim practice, she says no, I shouldn't go. On the round table, Mom has laid out the cut pieces of fabric for the skirt and blouse she is making for me. Plain blue for the skirt, pink and blue flowers for the blouse—my outfit for the first day of school.

As soon as my chores are done, I run to Debbie's house. She drags me into the bathroom so that I can show her. "Ah, that's not much," she says. "That's no big deal."

"You should have seen it before," I counter. "It was a lot."

Two weeks later and my period has stopped. It's afternoon again. Mom is out and my little brother sleeping. I take Volume M to my room, sit on my bed, and open it to *Male Reproductive System*. Peter has told me that Ray told him that his penis would get stiff and white stuff would come out of it. Yuck. Another discharge. A diagram shows a cross section of a man's lower body, with tubes and arrows going every which way, labeled with strange words— *glans, urethra, testicle.*

The door opens across the hall and Ray comes in half dressed in his undershirt and jeans. I am seized with fear. He isn't wearing glasses, and the look in his eyes chills me. Without speaking, without trying to be nice, he takes me by the hand and pulls me off my bed. Pulls me across the narrow hall and into his room. My bare feet feel the coolness of the shiny linoleum. Mom keeps the house so clean. I'm wearing new aqua shorts with white polka dots because I hope to go to Debbie's when Mom gets home.

He pulls me into the darkened bedroom. The window shades are down and yellow afternoon light filters in. I don't want to be in this room, something bad lies here.

Next to Mom's dresser, he forces me against his chest and kisses me, pressing his horribly wet lips and mouth against mine. My hip knocks against the dresser.

Silently, I plead for help from Mom's green scarf, her wooden jewelry box, her bottle of Yardley's English Lavender, her photos of us as babies. I beg her to come home.

He forces me backward onto the unmade bed, pulls my shorts and underpants down around my ankles. He pushes my shoulders to the bed and puts his penis against my crotch, against the soft part. His penis feels like a coat hanger, and I think how strange to have a body part that feels like a coat hanger. It sticks me and wants to go in.

I twist and struggle hard against the weight on me. I cry out and the weight relents. I jerk out from under him, rolling off the bed. I stumble across the floor, pulling up my underpants and shorts, and I run.

Running, running. I run toward the light, across the living room and past the doors leading to the backyard. I can't go outside. I run through the kitchen to the opposite end of the house, the new room, and throw myself down on the green sofa. The sprung cushions poke against my ribs.

My sobs come from a place so deep I feel I'm being turned inside out. I'm a bad girl, like the worst girls in my school. I'll get pregnant, my life is over. I'll be sent away. I grip the cushions of the sofa, grabbing at the green and black fabric. No one can help me, no one can undo this—not my mother or my brother, not my father or grandmother. Not Debbie or Miss Jensen. I am alone.

I don't hear him come in, but I feel him shake my shoulder. He bends over me, awkwardly rubs my shoulders, speaks softly. "No need to take on so, honey . . . mustn't cry like this."

Chapter 13

When my mother finishes my blue skirt and flowered blouse, I try them on and pose in front of the hall mirror. I should walk differently in junior high. No running, no sweating. A half yard of the blue cotton is left over, and I decide to sew a sleeveless top so that I have what *Seventeen* magazine calls coordinates. The machine sits under a window in the family room, an old black Singer in a mahogany cabinet. Mom threads the machine and shows me how to lift and lower the presser foot. "To start the machine, press here with your leg," she says. "Keep your fingers away from the needle."

Peter coaches me on junior high. "Your locker may be really far from your homeroom," he warns. He's two years older, an eighth grader, confident, even cocky. He uses Brylcreem to comb the sides of his hair back—like the Everly Brothers. Two girls walk by our house every afternoon, hoping to see him. He has a transistor radio, bought with money from his paper route.

Sometimes he lets me to listen to it: *Twenty-six miles across the sea, Santa Catalina is a waitin' for me . . .*

The pattern for my top has four pieces—a front and a back, a neck facing, and a sleeve facing. On Labor Day, I take the pattern pieces from the envelope and smooth them flat. I iron the length of blue cotton.

Shouting breaks out in the kitchen, and I stand the iron on its end.

"What the hell are you doing?" Ray's voice. I see him grab my brother's shoulder.

Peter stands in front of the refrigerator, holding an open bottle of milk.

"Are you an animal? Jeez. No consideration for anyone but yourself! You just put your germs on that milk bottle for the whole family to catch. Your little brother for Christ sakes."

"I'm sorry. I was thirsty."

"You're a slob is what you are. A heathen. Wash off that bottle good."

Mom comes in from the backyard, laundry basket in her arms.

"You can do without milk for a week," Ray finishes.

"What's going on?" she says.

Peter holds the bottle under the faucet.

"Your son just drank straight from the milk bottle."

Mom looks stricken; she hates it when Ray shouts at Peter. "How could you, Peter?" Then to Ray, "But can't you punish him some other way? He needs his milk, he's growing."

They move into the dining area, arguing, then come back in.

"Hand over your transistor radio," Ray says. "You'll do without it for a week. Maybe then you'll learn some manners."

"Get your radio," Mom says, more for Ray than Peter.

Peter flushes red, and his eyes tighten in anger. He mutters something on his way out.

Ray grabs his arm. "What'd you say?"

"Nothing."

"You'd better not say anything."

Later that afternoon, the newspaper truck stops in front of our house and I hear the thump of the bundle thrown onto the driveway. I finish pinning my pattern pieces and go outside to help Peter fold.

The paper comes folded in half. We fold it twice again, headline on top. Then we stretch a rubber band around it. We're kneeling on the grass next to the driveway.

Last night I woke up to see Ray sitting on Megan's bed. I smelled his pipe smell and heard the sheets rustle. Megan whimpered and turned away, tearing at my heart. I was frozen. I couldn't do anything.

"Sorry about your radio," I say to Peter.

"He's a bastard!" Peter throws the folded paper onto the pile. "I hate him."

"I hate him, too." I stop folding. "Can I tell you something?"

He looks up at me. "Sure."

I lower my head, and speak in a small voice. "Ray does nasty things to me."

Peter freezes. The color drains from his freckled face. "You're kidding."

I shake my head. "He took my clothes off and touched me. Megan, too. He tried to put his thing in me."

"Goddammit!" Peter says, his voice low and angry. His brow draws tight, and I know he's thinking hard. He shakes his head.

"What are we going to do?" I ask.

"We have to tell Mom."

The next day, Peter calls Megan and me into the dining area, next to Mikey's playpen, and tells us to wait. He calls into the kitchen where Mommy is washing the lunch dishes. "We need to talk to you, Mom." I look outside, wishing I were at Debbie's house, wishing I were not me.

Mom must hear something in Peter's voice. She turns off the water, wipes her hands, and comes in.

I stand close to Peter, feeling the tension in his body, the smell of cut grass and boy sweat. Megan clings to my side, her soft arm on mine. My bare feet rake the carpet.

"What is it?" Mom's eyes sweep our faces, the scared, shamed look on my face and my sister's, the frown on Peter's.

"Ray does nasty things to the girls," Peter says.

She inhales sharply and turns to me. Her eyes burn into me. "Is this true?"

"Yes," I say. I feel as if the earth may drop from beneath us. We're doing the unimaginable—telling on an adult. Worse, the telling is about sex.

I expect her to swear or get angry or yell at us. When she's really mad she screams "Goddammit!" But she is silent. Her face crumples, and she runs out of the room and into the hallway. The door to her room slams shut.

Megan and I look at Peter, expecting him to tell us what to do.

He shrugs and crosses the living room. "I'm going to Ronnie's," he says. Megan still clings to me, her freckled arms hanging limply at her sides. She's so young, and I'm supposed to know what to do!

After a minute, she tiptoes out into the kitchen and then the backyard.

I stay where I am, rooted to the carpet, waiting. I need to see if Mom is all right. I've seen that look on her face before.

A sound rises from down the hall, a terrible sobbing, an animal noise. It pierces the thin walls, charges the particles in the air. High pitched, out of control. I'm sure the house will collapse. We will all be lost, and it's my fault.

I take my bike and pedal it to the end of the street, to the barricade and row of poplars that borders the fields.

When I return, it's quiet, and I tiptoe down the hall. Through the open door of Mikey's room, I see Mommy bent over the crib, clutching him, sobbing still, but quieter. I don't matter as much as he does.

I back away wishing I'd never told. I stumble toward the other end of the house, to the table where my blue cotton is laid out. I pick up the scissors and begin to cut.

―

At breakfast the next morning, my mother pours orange juice for

Megan and me and stirs the oatmeal. She's not crying or acting weird.

"I'd like you to pack a toothbrush and pajamas," she says. "I'm taking you away for a few days."

"To Grandma's?" I ask.

"No, to Mrs. Edwards's."

I hardly know Mrs. Edwards. She's a teacher friend of Mom's, an older woman who lives alone on the other side of town. Why aren't we going to Grandma's? Her house is only an hour away, and we're always welcome! I see her on the porch, white-haired and square, in her black dress, watching for us to arrive.

Brushing my teeth, packing my things, the answer comes; Mom doesn't want Grandma to know about Ray.

Mrs. Edwards greets us on her front porch, tall and thin, with a dent in her skull behind one ear. It shows through her short, pale hair. She had an ear infection when she was young, Mom told us, before they had penicillin. She makes us chocolate pudding and lets us watch *77 Sunset Strip*.

That evening, she runs us a bubble bath and tells us that when her daughter was a teenager, she found her in the bathtub with all her underwear floating around her. "She was washing it," Mrs. Edwards said laughing. "Two birds with one stone!" It is strange to sleep in this house, in her daughter's old room. What if I were Mrs. Edward's daughter and had grown up here? As soon as the wish comes, I push it away. I wouldn't have Megan or Peter.

At home two days later, I find my pattern pieces on the oak table where I left them. School starts in five days—El Molino Junior High. Who will I get for a teacher? Gingerly I take the pins out. Peter says Mr. Eager is mean. Will the other kids like me? Will Debbie be in my class?

I pin the blouse front to the back at the side seam. Boys and girls have PE separately, Peter says. I carry the pieces to the sewing machine and sit. I find the little ruler under the presser foot, lay the cloth at the 5/8 mark, and lower the pressure foot. Slowly I push my thigh against the lever. The machine hums, the needle flashes up and down.

"Kate, stop!" Mom's voice is raised. "I need to talk to you." She stands in the kitchen doorway, dressed to go out in her green shirtwaist dress and the heels she wears to church. She looks stern, angry even. My heart skips.

Her voice lowers, but she doesn't move closer. "I need to ask you about what Ray did to you."

My stomach contracts and twists. I feel alone, no Peter to speak for me or tell me what to do. I search out her eyes, those stern, intelligent eyes I know so well. "Mommy, please!" I say softly.

"Did he—" she breaks off and looks away from me. "Did he penetrate you?"

The word shocks me. My brain races. She's speaking of his thing, his penis. Did it go inside me, into the place where the blood comes from? Again, I'm lying flat on the unmade bed, the yellow window shade down, my shorts around my ankles, his body on top of me. His thing pressing against the soft place.

"No," I say, in a stricken voice. I have no words to tell her more.

Her face and shoulders relax.

I want to cry out for help, to call her Mommy again, to ask her what if I'm pregnant, but she's gone.

Two days pass. I sew white rickrack around the hem of my blue top and try it on in front of the mirror. Ray is still living at our house. Nothing has changed in the rhythm of our days. On the day before school starts, Mom calls the three of us into the dining area, the same place where we told her a week ago. Ray stands braced against the kitchen door frame, his head down.

I feel the tension in Peter's body, the fear in my sister's that matches my own.

"Ray has something he wants to tell you," Mom says.

He lets go of the door frame but doesn't look at us. She forced him into doing this. "I'm sorry for what I did to you girls," he says, his voice low and hoarse.

"And?" my mother prompts sharply.

"And—" he mumbles, "I promise not to do it again."

He doesn't look or sound sorry. I don't believe him. I sneak a look at Peter.

Ray turns into the kitchen and goes out the back door.

"Is that all?" Peter asks. He tries to sound casual, but I hear the anger in his voice, his heart breaking.

"No," Mom says. "I need to say something, too. Don't discuss this with your friends. Or anyone else. This is a private matter. Do you understand?"

I nod. Ray is not leaving. What he did was bad but not so bad he has to leave. Or go to jail. It's because he didn't stick his thing inside me. Something else—the life of adults—is more important than we are.

Chapter 14

A few days later, I pick Debbie up, and we walk south on Miller until we come to the big cypress hedge, which tells us to turn right. Despite my new blue skirt and flowered blouse, I feel nervous. Debbie, wearing a pretty yellow dress, is quiet, too. More kids join us until we reach the massive U-shaped building that is El Molino Junior High. We know to enter the right side, which is the seventh-grade wing. Our names are posted with our classroom on a bulletin board. Some of the rooms have a *T,* meaning temporary. They've added portable classrooms. I find my name on *4T*—but not Debbie's.

My homeroom teacher, Mrs. Florian, has platinum hair and long mauve nails. She assigns us to write autobiographies. I pour out my heart in mine, writing poetically about the years in Southern California with Mom and Dad in a house where classical music played, and pansies grew in the backyard. I name my favorite record, *Scheherezade*. I want Mrs. Florian to notice me.

Before she can return our autobiographies, we're tested to see who will be admitted to the advanced math class. The Russians have just launched Sputnik and it's our responsibility to catch up with them. Mrs. Florian calls out my name. I gather my books and papers and cross over to the main building to Mr. Rasmussen's homeroom.

Abracadabra! As in *Scheherazade*, I am transformed. School takes over my life. New students, teachers, and school subjects catch me up in a whirlwind, making me forget home. They whisk me away from the girl crying on the green sofa. I am remade.

Abracadabra! I study algebra and good grooming. I model myself after Cecilia, a new friend, and listen reverently to Mrs. Mendès, our language and social studies teacher. She is beautiful, with ivory skin and black hair, and a yellow spot on her middle finger from smoking. She rules by wit and intelligence, teaching us about the four cradles of civilization—Mesopotamia, Egypt, Babylon and China. Above the blackboard stretches a timeline that my eyes keep rising to. All of history is captured there, immensities of time along a horizontal line, a great orderly progression, everything noted, everything remembered.

It is almost possible to believe that nothing bad happened to me.

Chapter 15

"It seems to me," Frances says, "that you were always expected to be older than you were. Your mother sent you to school early, she expected you to excel. She had you babysitting when you were only ten. When the worst happened to you she expected you to deal with it like an adult."

I nod, trying to digest this. Outside, a shining patch of magenta draws my eye. "I can't keep bougainvillea alive over the winter," I say.

She huffs.

I sigh and lower my head. "I got the message early, yes, that I was supposed to help my mother. When I was in first grade and my brother Peter seven, she left us alone. Megan was allowed to be a baby. And Mikey, too."

Frances takes this in silently.

"And look at me at the sewing machine! Teaching myself to sew!"

My chest tightens, my breathing stops, and I feel cold. Again, I feel my mother's presence behind me in the family room, telling me to stop sewing. I feel the pressure of her will, forbidding me from feeling, forcing me to give evidence. I've been over this with other therapists, but not one as demanding as Frances.

"What did you learn that day from your mother?"

"That no one would help me. That I had to hide my feelings."

"This is what we analysts call a soul death."

My arms have been wrapped around my midsection, and now I

clutch myself more tightly, fingers on ribs. If something like a soul death occurred that day, I've been fighting ever since to stay alive.

"Your mother didn't want to know anything else."

"She seemed relieved by my answer. I was giving her the answer she wanted. It meant Ray didn't rape me."

She studies me. "What do you think now? Did he rape you?"

I squeeze myself even more tightly, as if the organs themselves would fall out. Now I'm back in the bedroom with the shades pulled down, trying, trying to block out the figure of Ray. "No, not technically."

"What did it feel like to you, as a child?"

I want to beg Frances to stop. I want not to feel this agony. I squeeze my eyes shut, saying nothing.

"His pants were down and so were yours. You were a child!"

I shake my head back and forth. "I wasn't treated like a child. I didn't think of myself as a child."

"You felt it was the worst thing that could happen to you! You were afraid you were pregnant! How is that different from rape?"

"I don't want it to be true." I begin crying.

"I know." She takes a deep breath and we're quiet for a minute. "What did your mother do after this?"

"She went to our family doctor, with Ray, I guess." I wipe my eyes with a tissue, blow my nose. "He referred Ray to a psychiatrist in another town. Mom told me this later. Ray saw him just once and afterwards the doctor told Mom that Ray had said he wouldn't do it again. 'And besides,' he said, 'he says he doesn't have any money.'"

"So, life went on."

"She and Ray bought a new house!" I shout, almost jumping from my chair. "The solution to incest was a bigger house! Four bedrooms instead of three! Two bathrooms instead of one! I submit this to the tribunal as further evidence of her guilt. The purchase of the house."

"She could have stayed in the old house and thrown Ray out. She made a financial commitment with Ray."

"When I brought this up once, she insisted it happened a year later. No, I told her. I remembered walking from the new subdivision to my new friend Celia's and then to school. I went to the county records office in Santa Barbara and found both deeds of sale. And my sister turned up a letter she wrote to our dad mentioning the move. It was dated November 24, 1959."

"Proof positive," Frances says.

"Mom had to cash out her retirement account to make the down payment. That was against the rules, and she had to pay the money back."

Frances glances up at the clock, a sign we have about five minutes left. She sits forward in her chair. She'll sum up now, give me something to think about. "You learned that summer not to ask for help. You learned that feelings were dangerous. They led to hysteria and breakdown. Instead, you had to deny or repress them."

Always at this point, I begin wishing I could stay here, in this chair, forever. "I remember a high school teacher commenting on my poise, yes," I say. "My self-control. Before, in junior high, I was still myself. I had close friends and strong emotions. The damage took a while to sink in."

Frances nods, eyes fixed on me. "We'll talk about that next Wednesday."

Chapter 16

I look for Debbie in my new classroom, but she isn't here. I recognize Larry, Debbie's fourth grade boyfriend whose palm I read. Across the aisle sits a girl I've never seen. Her name is Cecelia, white and green in my mind, because *C*s are white and *L*s are green. She's tall and willowy, beautiful.

I keep sneaking looks at her. Her wavy brown hair is cut in a grown-up style, like in the magazines. Her figure is grown-up, too. She is poised, reserved, and I am careful in my approach.

At recess, everyone surrounds Larry. He grins at me, eyes bright behind glasses. "I know you. You're Debbie's friend. We played touch football together."

"You came to our school carnival, too!" I say, smiling. "I read—"

"You said your hair was blond because you drank peroxide when you were a baby."

He turns to a big hulking boy named Ron Izzi. "Izzat dirt on your upper lip?" He points to Ron's mouth, where a mustache creeps.

Larry notices everything, lightning quick, and he makes fun. I like him.

On the third day of class, I ask Cecilia for a sheet of graph paper. When class is over she says, "You can call me Celia."

"What school are you from?"

"I'm not from here. I'm from Atascadero," she says, blushing slightly. *Is she shy?*

"Atascadero!" I say, nodding, as if it's exotic. "I've never been there."

She brightens and asks how I like Mr. Rasmussen. "This math is weird, isn't it?"

We're learning set theory. Our texts are lemon yellow, paper-bound books from Yale University that look like they've just been run off on a mimeo machine. *School Mathematics Study Group*, they say, and they teach math in a new way.

In November, my family moves to a four-bedroom house on the other side of town, with Dutch-style trim and diamond-paned windows. Supposedly it's nicer than Pony Street but the front and back yards are bare dirt, no grass or trees. At the end of our street is a farm with a water tower, and beyond it fields of broccoli and cauliflower stretch all the way to the dry bed of the Santa Maria River.

I set out for school in the cool foggy mornings, passing houses that look like ours, all with smooth, curved driveways. I turn onto El Molino Avenue, and three blocks on Celia waits for me. I carry my binder and books the way she does, cradled lightly in front of me. Boys sling them under one arm. The binders are covered in blue cloth, divided by subject. In the morning, we have math and science with Mr. Rasmussen; in the afternoon, language and social studies with Mrs. Mendès.

We walk home in a pack of other kids, passing the tall cypress hedge. Sometimes I see Debbie and Pammy and feel a pang of guilt; they turn off toward my old neighborhood. Celia and I stop at Forrest's Drugs on Broadway to buy a Mounds bar for her, an Abba Zabba for me. Alone now, under pepper trees, we gossip. We feel special, singled out, known at school as being with the smart kids. We have crushes on both our teachers. We were thrilled one morning when Mr. Rasmussen grabbed Ron Izzi by the collar and threw him out of the classroom.

"Mrs. Mendès smokes, you know," I say. "You can see the nicotine stain on her finger."

"Do you think she's divorced?" Celia asks.

"No." She has one little boy. She graduated from Emerson College in Boston, which accounts for her accent and nice manners. "She can't be divorced. Her husband must be off at sea or in the military."

When we reach Celia's, her mother, a smiling, broad-hipped woman, makes a fuss over us. "What a lovely plaid," she says, fingering my red pleated skirt. "I could run up one for you, honey."

"No, Mother, I have plenty of skirts," Celia says. "It would make my hips look big!"

In the bathroom we comb our hair and try on lipstick, which I wipe off before leaving. "Your haircut makes you look too young," she says. "Get it cut like mine." Hers is called a bubble.

In social studies, we advance along the timeline, from Egypt to Ancient Greece. Mrs. Mendès asks us to write reports on our favorite Greek god.

"Who have you chosen, Kate?" she asks in class.

"Artemis, goddess of the hunt."

"And shunner of men!" Larry shouts. "Kate doesn't like boys."

Mrs. Mendès gives him a challenging look. "And you, Mr. Hohlman?"

"Bacchus," he says. "God of wine and orgies."

"A minor god," Mrs. Mendès says dryly.

"My dad takes me to plays in Los Angeles," Larry brags one day after lunch. We're sitting on a bench outside the seventh-grade wing.

I've seen a lot of plays, too, I tell him, also in LA. Back in our desks we make lists to see whose is longer. We both like *Guys and Dolls*.

Larry's mother is called in for a conference about his conduct. Celia and I spot her on our way past the classroom, sitting opposite

Mrs. Mendès at a student desk. Later, Greg, Larry's best friend, tells us what happened. "Mrs. Mendès said Larry has a very high IQ, one-forty-five, genius level!"

"Wow!" we say.

Greg, friendly and bearish, shakes his head. "He's gonna be thrown out of special math if he doesn't shape up."

Celia labors over her drawings of Aphrodite, pastels of the goddess emerging from the sea in silky garments. Celia's handwriting is delicate and even, tall narrow loops, slightly withholding, blue ink on white paper. No cross-outs. Her fingers are tapered, the nails buffed ovals. She doesn't need any of the lessons on grooming we're getting in Home Ec.

At seven on a Friday night in November, we huddle in a packed circle in the auditorium of the Veterans Memorial Building. When the DJ plays "Poison Ivy" and "The Hokey Pokey," we dance, the girls anyway. Then the first slow song comes on, "Mr. Blue." Jeff, a tall, handsome boy not in special math, asks Celia to dance. He asks her on the next slow dance, too. Chaperones circulate, on the lookout for cheek-to-cheek dancers.

When no one asks me, I look around for a friend. Larry lurks at the edge of the dance floor, eyes down. I don't go to him.

When the last dance is announced, "Put Your Head on My Shoulder," Jeff and Celia dance again, two tall, handsome gods, cheeks close but not touching. I feel a tap on my shoulder. It's Jerry, a classmate with fair hair swept back from his forehead and curly eyelashes. He asks in a husky whisper.

That night, I stay over with Celia in her lavender bedroom and we play a game we call Hogan, named after Indian dwellings. We crawl under the covers and stand up to form posts, then fall onto the mattress, knocking into each other. So she can be silly, like me! She wears a bra under her nightgown, and her legs are smooth and brown, shaved.

The next day, we go out walking in the rain past my house to the farm and along a dirt road.

"We're thirsty!" I cry, my mouth open. It's the first rain of the season.

"Who do you like?" she says. Our tennis shoes squish. She smells of her mother's Charles of the Ritz oil.

"Jerry, I guess," I say. "Who do you like?"

"Jeff," she says, matter-of-factly. Then she pauses and gives me a sidelong glance. "But who do you *really* like?"

I blush. "Larry."

She spins around. "So do I!"

We burst into laughter and run back, splashing each other, exultant.

—

The following Monday, I get my period for the first time since August. Does this mean I'm not pregnant? Four napkins are left in the box my mother got me, and I use them that day and the next. On Wednesday, I wake up to find the napkin soaked to the edge.

My mother's Kotex sits on the top shelf of the linen closet. I stare at it, but I don't dare touch it. Touching and taking are forbidden—stealing. She's in the kitchen cooking. I try to imagine myself asking. Impossible.

I stuff thick layers of toilet paper into my underpants and go to school. When Celia has her period, we call it *Glockamoora*. She's had hers for a year. In the girls' restroom after lunch, she calls into my stall. "How are things in Glockamoora?"

"Not good," I say. "Do you have a nickel for the Kotex machine?"

"No," she says, and the warning bell rings.

Panic seizes me; I pull out as many sheets of the slick brown paper as I can. I stuff them into my underpants and walk stiffly to Mrs. Mendès' classroom, the paper scratching. I keep my coat on over my red plaid skirt. My seat is in the second row.

"How was Rome governed?" Mrs. Mendès asks. She's playing with a long double string of pearls.

We talk about the first republic and the council and Julius Caesar. "Today we're going to act out the killing of Julius Caesar," she says. Her necklace breaks and pearls scatter. I stay in my seat, too frightened to help.

Mrs. Mendès calls on Larry to play Caesar.

"Do I get to say, *Et tu, Brutus?*"

I feel the blood soaking through into my underpants and skirt. There must be something wrong with me, to bleed so much. It's because of what Ray did to me. After social studies, the minutes of language arts tick by. We read "The Lady and the Tiger." Finally, the clock strikes three, the bell rings, and I hurry from the classroom.

"What's the matter with Kate?" I hear Larry ask Celia.

At Forrest's drugstore, with babysitting money, I buy a box of Kotex. At home, I lock myself in the second bathroom, strip off my skirt and underpants, and put clean things on. I wash my skirt in cold water. I spread the pleats out on the lid of the toilet and scrub and scrub until the water runs clear.

A few weeks later, before leaving for school, I open the hall closet and pull out my coat.

"What is that?" Mom cries. She grabs the camel wool coat, opens it and gasps. On the lining, a large, reddish-brown stain that looks like South America.

"What *is* this?"

"My period," I say. I didn't think of cleaning my coat. "I didn't have any Kotex."

"Why didn't you tell me? Why didn't you ask?"

I begin to cry, vaguely aware of unfairness. Shouldn't *she* have remembered? If she had, I would know she wasn't mad at me. "I don't know!" I sob.

"Are you still bleeding?"

"No."

"This will have to go the cleaners. Today."

After this, Mom remembers, or I ask.

At Woolworth's, Celia and I buy each other the same Christmas present—a gift box of twelve packages of Life Savers. That night, we sit on one chair at the desk in my bedroom.

"You have to change your handwriting," I say. "He'll recognize it."

"I'll print, in a really messy way. I'll use my left hand." Her hand is poised over the Christmas card we bought, also at Woolworth's. "What shall we say?"

"*Do you know you have two secret admirers?*"

"Too sappy," she says. "It has to be funnier. Dirtier."

"*You're quite a suave guy and maybe you want to meet us*"—I hesitate.

"*In the place you know, in the alley behind the American Bakery,*" she says, giggling.

"That's really dirty!" She and I have heard boys talk about a whorehouse there.

"He's not going to know it's from us. See, I'm making my writing really strange." She writes again. *I'm sure you know the place well.*

"We can end by saying, *From your secret admirers.*"

"*From your admirers, who know all your secrets!*" We burst into laughter, and I tumble off the chair.

We get Larry's address from the phone book. I put a stamp on the envelope, and we run to the mailbox.

The bluffs along the river have turned green—an undulating line of spring above dun-colored rock—and Celia and I walk to see them. Our favorite song is "Greenfields," a sad song in a minor key.

Once there were green fields, kissed by the sun.

The next Saturday we meet Debbie, my old friend, at Ruth's Fountain downtown. We drink cherry Cokes and take turns choosing songs on the tabletop jukebox. We're going to the city pool afterward and wear our bathing suits under our clothes.

Outside, walking three abreast on Main Street, Celia blurts, "I'm the prettiest, Kate's the next pretty, and Debby's the least pretty."

Debby's eyes widen, and she breaks away from us, sobbing. "I hope you have fun at the pool!"

Celia and I walk on, giggling. I feel ashamed and happy at the same time—ashamed because I didn't stand up for Debbie; happy because I'm the second prettiest!

Celia decides it's too cold to go swimming, and I invite her back to my house. Will Ray be home? He hasn't bothered me or my friends all year.

When we get home, Mikey is napping and Mom is grading papers in her room. Ray must be at work. We decide to take a shower together in our suits in the small bathroom, which has a tile stall. I'm still wearing last year's bathing suit, small on me now, riding up on my butt. Celia's is mauve, draped and tucked across her bust.

I turn on the water and we step into the warm spray, Celia holding her head back. "Should have worn my bathing cap!" she squeals.

The stall is small, and we can't help but bump up against each other, slippery thighs and arms against each other.

"I like your hair short," she says, cupping my chin. I had it cut to look like hers.

We stretch out our arms and legs to compare them. She lifts my chin and we kiss, making me shiver. I've so admired Celia, so wanted to touch her skin and face, but the actual doing scares me.

Chapter 17

Summer comes, and Peter, Megan, and I visit Dad and Sally in Los Angeles. This time, Megan and I stay at their apartment in sleeping bags in the living room. Grandma has moved into a care home because she had a breakdown, Sally tells me. We're not allowed to see her.

In August, back at home, we crowd into the Pontiac with Mom, Ray and Mikey to drive to Sequoia, Mom's favorite place. It's the first time we've been there with Ray. Our tent cabin perches on a slope near a huge granite boulder. During the day blue jays squawk in the piney heat, and Megan, Peter and I walk to the general store to buy cherry phosphates. Ranger Steve, handsome in pressed khaki and a broad hat, leads us around Bearpaw Meadow to John Muir's cabin, made from a hollow log. At night, Megan and I scurry in the dark to the restroom to brush our teeth, afraid we'll run into bears. The stars hang low, pulsing brightly.

A different ranger takes us into the giant sequoia grove where the ground is soft and spongey under my feet. The trees cast a spell, their elephant feet gripping the ground, trunks glowing reddish brown in the filtered light. "Touch the bark," says the ranger. It's thick and hairy under my fingers, alive. The bark protects the tree from lightning, he says. They're as old as the Greeks and Romans.

Ray doesn't go on the hikes. He reads Westerns on the porch, smoking his pipe.

On our last night, all of us except Ray go to the evening campfire where we sit on stumps and listen to Ranger Steve talk about bears and stars. He leads us in singing "Mares Eat Oats" and "Row, Row, Row Your Boat" in rounds. After the singing, in the dark, we toast marshmallows over the embers. Peter and I meet two other kids our age and stay longer than Mom and Megan.

"Where in the hell have you been?" Ray shouts when we come back.

Peter shrugs dramatically. "The campfire! Where do you think?"

"Don't get smart with me! You met some kids, and you drank booze. I can smell it!" He grabs Peter by the shirt.

"Asshole!" Peter says.

Ray slaps him. Mom grabs Ray's arm and he whirls toward her. Megan starts crying in the corner.

A man bangs on the screen door. "What's going on in there? You're disturbing the whole camp!"

Mom goes to the door. "I'm terribly sorry," she says to the man. "There'll be no more shouting." Back inside, she hisses at Ray: "Look what you've done!"

After everyone else goes to sleep, Peter and I sneak outside and huddle next to the boulder, which still holds the heat of the day. "I want to kill him!" Peter says.

"I do, too," I say. A new feeling takes hold of me, squeezing my heart. Rage. Hatred.

———

"Not you two again!" Larry says on the first day of school. We're in the eighth-grade corridor. His eyes drop to Celia's neckline, low cut and flowered. He doesn't see me in my new dress, a green shirtwaist with a white portrait collar.

I stand with my back to his. "I've grown," I say. I measure five feet, three inches, Celia, five-six. Larry hasn't grown.

"I see you shaved your legs. Badly." Forgotten bits of toilet paper cling to cuts on my calves. Mom finally relented.

In the classroom we three are seated near each other along the west facing windows. We immediately dislike our homeroom teacher, Mr. Keck, a short, bald man, red faced, who tells stories about being a US Marine in the South Pacific. Missing Mr. Rasmussen, we roll our eyes and pass notes.

Everyone argues about the election—Nixon vs. Kennedy. "It's the end of an era," says Mr. Poulsen, our social studies teacher. At recess we line up on opposite sides of the corridor, Nixon supporters—most of the class—-on one side, and Larry, Greg, and me, on the other.

A week after the election I'm halfway to Celia's on my way to school when I realize I left my social studies report at home. I run back, my binder banging against my chest, knowing I'll be late. Will Celia wait?

I burst in through the front door and stop, frozen. On the couch, Ray lies on top of Megan kissing her, his sun-darkened arms grappling, her white petticoats fanned out, pale, freckled legs exposed.

Ray's head jerks up and he looks at me.

Last month he grounded me for wearing lipstick. One day after church, he said, "You look like a hussy in that skirt." Then on a night Megan was gone he came into my room and trapped me against the dresser. Kissed me, his mouth wet and flabby. He unbuttoned my pajama top.

When I see him with Megan, I'm seized by fury.

I run into my room, grab the folder from my desk and come out again. Ray is standing and Megan is bent over, putting on her shoes. I scream, "You can do anything you want to me, but leave my little sister alone!"

I slam the front door. By the time I reach the sidewalk, I am sobbing.

I think of all the work I put into the report I'm carrying. "I expect to see your name as a writer someday," my teacher, Mr. Poulsen, said. What use will my talent be if I come from a bad family?

Two blocks from Chapel Street, I try to forget what I've seen. I push away the awful scene and silence my fury. I can't let Celia see.

"What happened?" Celia wears the collar of her white Ship 'n Shore turned up in back, like Doris Day.

I struggle to keep my voice even. "I had to go back for my report. Sorry!"

I receive a pass asking me to report to the office of Mrs. Mendès, who's been promoted to girls' dean. Wearing her usual long string of pearls and a black sweater, she sits behind a desk smiling and asks me to take a seat. I breathe in her smell of perfume mixed with tobacco.

"I think highly of you," she says. "I would like to see you run for student body president."

I blush, embarrassed and pleased at the same time. I've never wanted to run for office. That's more in my brother's line. I just want to do well in my classes and be liked.

She smiles again, her lipstick a vivid red against her fair, lightly freckled skin that reminds me of buttermilk. "I see you haven't considered this before. You underestimate yourself, Kate. I know you can do it."

I leave her office, turning her words over in my mind. I walk past every other eighth-grade classroom on my way to mine. Of all the students, Mrs. Mendès has chosen me. President of the student body. It's a new path forward, away from home.

"Dean's pet," Larry and Celia call me after I win the election. They trade meaningful glances when I'm called out of class for meetings. Worst of all, at the December school dance, I have to make a speech, so I'm not on the dance floor when partners form. I stand alone and conspicuous.

I double up on my efforts to fit in. I start a new list of plays with Larry and pass notes to Celia about Frank, her current beau. At recess, as the kids gather on the basketball court, Larry teases me, and I chase him and swat at him. We run across the field away from the others to the cypress hedge. He spins me so my petticoats show and grabs me, his eyes locked on mine. The underarm of my new dress rips. He doesn't once look back to the basketball court and his friends. After this day I know that he knows I like him. Does he like me?

On a Saturday morning in December, I arrive at Celia's house, as planned.

"Do you want to go downtown?" I ask. "You can help me shop for a new bra." I've saved up my babysitting money.

She sighs. "I guess so. There's nothing else to do."

Moody, I think, as she gets her sweater. Larry and I agree on this description of her.

At Colliers Apparel, I poke my head out of the dressing room curtains and ask her to come in. "I finally fit into a real size—32A!" I say. The bra is white and lacey with pointed cups.

"I never buy the size that fits me," she says, hardly looking. "I buy a size too small. When you wear a low-cut dress it looks really sexy."

A feeling like distaste runs along my spine.

Sandy opens her door with a big smile. "Hello you two!" Celia and I enter her warm foyer out of the winter night. Sandy's house is in the nice neighborhood, where doctors and lawyers live. We follow through the kitchen and into a dimly lit rec room. Larry, Greg, and Frank stand around the punch bowl wearing slacks and sports shirts. The girls in their party dresses crowd the record player. They pull 45s out of their paper jackets and argue about the order. Then Meta, a good dancer, stacks them on a fat spindle. "Yellow Polka Dot Bikini," "Poison Ivy," followed by "Summer Place" and "Greenfields."

When "Greenfields" comes on, Jerry asks me to dance. His shirt has short sleeves, and his arms feel solid and warm against mine. "Once there were green fields, kissed by the sun." He nuzzles my cheek, then slowly turns his head to find my mouth. He kisses me. His lips are soft and full. The tip of his tongue darts into my mouth, startling me. Out of the corner of my eye I see Larry on the floor, watching.

After the dance ends, Greg finds me. "Larry just said, 'Where did Kate learn to make out like that?'"

I feel proud.

At the punch bowl, Sandy whispers with two other girls and I come over.

"Did you see?" Sandy says, frowning.

"Really cheap. Bad," says Meta.

On the couch, Celia and Frank are practically lying down, locked in a long kiss. One of her shoulder straps has slipped down.

"Her dress is so low!" Sandy says. "How could her mother allow it?"

I know that Celia doesn't pay much attention to what her mother says anymore.

Two more girls rush up, and Celia must notice. She jumps off the couch and runs out of the room, her hands covering her face. I follow her, down the soft carpet of the hall, Sandy and another girl behind me. We hear the bathroom door lock.

"Celia," I say. "Let me in."

"It's all right, Celia," says Sandy.

After a few minutes, Celia opens the door. Her face is pink and puffy but still pretty. "Just Kate."

"What were they saying?" she asks after I close the door.

"Never mind. They're jealous." I'm proud to be the one she lets in, but I'm worried. She asks for her purse so she can comb her hair and put on lipstick. I go, but I feel a distance open between us. There are rules. Lying down on a couch with a boy is not okay. My stomach clenches as I remember my sister and Ray on the couch.

I feel her going another way, spoiling our friendship. The words in our song come to me; *Green fields are gone now, parched by the sun.*

"I know you like Larry," Greg says. "I think he likes you, too." Greg has begun calling me, I hope at Larry's urging. On the Friday before Easter vacation, he invites Larry and me to his house in the evening. We sit on twin beds in his bedroom and play an LP of the comedian Shelly Berman doing a monologue about a lady hanging from a department store window by her bra strap. Then Greg turns down the lights and puts on "The Theme from A Summer Place." Larry and I stand, and he puts an arm around my waist and takes my right hand in his. I hunch to make myself shorter. We shuffle our feet back and forth on the carpet. I put my cheek close to his. When the song is almost over, he kisses me. It's a timid, dry kiss, nothing like Jerry's, but it's done. Larry has kissed me.

In April, because President Kennedy said we should, we endure a week of physical fitness tests. "Ask not what your country can do for you, but for what you can do for your country." It's like Sputnik and special math.

Boys and girls have PE on separate fields, divided by the cypress hedge. It's day three and we're doing the standing and running broad jump. I did well on the first two days, but I excel at jumping. The teachers compliment me, showing me the measurements they've entered on their clipboards. I'm sweaty and disheveled and happy.

Debbie runs across the field toward me, alarm on her face. "Celia is saying bad things about you! She says you bad-mouthed her to Larry." She points to the group of girls near the hedge. Celia's in the middle, a cardigan draped around her shoulders. I feel as if I've been stabbed.

I follow Debbie back across the field, letting the others, including Celia, get to the classroom wing ahead of me. It's not just my being student body president or winning at broad jump, I know. In the competition over Larry, I've inched forward. Larry and I have shared rumors that Celia is going out with high school boys. We've called her "fast" and "cheap." We snickered in class when she mispronounced a word. And there was the invitation to Greg's that didn't include her.

I take a long drink at the water fountain in the corridor.

After school, I avoid her, staying in the office until the sidewalks are empty. She and I don't speak again for a week.

Late in May, everyone in our class is invited to a swimming party and barbecue at the Brown Ranch. Jimmy Brown is a quiet boy, but Larry and Greg tell me his family is an old one. "Pioneers," Greg says. A school is named after the first settler.

In a station wagon driven by Mrs. Brown, I watch as we cross pastureland and then hill country. The road narrows as we go into a canyon shaded with live oaks—ancient, sheltering trees, like the ones Artemis hunted in. I haven't forgotten my mythology. In my bag is a towel and a new two-piece bathing suit sure to impress Larry.

At an entrance gate, Mrs. Brown turns around. "If any of you girls have your period, please place your used sanitary things in the wastebasket, not the toilet. The ranch is on a septic system and it's very delicate. Thank you."

How easily Mrs. Brown says this! She's a small, pretty woman, and so polite.

"Of course, Mrs. Brown," we all say.

Ten minutes later, we crowd into a small changing room. "Oh

no!" Meta says. "You can't go in the water!"

"Oh well," says Celia.

I can't help feeling glad. She'll have to stay in her shorts and one of those sleeveless white blouses that are getting old.

She and I are polite; we speak, but we're not best friends anymore. Her parents have bought a house in a new development south of the high school. They'll be moving soon. She and her sister will occupy the master bedroom, with its own bath.

"You have a two-piece!" Sandy says, and everyone turns to look.

"I got it in Santa Monica," I say. Sally helped me choose it. "The colors bring out your skin tones," Sally said. It's orange and yellow.

The pool shimmers in the morning light. It looks as if it's been there forever, a green rectangle carved out of the woods and partly shaded by trees. The water is dotted with oak leaves. Along with the first boys, I dive in. "Yikes!" someone says, because the water is cold. It tastes of grass and leaves. "It's spring fed," I hear Mrs. Brown tell a mother.

We swim and splash each other. Transistor radios come out and the boys snap towels at each other.

I get out of the water and find a sunny spot on the concrete to sit in. I wrap myself in my towel. Larry comes over and sits beside me.

"Neat suit. You look like Sandra Dee," he says.

"Thanks. I got it in LA," I say. Is he thinking of our kiss? Could there be another today, a better kiss, before we leave this place? The hillside above us is steep, covered with oak trees.

We talk about Los Angeles and the new amusement park in Ocean Park, and whether he'll go there with his family this summer. I take the towel from around my shoulders and spread it beside me, stretching out my legs. Larry says he's going to take drama next year.

"Are you worried about high school?" I ask.

"I don't know. I just wish I'd grow." He breaks off and nods in the direction of the dressing rooms where Celia sits with another girl in shorts. "Celia's not swimming. Is she in one of her moods?"

"Probably."

The diving board groans and clanks as Ron Izzi bounces up and down, his weight testing the old spring. All the boys start doing cannonballs and the girls scatter from the edge, shrieking. The mothers have left the pool area; they're setting tables on the screened porch. I smell hamburgers and hot dogs being grilled.

After his third cannonball, Ron bounces at the end of the board and shouts across the water. "Celia and Lotte! What're you doing over there?"

Jerry joins in. "Are you too good for us? Don't want to get your hairdos wet?"

All the boys, including Larry, turn to look at the girls on the bench.

Jerry dances closer to them. "Celia, we miss you! No fun without you!"

"I have no interest in going in," she says, blushing.

Larry jumps to his feet, eyes alight. He sidles over to Jerry, singing a song we learned from *H.M.S. Pinafore*.

"Gaily tripping, lightly skipping
Come the maidens to the shipping."

The color rises in Celia's cheeks, her eyes blaze. She stands, clutching a towel around her hips. "You think you're so smart, little man!"

"Just put your feet in! Your cute, little painted tootsies!"

They're bright pink.

Larry grabs a corner of her towel and pulls. She locks eyes with him, smiling.

I know what's coming and I pray. I pray that Artemis or the god of the oak trees will stand by me. But Larry pushes Celia in then kneels to watch her come up. I want to run away. I want not to see. She stands in the water waist deep, her cotton blouse and bra plastered against her body. The water runs in rivulets over her beautiful breasts. She laughs provocatively and makes her way toward him. She pulls herself up out of the water, her shorts clinging to her long, shapely legs.

A bell rings from the ranch house. "Food's on, kids!" shouts Mrs. Brown. I join the others as they leave the pool area and move downhill toward the ranch house. I concentrate on my footing over the slippery oak leaves. My heart is bursting, but I hold back my tears. I can't let my feelings show. I hold my head up, imagining I'm a wounded queen.

I serve myself a meat patty, a bun, and potato salad. Greg beckons me to his table, but I take the first place I find, not wanting his sympathy, which will make me cry. When I bite into my hamburger, my throat closes. On the hillside above me, Larry and Celia sit under a tree, talking. The late afternoon sun streams through the dark branches and leaves, dappling their bodies.

Chapter 18

It's December, and Frances is knitting. Folds of soft, heathery wool hang from her needles.

"What pretty yarn!" I say. "Where did you get it?"

"Online."

There's the reminder. We're not here to talk about knitting.

"I want to tell you about a dream," I say after a minute. "It's a dream I have a lot. Not quite a nightmare, but almost. I'm with other people usually, in charge of them, and the house—whatever house I'm in— is a mess. The sink and counters are overflowing with dirty dishes and pots and pans. The laundry room is knee deep in dirty clothes. There's no way I'll ever get it all washed and put away. It's a scene of overflowing chaos. As if these things have risen up, and they're going to smother me. I have a feeling of being—" I stop, unable to find the word.

"Overwhelmed?" Frances says.

I nod. "Drowning. I've never lived in a house like that. My mother was a meticulous housekeeper."

"That doesn't surprise me."

"And I am, too. Compulsive even."

She smiles. "It's not about laundry and dishes, Kate. The dirty laundry and all, those are feelings."

"Huh," I say, floored. Does she mean the feelings I don't even know are there? As naked as I feel in this office, it's never enough for Frances. I shake my head. "I don't know. The whole mess is so threatening."

"Think how overwhelmed you felt after Ray assaulted you. When you were crying on the couch. That's the state I'm talking about. You had no names and no understanding of the thoughts and emotions that came over you."

"I thought I should be able to handle it."

"Now, wrapped up in your mother's decline, the onslaught is heightened."

I picture a battle, a rain of arrows, horses charging, which is what the dreams feel like. "I'll have to think about that."

Sometimes Frances wants me to take something further, and I can't. I hit a dead end. Like now. My eyes wander to her bookcase, and again I wonder what the titles are. Probably Freud, and Jung and Adler.

"Last time we talked about your friends in junior high," she says. "You had strong feelings for Celia and Larry. Deep and genuine feelings." Frances knits rapidly, purling now, her steel needles clickety-clacking. My hands itch to do the same.

"Both of my friends hurt me," I say finally. "Celia especially."

"That comes with the territory." In the calm of her voice, I feel the pleasure she feels as the yarn travels through her fingers.

"When I remember myself then, in the seventh and eighth grade, I like myself. That girl is me. She connects with the me I knew as a child. After that year, though, I got scared, I closed up. I didn't let people see how I felt. The change happened fast. I remember after we graduated, Celia invited me to a slumber party for her birthday. There must have been a dozen of us. I wasn't special anymore. This was in her new house, where she and her sister had the master bedroom and bath, like they were more important than their parents. At the party, Celia and Sandy were curled up together on a porch swing, talking. I sat down next to them and told them my Grandma Lily had had a breakdown and been put in a home. I worked up some tears, trying to make them feel sorry for me. This was my dad's mother in Santa Monica. But that's not what I'm getting at. I used Grandma. I was putting on an act. It didn't even work. They started talking about something else."

"Slow down. What happened to your grandma? Did you see her again?"

"A year or two later, she moved in with Dad and Sally."

"What about her apartment?"

"Gone. I never saw it again." The pretty rooms and the paperweights and the balcony looking over the lawn—taken away.

Frances sighs. "Another loss." She takes five or six stitches, not seeming to count. "Are you aware that Celia carries a special charge for you?"

"Oh yes. It's like I was in love with her. And she disappointed me, she betrayed me."

"Attachment and cruelty. Love and abandonment. Who else does that remind you of?"

I look around the room as if the answer is on the wall, or outside on the tiny patio. Maybe a bird would fly by with a banner in its mouth. *What is Frances getting at?* I wonder.

"Oh," I say. "My mother."

"Unconsciously, you chose someone who was like your mother. Someone powerful, whom you want badly to please."

"Mom is everywhere. I can't get a break."

"Unfortunately, no."

"Tentacles everywhere, like an octopus. My kids had a joke. 'What did the octopus say to his girlfriend? I want to hold your hand, hand, hand, hand, hand, hand, hand, hand.'"

France smiles, and that makes me happy. "Celia dominated me," I say.

Frances shrugs. "For the most part. You were beginning to show some independence."

"She threw me under the bus."

"As your mother did. And something else I noticed in your telling. You imagined that this swimming party at the end of the year was a decisive event. She won and you lost. But that's your version of things, Kate, a construct you imposed. I doubt she and Larry saw it that way."

I remember driving home in Mrs. Brown's station wagon, the twilight settling in. I remember wondering whether Larry and Celia were in the same car. I remember a feeling of deep sadness and loneliness. "You mean they probably felt things less strongly." The truth of this settles over me, like a clean sheet falling softly onto a bed.

"Your mind can get you into trouble," Frances says and steals a glance at the clock over my head.

—

The following Wednesday, Frances is knitting again, joining the sleeves to the body of her heathery sweater. I wish she'd look up.

"I'm really mad at Brookvale," I begin. "My mother fell Saturday night and was taken to the ER, and I didn't find out until yesterday! The aid called my cellphone—in the middle of the night—using her cellphone. I ignored the call because it was an unknown number. I've told them to use my landline. I'm not like other people. I don't live attached to my cellphone!" I let out a long sigh.

"Was she hurt?"

"Yes. In the ER they closed a long skin tear on her arm with staples. As soon as they left her, she pulled them out. So, they put in stitches and a thick bandage to keep her from hurting herself."

"Oh, dear," Frances groans.

"Richard said that's what dogs do, pull out their stitches. I can't stand it that I wasn't there!" A knot of anger and guilt builds inside me. "I could have helped her."

"You want to save her dignity."

"The last time she fell she fractured her pelvis, and I assume they did an X-ray again this time." I shake my head. "Sunday went by, Monday. I don't know why no one asked, 'Has her daughter been told? Where is Kate?'" Again, I sigh. "When I finally saw her, she lay on a recliner in the common room—usually she's in a wheelchair—under a blanket, looking weak and confused. She said her hip hurt, and I asked the staff if she'd been given an X-ray in the ER. No one knew. It was a shit show. Sorry."

"It's okay."

"I took Mom's hand and bent very close. Her grip was so weak. She looked around the room and then asked me, 'Is Mother here?'"

"Her mother?"

I nod. "Her eyes were so . . . pleading. Needy. I couldn't help it. I imagined Grandma there, too. I wanted her."

"Yes," Frances says, looking up at me. "She was with you." She lets a long minute go by. "I've been thinking of something you brought up last week. Your grandmother Mimi had a breakdown, and your father had to move her out of the old apartment. What about your father? What role was he playing in your life then?"

"We kept visiting. We crowded together in the apartment on Barrington. Then, a year or so later, he and Sally moved to a bigger apartment so they could take Grandma in."

In a letter, Dad sent the floor plan for the new apartment, which had three bedrooms and a balcony. It was more modern than Barrington, but it lacked the charm of the place he shared with Grandma on Second Street. The balcony looked across a driveway into the windows of the building next door. Grandma had a few pieces of furniture with her, but she was peevish, complaining a lot.

"I don't think Sally and Grandma got along too well. I felt tension in the apartment."

"And your dad?"

I take a deep breath. "How can you concentrate while you're decreasing?"

"Would you rather I didn't knit?"

"Yes."

"All right." She folds the sweater and puts it and her needles in one of her tote bags.

"We only visited that apartment once, in the summer, when I was fourteen. One afternoon, Dad called the three of us—Peter, Megan, and me—into the living room. He was sitting in Grandma's Windsor chair. I was scared about what he might say, like that he and Sally were breaking up. No, he asked us a question. It was hard for him. 'Does your stepfather treat you all right?'"

"Thank God," Frances says.

"We said no."

"What did he do?"

"He started crying," I say.

"And that's all? He didn't ask you anything else?"

"I was just happy that he cared. No one else cared."

"But he did nothing? Nothing changed?"

I shake my head, still wanting to defend him. "He had Grandma to take care of and Sally's boys. A few months later, Sally did leave him."

"No, Kate. He could have done something. He should have."

I start crying. "He felt so bad!"

"You had a very deep need to believe in him. But now, you can see his failure, can't you? What if now you learned someone hurt Julia?"

I shake my head rapidly, hating her question. "He loved us. I don't think he could do more."

Chapter 19

At noon, I find Mom behind the librarian's desk in the Nebraska Historical Library, talking excitedly on the phone. The librarian, whose name plate says Gabriel Perez, explains. "Your mother was asking about material on a lynching that took place in Omaha in 1919. She told me her parents had witnessed it. A professor I know at the university is writing a book about the same subject, so I put them in touch."

Mom's face is shining with excitement when she hangs up. "Isn't that wonderful? He wants me to send my chapter as soon as I finish it. And he gave me more information about the lynching."

After she packs her notebook and pens into her briefcase we leave the library, taking the path that leads to the Parade Ground. "It was September 19, a Sunday afternoon, and Mother and Daddy were seeing patients in his office. This was before they married. His office was on the fifth floor of a building just half a block from the courthouse. They heard a terrible uproar coming from down the street. Mother called it 'unearthly.' Daddy said, 'The courthouse.' It was the mob gathering, six thousand people eventually, Mr. Harkins said. My parents locked up the office and hurried to Daddy's car."

Mom is breathing quickly, anger in her voice. "A Black man had been accused of raping a white woman and he was being held in the jail. One newspaper called him a 'Black Beast.'"

"How did your parents feel about it?"

"Why they were horrified, of course! They were proud of their city but ashamed that so many were *backward.* That was the word my father used."

This is her good side, I think, as we cross the grassy field. She's been an outspoken liberal all her life, a pacifist briefly in World War II, a civil rights advocate in the sixties. After I left home, she hosted a Black teenager from a Chicago slum for five months.

"Good for you, Mom. You're making a contribution to history."

A cluster of contemporary, brick buildings rises in front of us.

"Well," she says, "my work is cut out for me. I'll revise that chapter as soon as I get home and send it off to Mr. Harkins."

I spot the clock tower.

"I was also looking for records of my mother's work at the Nebraska Nursing Association. Mr. Perez told me I'd have better luck at the University of Nebraska Medical School. Apparently, they have a library, too, the McGoogan Library. As soon as we get back to the hotel, I must call them."

"The Nebraska Nursing Association," I say slowly. "The 1930s."

"Mr. Perez said the McGoogan might keep limited hours. That's why I want to call."

"But do you honestly think there'll be a record of her work there?"

"I know she wrote reports for the state." Mom is making a beeline for lunch, as she always does. We share this trait, always famished at eleven. Not a good time to challenge her.

"Isn't that like me going to Contra Costa College and asking for copies of your old course outlines?"

"These are far more important, I would think," she says heatedly. "It is the *state's* medical library." She pauses to catch her breath.

"I mean, what will they tell you about Grandma?"

"I don't know why you're questioning me. Surely, I get to decide what goes in my book."

"But I have to drive you there. And tomorrow we leave for Grinnell."

"We may have to put off our trip to Grinnell."

I stop on the path, shaking my head. I wanted to go to Grinnell. She and Dad met there. They worked on the literary magazine; they went on picnics and read A.E. Housman. "Loveliest of trees the cherry now." When I was eleven, I found a copy of *A Shropshire Lad* in our bookcase, inscribed *To Lizzie, Love Phil.*

"I don't want to put off going to Grinnell. We don't have time. We leave for home on Sunday."

"Why is Grinnell so important to you?" Mom asks.

We're still stopped. My wish has more to do with Dad than her. I want to find some remnant, something I can see or touch, of *his* time there. He went to Grinnell because his uncle, a music professor, lived there with his wife and four daughters in a big house near campus. Dad and his brother lived with their mother, sister to the uncle, so Grinnell was family and home.

I start walking again and speak cheerfully. "I want to go because you made Grinnell sound so beautiful."

"Let's discuss this at lunch."

We cross the street, then follow a walkway to a plaza where tables and umbrellas are set up. At the cafeteria entrance, Mom struggles with the heavy glass door, not built for an eighty-five-year-old. I pull it open.

"I hope they have soup," she says.

"Cafeterias always have soup."

At the salad bar, I gather sustenance: spears of romaine, wedges of tomato, kidney beans, chunky tuna.

We find a table outside. Nearby a fountain splashes. Around us, students eat, read their textbooks, peer into laptops. A group of nursing students sits next to us, wearing scrubs, chatting, laughing. They look like the community college students I used to teach—early twenties, all women, except that these students are all White.

My mother has chosen split pea soup, a corn muffin, and coffee. "I had a choice between a Parker House roll and a muffin," she says cheerily.

After she has taken three or four spoonsful of soup, I start.

"You talked so much about Grinnell when we were growing up. You said the campus was so beautiful. And you and Dad met there. Isn't that more important than some archives you may or may not find in a medical library?"

"I don't know what you're going on about. I came here to research my parents' lives. I would like to see these reports."

I cut into a tomato wedge. "Didn't you already pay for our room at the bed and breakfast?"

She pauses, soup spoon in hand. "Perhaps I did." She sighs. "Oh dear, I suppose it can't be canceled. Maybe we can go to the McGoogan when we get back."

I should quit now, but I don't. "There's something else I want to say. You're writing your book for us, right? I love it when you write about what you actually remember. I'm not interested in Grandma's reports."

"Other readers may be."

"Like who?"

"Historians, perhaps. Nursing scholars. And your sister Megan. She's a nurse."

"I doubt it."

The table of nurses breaks into laughter, and for a second I think they've overheard us. I lay my fork down. Mom is quiet, so I know I've hurt her. She still has soup left. She is beginning to eat more slowly. She raises another spoonful, swallows it noisily, and begins to cough. I pat her on her back, offer her my water. The spasm eases, she drinks, holds herself still. She's been doing this more lately.

"You're a good writer, Mom. Don't get me wrong. But you have limited time. Remember the old maxim, write what you know? Maybe you should write more about yourself."

"Like *you* do, you mean," she says pointedly. "You want me to write about things that are painful."

The nursing students rise from their seats and sling on their backpacks. On their way past the fountain, one skims her hand across the water. I look for my mother's eyes. "Your memories might be less painful if you wrote about them. Or talked about them. Have you asked yourself why you spend all this time writing about your ancestors' lives?"

She slams her napkin down. "I can see where this is heading. Once again, you want to discuss *my* failings as a mother." She stands, picks up her tray. "Don't you think this is too public a place to have such a conversation?"

I look around. "There's hardly anyone here!" She strides off toward the busing station, and I follow.

We walk back across the parade grounds in silence. The sky is a solid blue now, the clouds have moved eastward, and the hot sun beats down on us. After we're buckled up, she takes off her hat and pulls lip balm from her bag. Signs of recovery. I pull away from the curb, out of the deep shade of trees and into the roadway. "We take 30th Street toward downtown," Mom says. "To get back to the hotel."

No need to tell me since I got us here, I think. I squelch my anger and drive.

Chapter 20

"Mom did eventually write about her own life," I say, laughing. "It was kind of funny." I keep laughing though I know Frances doesn't understand.

"Why are you laughing?" she asks. A vase of daffodils sits on her bookcase—from her garden, I'm sure. It's February, early spring in California.

"I don't know. She was just so serious. We could never tease her. When my sister and I get together now, we tell stories about her and laugh."

"Such as?"

I think for a second. "Little things. The vocalizing exercises she used to do at home. *Oooo-aaah*. Or she would put her hand on her diaphragm and pant in the most embarrassing way. Or the tiny meals she served us." The last time we did this, Julia scolded us. "There may come a day when we talk about you like this!"

My head falls back against my chair and I close my eyes. "Mom was a good writer. She would sit down at her computer every morning at nine and write for two hours." I see her in her upstairs office, sitting at a table the height of a child's, and typing away at her old, desktop Mac.

"She wrote her way to the midpoint of her mother's life and decided to publish those chapters as *Book I*. Maybe she worried she wouldn't finish. She was nearly ninety. She'd show her work to her writers' group and to all of us, too, one chapter at a time. She started into the second book, still focused on Grandma. Then suddenly, she jumps the track. When she herself goes away to college. Suddenly the young coed is center stage. She tells us all about the men she dated, picnics, professors, and Gerald, the boyfriend who went off to war without proposing." I'm laughing.

"Why is this funny to you?"

"She was always so repressed. She was such a disciplined writer."

"But weren't you glad?"

"Yes. All her readers were. Let her rip."

Frances smiles faintly. "This was probably the beginning of her dementia. She was losing inhibition."

"She wrote about how she almost dropped out of Grinnell to marry my father. She spent the summer before senior year with him in LA, having sex in Grandma Mimi's apartment. She continued with her own life—wedding, babies, our first years in Santa Monica." These chapters were sweet, stories of running after toddler Peter who was streaking into the ocean, giving birth to Megan in the car because the third child came so quickly.

"By this point, she'd noticed problems with her memory and gotten a diagnosis of early dementia. She started writing about the breakup of her marriage to Dad and the months we lived in Santa Barbara with Grandma. She wrote about her breakdown and hospitalization. She agonized and labored, draft after draft. It took everything out of her."

Outside France's window, a flicker streaks by, its cream and brown spotted breast bright against the redwood tree.

"She was so anxious about how we would take it. But we all praised her, we reassured her, and so did her writers' group." Frances listens intently.

"That was her last gasp. After that she'd sit down to write every morning and produce just a few sentences or an anecdote. I went with her and her husband to a specialist, a gerontologist, Doctor Baretta. Karl asked if there was a medication Mom could take to help her finish her book. Doctor Baretta turned to Mom. 'What's it like when you sit down to write?' 'It's as if I'm beginning all over again,' Mom said. 'I don't know where to start.'

"So kindly, with such respect, the doctor explained all the operations that had to go on in the brain before anyone could write a word. 'You'll need to ask your family to help you finish,' she said."

"You're speaking about your mother now with such sympathy and affection. More than I've heard from you before."

"I felt terribly sorry for her. I knew what she'd lost. It was maybe the best part of her."

"And maybe you felt stronger than her?"

"Yes. I was the mother, and she was the child."

"And did you help with the book?"

"Megan and I did. Mostly me. It was a lot of work just making sense of her files. Her desktop was a storm of little Word icons. I organized them and imported the files onto my computer."

"Coming into your domain she was, crowding you out. Again."

"Part of me felt proud. Look at me, the good daughter, preserving my mother's legacy. The other part, the writer in me, was raging. I felt my own time ticking away."

Frances nods, a sad smile on her face, and we share a moment of quiet. She knows.

"My sister and I went back to telling Grandma's life, wrapping it up. Once, visiting Mom to go over a chapter, we went for a walk. I brought up a part of the story she had left out. It was when we lived at Grandma's at second time, when I was six and Mom was pregnant. We were walking on a concrete path in her neighborhood between hedges. She didn't answer, and I thought she didn't understand. I added a word or two, maybe the date or the word *baby*. Her face just closed. It was like a steel door clanking shut."

"Meaning?"

"I was not to inquire further."

"How did you feel?"

"Slapped. She could still be so strong!"

"As in, how dare you!"

"It would have been so good to talk about that baby!"

Frances leans forward. "This was perhaps the deepest wound of her life." She glances at the clock. "You could look for the child now, with DNA matching."

"I know."

"Or he could find you."

Two weeks later, as soon as I sit down, I burst out. "I'm so angry!"

"What's the matter?" Frances asks.

"The Mueller Report!" Attorney General Barr has announced that Trump committed no wrongdoing. Neither colluding with the Russians nor obstructing justice. I want to hammer my fists into my knees. "We so had our hopes up! They were taking a long time but that was a good sign. There were no leaks and that was a good sign! We could trust Mueller."

Frances nods.

I put my face in my hands, crying. "What am I to do with all this anger?"

"A lot of us are angry. Everyone's anger is personal, though. You had flawed authority figures in your past, and you were angry with them."

"And Trump is a sexual predator, like Ray."

"More reason for anger." She lifts her chin, fingers one of the rings on her chain. "As a child, you were angry but powerless. You were unable to change anything. The same as now. Trump is the harmful authority figure."

When Frances refers to me as a child, I feel soothed because I was never allowed to think of myself as one. "Once, my sister and I were packing to go to Dad's. We were in front of our open closet, and Mom came in. 'Now don't go around half dressed in front of your father,' she said. I got so angry! Dad would never, never have done anything like that! And it was so hypocritical of her! Her own husband . . . in *our* house!"

"Did you say anything?"

"No. I might have stormed around the room or said something to Megan. After."

"Your anger toward Ray was worse. You told me about that time in the mountains."

"When I told my brother I wanted to kill him."

"Anger and helplessness. The same, isn't it?" Frances asks.

"I felt hatred too. It was terrible to live with hatred for so long." Tears come to my eyes.

Frances says nothing, just fixes me with wise, knowing eyes.

Chapter 21

Mom and I get back from Fort Omaha in the early afternoon. In the elevator of the Marriott, she tells me she'd like to rest. At home she takes a nap every day, and I've been surprised she hasn't wanted to on this trip. I chalked it up to the adrenaline of travel. Today is different. After our blowup at breakfast, the excitement at the library, and my pushing her at lunch about her writing, she's worn out.

So am I.

I follow her to her room looking out to the river and pull the heavy gold drapes closed. She sits at the foot of the bed and takes her shoes off. Her movements are slow, her shoulders slumped, her face pale and slack. With a soft groan she lifts her feet and legs onto the bed and drops heavily back, face up onto the pillow.

I pull the throw blanket up over her small body.

"Shall I give you an hour or so?"

She nods.

What to do? What to do? I ask myself once I'm in my room. A familiar twining of anxiety and self-doubt tightens around me. Maybe she's right; maybe I am being unfair. I hear her words again and see the anger contorting her features. I think of Oedipus, who couldn't bear the light, the public shaming. What right have I to upset her hard-won equanimity? To hack away at her defenses?

The Bank of Omaha sign outside my window says it's eighty-four degrees outside. Fear no more the heat of the sun. *Get out, get out,* I tell myself. On my dresser sits the full-color brochure I was given yesterday: *Discover Omaha!* The cover photo shows the Old Market District, its worn brick fronts, a raised sidewalk and a carriage drawn by horses. I'll go there. Anything to stop thinking.

I pull off my cotton slacks and look for something cooler—the skirt I brought to wear to dinner. Digging through my suitcase, looking for crinkly red cotton, I hear Mom's voice again, that sharp rise, edgy, strained. *"I can see where this is headed. You want to discuss my failings as a mother."*

Our old struggle lies so close to the surface! It doesn't take much to lay it bare. I kick off my sneakers and search for my sandals. Buckling them, I remember every word she's ever said or written on the subject. Worse, I hear the things she doesn't say. That I have no right to complain. That I've been lucky. My life has turned out so much better than hers. How can I say I've suffered?

Get some perspective, I tell myself. *She was formed by the Depression, her father's death, and Calvinism. She learned a little Freud in college and later Doctor Spock, and that was it in terms of psychology. She lacks the language, the tools for looking into herself.*

I run a comb through my hair and splash my face with cold water.

Why does she have this power over me? I remember a scene in the public library when I was a senior in high school. I was depressed—maybe the first acute depression of my life. My brother and the boys I'd been dating had gone away to college. I'd gained weight, done poorly on the SATs, couldn't concentrate.

That day, Mom stood next to me as a librarian explained the reserve book procedure. I asked a question indicating I hadn't heard or understood. Walking away, Mom scolded me. "Why didn't you understand? What's the matter with you?" She was embarrassed by my stupidity.

I pick up the brochure, feeling a flush mount from my spine to my chest and shoulders. I make sure I have my room card and grab my purse. I close the door behind me. *Every city has its old town these days,* I think with deepening cynicism. They tear down skid row and abandoned warehouses and then, out of nostalgia, recreate a past that never was.

In the elevator I press *L* for lobby, still hearing my mother's aggrieved tones. How can I complain? I've been married to the same man my entire adult life, a man who earns plenty so that I work as little or as much as I like. My only child loves me. I lean against the stainless-steel wall. *Except, except!* Except that sometimes I think about killing myself.

I cross the thick carpet of the lobby, where the woman at reception smiles and wishes me a good afternoon. I manage a half smile then pass through the revolving door into the humid afternoon. The humid air envelops my body.

I shade my eyes against the blinding glare of the sidewalk, then look up to get my bearings. My map tells me to proceed west on Dodge and then turn right. I cross into the shade and make my way past modern storefronts and office buildings, then turn onto 13th Street.

The last time I felt like ending my life was when Julia got so depressed in college that she dropped out. The beautiful, happy child disappeared and in her place was a thin, frightened creature, unrecognizable. When I saw a child on a bicycle, happy and strong, I wanted to shout to the parents, "Don't get too attached! This happiness won't last! Your child is headed for trouble!" Terrible adult trouble. Estrogen and testosterone brought darkness and turmoil. All my work and love—everything I'd striven for—had come to nothing.

I turn onto 13th Street, barely noticing that the street is getting busier, the sidewalk more crowded. A little boy collides with me, and his mother scolds him. "It's all right," I say. "I wasn't looking."

Don't be angry at your little boy, ever, I want to tell her.

I'm in the Old Market District now, merging with the tourist crowd. Weathered brick warehouses line the street, and baskets of petunias hang from iron lamp posts. A metal awning over the walkway, edged in fretwork, makes a graceful curve around the corner. Families and couples smile and laugh, holding hands, eating ice cream cones.

The men wear shorts and T-shirts, the women, halter tops, and floaty skirts—neon pink, yellow, turquoise. Their arms and legs are tan, and some wear jeweled sandals, toes painted in metallic colors. The fashions of the Coasts have come to the Midwest.

In front of me, a girl with long blond hair jumps on and off the sidewalk. She wears denim shorts and white sneakers; thirteen, perhaps, newly grown into her full height. She reminds me of Julia, who was a dancer, like me. She takes hold of a post and leans out into the street.

Is Julia all right? I wonder. *Is she adjusting to her students? Making friends in the new house?*

Across the street in a dusty square, people are climbing into a horse-drawn carriage—a surrey with fringe on top. A pair of horses drink from a water trough. "All aboard," the driver calls, and shakes the harness bells. I watch as the carriage pulls out, its passengers wearing that special, expectant smile tourists wear.

Across the square, a large willow tree surrounded by a bench offers shade. It's 2:30 on the West Coast. Julia will be out of class. I sit on the bench and pull out my phone.

"Hello, honey," I say when she answers.

"Hey, Mom." Her voice is low, even hoarse.

"Classes going better?" Ever the optimist!

She bursts into tears.

"What's the matter?" I think I know but ask anyway.

She keeps crying. A dog whines in the background.

"Where are you?" I ask.

"I'm home."

"In Napa? But it's a Tuesday! You should—"

"I just couldn't take it anymore!"

Images and feelings from the past crowd into my mind—reminders of phone calls and sudden journeys, eight years ago when

Julia dropped out of college. *But she's an adult now,* I tell myself. *She graduated, she's had jobs, and earned a second degree.*

"I know, honey," I say. "I know you've been having a hard time."

Three older women in sun visors approach the kiosk where tickets for the carriage ride are sold. Did Julia call in to say she wasn't coming in? I can't ask her that. "Did something happen?" I say instead.

Yesterday her supervisor called her in for a conference. "That was the worst. It was so embarrassing."

"It was probably just a routine thing."

"No, no. I snapped at the kids last week, and someone must have complained because she—"

"Who?"

"The supervisor came in for a second observation. I just can't do this, Mom!"

I picture Julia in the kitchen, dressed in jeans and a T-shirt, her blond hair flyaway and lovely around her face. She is so graceful and gifted. "Did you think of calling anyone? Your old therapist?"

"Dad said the same."

"Do you think maybe you could?"

"Maybe."

According to Dr. Brazelton, the reigning childrearing expert in the '80s, children misbehave in three different ways—by rebelling, seeking attention, or falling apart. Julia was the latter.

"Maybe I could take Zorro to school," she says.

Humor. Good, I think, *except she probably means it.* The women in sunhats, tickets in hand, approach my bench. I move to the other side.

"You've only got a couple of weeks, right? Hang in there. You can't let the school down."

She starts crying again, and my heart grabs. She has no fight left in her. When she was afraid at five or six, I used to quote a line from a record we listened to, of *The Hobbit.*

"'This will be the bravest thing you ever do.' Do you remember?"

She stops crying.

"Who said it?"

"Gandalf."

"Do you want me to come home?"

"No, no. I've got Dad. And Zorro." She blows her nose. "How *is* Grandma?"

I tell her a little about our day, and we finish by saying "I love you."

Chapter 22

I find my mother in the crafts room, sitting at a table with others making May baskets. The table is covered with pastel-colored construction paper, ribbons, stickers, and glitter. Some of the women construct their own baskets. Others, like my mother, are given a folded and stapled basket, which they decorate. I pull up a chair next to Mom who's struggling to tie a green ribbon.

She turns to me, a stricken look on her face. "I've had terrible news. Peter is in jail."

Thirty years ago, my brother was in jail. He was arrested and charged with selling cocaine. Later reduced to possession. The judge urged him to leave town and start a new life—and Peter did. He moved back to California and started a master's degree program in painting.

"No, no, Peter is fine!" I say. "I just talked to him!" This isn't true, we haven't talked in several months.

"I'm afraid you haven't heard the news yet. I have. The president told me."

She means Jean-Pierre, the director at Brookvale. She thinks she's in a university and he's the president. I pull her wheelchair away from the table.

"Peter's doing well, Mom. He lives in Boulder, with his wife Willie, whom we all love so much. Remember their house? He's painting. Remember his gallery and the show we saw there?"

The following day, a few minutes after noon, I tell Frances, "Usually, I can talk her out of her delusions. But not this time." I reach around to massage the crick in my upper right scapula—the spot where all tensions meet—my own love and anger toward Peter, Mom's true disappointments and delusions.

"A very old anxiety has taken hold of her," Frances says.

A silence settles between us. We seem to share an awareness of just how close we ourselves are to my mother's stage of life, how soon we may lose our hold on reality.

"When I find her in the common room, she's always in the same place, her wheelchair parked next to two other silent ladies. There she is, with a blanket over her, looking so small. She's listing toward the left. The staff put a pillow next to her to prop her up. Our doctor thinks she may have had a small stroke."

"Resulting from her falls, perhaps."

Frances is dressed in her tennis outfit today, a sweatshirt and a short white skirt over gray leggings. She asked me to send an email once to make sure we have each other's address and her response was, "Back at you." I picture her whacking the ball, then pull my attention back into the little room.

"I look at my mother and wonder if the woman I see now is the same person I knew before. When she hurt me."

"Does it matter?"

"I don't know. I can be nice to her because of the way she is now. I feel sorry for her. She's so dependent and needy! There's so little of *her* left. When I take her into the garden and we watch for birds at the feeder, I see a spark. In her room, I see certain objects, her address book or her clothes, that give me a sense of her old self. But the rest is gone."

"The mother who raised you is gone, yes. Yet her imprint remains.

The feelings remain. I think you understand that after all this time." Frances fiddles with a ring—*her mother's?*— hanging from a thin gold chain around her neck. "Speaking of time, I want to bring something up. "We've been seeing each other for what? A year, yet you've never brought up sex."

She keeps her tone light, so her question seems without pressure. "Most survivors of sexual trauma report having difficulty as they grow up and attempt to have healthy sexual relations."

Frances crosses her legs—nicely shaped legs below the white skirt. Not for the first time I wonder about her sexuality. *Is she straight or gay? Living alone or with someone?* She's attractive, yes. I would be attracted to her—if I were gay.

"I've talked about sex *ad nauseum* with other therapists! Starting with Dr. Abrams, the human-potential guy. So no, I don't want to talk about it."

The corners of Frances' mouth twitch.

"He made me imitate the noises my mother made with Ray. He jokingly threatened to coach my boyfriend and me. I've talked about it a lot."

She raises her eyebrows. "But not in here."

Again, analysis is different than other therapies. It's long, for one thing. And wandering. And ever searching.

"Okay," I say. "It's complicated. When I went out with boys at fourteen or so and we made out, I responded very strongly. I loved it. Then I think I got scared. I pulled back. I had a long relationship with a boy who was asexual or a closet gay. Very disturbed." Inwardly, I shudder, remembering Hurst, who harassed me when I broke up with him." I remember locking myself in the house while he pounded on the door. "I figured out how to give myself pleasure, though. I remember my mother telling me once I was in the shower too long."

Frances nods, knowingly.

We let a silence settle between us. My session is at noon, so the sun shines straight down on the little patio, through the redwoods that grow along the fence. The bougainvillea is against the building, grabbing all the sun it can.

Chapter 23

My eyes take a minute to adjust. The theater is dark and quiet after the glare and noise of the parking lot. I've walked to the junior college from my high school, where I'll graduate in two weeks. I've been accepted to UC Berkeley and won two scholarships, plus the award for best liberal arts student.

The theater is shaped like a shoebox, the walls lined with rough wood, the stage a simple platform, with an upper level, Elizabethan style. The tiers for seating rise sharply. They're bare now, the chairs stacked on the top row. I step onto the stage and imagine myself in a long skirt, playing the lady in the Molière play I saw last week.

Above me, I hear footsteps on the upper stage. Larry peers down at me, wearing baggy chinos and Keds. We stare at each other.

We haven't seen each other much in high school. I went out with upperclassmen. At the start of sophomore year, he found me outside the math building. "Look what I've been doing all summer!" He meant growing—he was taller than I was—but I ignored the hint. He took drama and acted in all the plays but didn't try hard in other subjects. By senior year, he'd become moody and distant. If we met when no one else was there, we exchanged a silent greeting as if to say, "I know you and you know me, and we still matter to each other."

"Have you seen Mr. Charlesworth?" Larry asks me, now.

"No."

We continue to stare at each other. "Are you signing up for

summer theater?" I ask.

He nods. "You?"

"I think so."

"You do that in the administration building."

He turns and leaves through the same door.

On the way to the administration building, I imagine finding him at the grad night party. We're in the cavernous Veterans Hall where we had dances in junior high, and I'm wearing the fitted blue dress I've sewn for graduation. He wears the mandatory white dress shirt and black slacks for boys. The Rolling Stones are playing. I ask him to dance.

"It's not a school-sponsored party," Mom says. "I won't let you go."

I stare at her. We're in the kitchen where I'm ironing my graduation dress. "You're kidding."

"Vanessa said there's a lot of drinking."

Vanessa is another teacher. "You let Peter go."

"Peter's a boy."

I stare hard at her. "That's not fair!"

"Vanessa said that last year there was so much spilled beer that boys slipped on the dance floor!"

"You think I'm going to drink?" I yell. "No, you think some drunk boy is going to take advantage of me."

"It isn't proper. Ray and I will take you to dinner."

This is the worst punishment I can imagine.

The ninety minutes of dinner with Ray at the Vandenberg Inn are an agony. He stands when people come by to congratulate me. "You must be so proud!" they say. As if he had anything to do with my success.

"Why weren't you at the party?" Larry asks. We're outside the theater on the steps, taking a break from our first rehearsal.

I groan. "Mom wouldn't let me. She was worried about the drinking."

He chuckles. "There was a keg or two. Too bad. We missed you."

"Who?"

"Celia and Greg and Debbie, too. All the cliques and divisions fell away. We were just old friends."

"Mom made me go to dinner with her and Ray."

"Ugh," he says giving me a searching glance.

"I hate him," I say, surprising myself.

"I know," he says.

Mr. Charlesworth calls us back inside.

Five of us sit in a small circle on the stage, lit by work lights, Mr. Charlesworth and the four of us cast in the first play of the summer. We're doing a read-through of *The Glass Menagerie*. I'm Laura Wingfield, and Larry is Tom, my brother. Mr. Charlesworth's wife, Helena, plays Amanda, and the Gentleman Caller is acted by our professional actor-in-residence, Paul Jenkins.

We're reading out of small, soft-covered blue books where I've underlined my lines. The book feels holy in my hands. Why has Mr. Charlesworth cast me as Laura, the gentle, damaged daughter? He knows our family. Does he guess our secret?

On another day, I watch from the seating area as Larry rehearses his opening monologue. Larry leans against the railing of the Wingfields' fire escape, a shock of dark blond hair falling across his forehead; the bones of his face are sharp, but his mouth is soft. "The play is memory. Being a memory play, it is dimly lighted, it is sentimental, it is not realistic." The words, spoken in a warm baritone, thread their way into my heart.

On Friday afternoon, Larry catches me outside the theater. "Want to go for ice cream?" We get into his car, an old white Comet, and drive to a nearby shopping center. Larry pays, making it an actual date, and we take our cones to a bench outside. He's got strawberry; I've got chocolate chip, both in sugar cones.

"I never thought I'd be doing something so fun and normal with you," I say.

"You don't think I'm an all-American boy?"

"No." Are we flirting? My mother shops at the grocery store next door, and I hope she won't see us.

"You see me as a mole, living in the dark? I love sunshine. I love ice cream."

"So do I." I blush, thinking about my weight. In scene six, Laura faints at the dinner table and Tom has to carry her into the living room.

Larry takes a bite from the end of his cone. "What happened to that tall guy you were going out with?"

I bite the end of my cone, too. "He fell in love with long distance." I giggle. In our play, this is how Tom Wingfield explains the long-ago departure of his father, a telephone man. In fact, I'm over the tall boyfriend.

"How do you like your gentleman caller?" he says.

"He's fine," I say, trying to sound neutral. Paul Jenkins is a wiry Texan in his late twenties, very subdued until he's onstage and bursts into life. "They're making me special shoes so that I limp. And I have to bind my breasts."

Larry looks sideways at me, eyebrows raised. "So you'll look maidenly."

He drives me home, taking College Avenue north, formerly empty fields where new developments are being built. Santa Maria has tripled in size since my family moved here.

"More ticky-tacky houses," Larry says.

He pulls up to our house and turns off the engine, drums his finger on the steering wheel. They're expressive fingers—spatulate in shape, the nails bitten. "Is your stepfather going to harass me?" he says.

"What do you mean?"

"I hear he comes out and shines a flashlight into your date's car."

I redden. "Yeah. Sometimes. But it's daytime. And——-" I stop.

"We're not making out."

I smile. "Right." I open the door and get out. "Thanks."

"See you Monday."

"No dating among cast members," Mr. Charlesworth announces on Monday. "It interferes with our work." He's a benevolent dictator we wouldn't think of defying. Rehearsals go on. Scene three begins with me alone on stage, dusting my glass animals and playing an old record on the Victrola. When I hear Amanda at the door, I rush to the Victrola, take the needle off the record and sit before my typing chart. I limp, one leg longer than the other. My mother enters, her face stripped of its usual cheer, her step heavy. "Deception, deception, deception," she declaims, and I feel slammed by the weight of her anger and disappointment—in me. "Mother, please," I beg.

When we do this scene, I imagine being shamed by my mother; I decide that Mr. Charlesworth cast me as Laura because of that.

A later scene brings Larry and me together, alone. He comes home late and drops his key down the fire escape. In my nightgown, I let him in. He confides in me, telling me about his night out, halfway confessing his drinking. He's been to the movies, where a magician performed tricks. He turned water into beer, then wine, and finally whiskey. I listen, rapt, in love with him. "He gave me his magic rainbow scarf. Here, you can have it, Laura," he says and drapes the shimmering fabric around my shoulders.

Now I think Mr. C cast me as Laura because of my imagination, and my feelings for my brother, Peter. I cherish the moments when other characters touch me—Tom placing a scarf around my nightgown clad shoulders or carrying me to the living room; the Gentleman Caller kissing me lightly on the lips. Most of all, when Amanda holds me at the end of play, sitting on the floor in front of the candelabra.

I cry a little, enough to stain Helena's bodice with mascara. Mr. C. wants me to cry, and at dress rehearsal I shed real, visible tears.

———

Our play is a success. When it closes, I wait for Larry to ask me out again. He spends his time with another company member, Keith.

I run sound for the next play on a reel-to-reel tape recorder that terrifies me. One day, up in the sound booth I hear two girls from the company talking below me. Larry and Keith have just come in by the side door, wearing identical sunglasses and hats.

"Are they fairies?" one girl says.

The other raises her shoulders dramatically, as if to stay, *Who knows?* "Larry's kind of effeminate," she adds.

Are they right? Is Larry a homosexual? Is that why he's ignoring me?

A week after we open, I invite the company over to my house for crêpes. The rest of the family is in Santa Barbara where Ray is having a procedure, something to do with his prostate.

Keith and Larry mix vodka and orange juice and hand the drinks out. I fry crêpes and serve them. The house is alive with voices and laughter.

"I can't believe Kate Laidlaw is throwing a booze party!" Larry says.

———

At the end of August, on our last night together, the Charlesworths invite the company to their townhouse for a party. Mr. C. has allowed beer—no hard liquor—and Helena makes enchiladas. "Tex Mex," she calls it because she's from Austin. After we eat, everyone sits on the floor telling stories and laughing. I slip away to the bathroom, up a half flight of stairs. When I come out, Larry is waiting for me.

"Want to take a walk?" he asks.

We tiptoe out the front door and down the steps. Their condo is one of twelve or so stylish, new units, two-storied, and arranged around a garden and pool. Each has a tiny courtyard in front. Larry opens the gate to let us out.

Is this another date, finally? It's dark, end-of-summer dark. Yellow light spills out from the neighboring condos onto a concrete path. The nutmeg scent of star jasmine rises from the ground, and I follow Larry into the lawn in the middle. The pool, surrounded by a metal fence, glows an eerie blue green. Larry unlatches the gate and sits cross-legged on the deck. I do the same, legs to one side. I'm wearing a new dress to start school in.

"Are you glad to be going away?" he asks.

I'm close enough that I can smell beer on his breath. "Yeah," I say nodding. "Peter is driving me up next week." Peter and Larry have been friends since they acted together in high school.

"Neat." He pulls out a cigarette from his shirt pocket.

After he smokes it, will he kiss me? Ask me to go home with him? He lives in a cottage behind his parents' house, not far from here. I came with my friend, Janet.

Larry cups his hands around the match. "It's good you're going away from home."

Peter has been telling me that I'm too straight, that Mom has too much control over me, and I assume Larry means the same thing. "Mom can be a pain, yes. I'm dying to leave!" Then I remember . . . Larry isn't leaving. "Sorry."

"It's okay. My parents leave me alone. I'm only staying because of Mr. Charlesworth."

This isn't true; Larry didn't earn the grades to get into a good school or win a scholarship, which his family would need.

He stubs his cigarette. "I don't just mean your mom. Peter told me about Ray. About what he's done to you."

I gasp and a wave of shame passes over me. Images of Ray's mouth on mine, his fingers unbuttoning my blouse, touching my breasts, invade my mind. Tears prick at my eyes. "It's okay. It's not that bad."

"Kate! It's completely shitty. How in hell can your mother stay with him?"

I'm crying now; I've never talked to anyone about this. He scoots over closer and puts his arm around me.

"I don't want you to feel sorry for me," I say.

"It's okay," he says, squeezing my shoulder. "Just get out of that house and stay away."

But if I leave, I won't see you, I want to say. Has he taken me out here only to give me brotherly advice?

From the other end of the garden, voices and the squeak of a gate opening.

"Larry, where are you?" a man, probably Keith, calls.

Larry and I get to our feet. "Take care of yourself," he says.

"You, too."

Chapter 24

A week later, in the back seat of Mom's Pontiac, Megan and I trade worried looks. We're on the way home from a week in Laguna Beach, and we've asked Mom to stop at Dad's to drop off a birthday present. Mikey's in the front seat next to her. Dad has just moved to a new apartment in Santa Monica off Wilshire.

Megan and I haven't seen him all summer. I asked him to come to my play, but he couldn't take the time off. After she parks, Mom lifts her face to the mirror and carefully applies lipstick.

"Are you sure you want to go in, Mom?" I ask. "Megan and I won't be long."

"Of course I want to go in. It would be rude not to say hello."

Dad is getting married soon, his third time, to Hilary, a young woman we like. She's likely to be in the apartment. The meeting will be embarrassing for everyone.

Mom runs a comb through her hair. "All right?"

We get out into the hazy glare of August in the Los Angeles basin. The apartment complex is new, with balconies upstairs and a courtyard planted with small palm trees and ferns. Mikey skips up the path, and we find the stairway leading to Dad's number. Our birthday present, a record, is more than two months late. My sister and I didn't know how to mail it safely, but more than that, we want to see him.

Mom knocks and Dad opens.

He takes a step back. "My, you've *all* come!" His hair is neatly cut and shorter than usual. He's dressed in shorts and an old blue T-shirt. In the living room beyond, kneeling beside an open carton and piles of books, is Hilary.

I hear a sharp inhale from my mother and rush forward, noisily, to hug Dad. "Hi, Dad! We're here!"

"Hello, Philip," Mom says.

Hilary is blushing, and the two women say hello.

Hilary is a slim, shy young woman from New England who usually dresses modestly, but today she looks like a floozy. Her hair has been sculpted and teased into a bouffant; she's been to the hairdresser. She wears a sleeveless top and pink short-shorts. Mom, some ten years older, has on her old khaki Bermudas and a plaid shirt.

The wedding must be tomorrow. We haven't been invited.

"Have a seat," Dad says. Hilary offers lemonade.

"Can I look at your Peanuts books?" Mikey asks.

Hilary digs into one of the cartons and, smiling now, hands the book to Mikey. Megan and I perch on the edge of a new blue couch. We hand over our present, a recording of the musical *Oliver!* Dad exclaims over it.

"I like the song 'Who Will Buy?'" says Megan.

"She's been playing it *all* the time," I add.

She and I take up the burden of conversation, telling stories about summer theater—how late we stayed up striking sets; how cranky the spectators were when Megan ushered; how exciting to work with professional actors.

"One night," I say, "on stage, in the middle of a scene, my garter belt came undone. It was the 'Deception, deception, deception!' scene.'"

Dad chuckles. "Oh dear. What did you do?"

"I stayed behind furniture. I played the whole scene imagining me on stage with my stockings around my ankles."

Mom gets up from her chair and goes to the bookcase.

"I'm sorry I couldn't come to your play," Dad says.

"It wasn't a long run." In truth, I cried when I got his letter. He'd come to see Peter in his play the year before.

"We're doing a Williams play this year," he says.

Mom waves a worn, red book. "This is my book."

"Which book?"

"Gerard Manley Hopkins. I wrote a paper on him."

"I don't think it's yours, Elizabeth. I wouldn't take your book." He goes to her.

She hands the book to him. "I think you gave it to me! At Grinnell"

He turns a page or two. "No inscription."

"That doesn't prove anything."

They argue. I expect Dad to give in, but he doesn't.

I get up. "We should be going. You have all this unpacking to do."

Dad rests the book on top of the case "Are you driving to Santa Maria?"

"Santa Barbara," I say. "We're stopping at Grandma's."

Hilary hugs me and asks when I leave for Berkeley. I miss whatever passes between Mom and Dad at the door.

"Goodbye, Thumbelina," Dad says to Megan. "Thanks to you both for my present." Mikey asks for a hug, too. "You can have the Peanuts book," Dad says.

"'Listen to the record!" I call out going down the stairs, still trying to lighten the mood.

We get into the car and Mom shoves the key into the ignition. "Why didn't you tell me she would be there?"

"We didn't know," I say in a small voice.

"Really, we didn't," Megan says.

"She *shouldn't* have been there! They're not married yet."

Hilary with her New England prudishness is probably upset, too.

"Oh, Mom," Megan says wearily. "Just drive."

She begins sobbing as soon as we reach Highway 1. She cries loudly, uncontrollably, as we continue north through Malibu, stopping at long traffic lights, happy beachgoers crossing the road in front of us. I'm afraid she'll run over someone. She is still crying at fifty-five miles an hour along the curvy stretch north of Malibu. "I made such a fool of myself! Why did you let me?"

Megan and I squirm. Mikey gives us anxious looks from the front seat.

"Slow down, Mom!" Megan yells once.

I'm mad. Mom stole our precious hour with Dad, the only time we had with him this summer. He listened so closely when I told the garter belt story and laughed, yes, but in such an understanding way. Then Mom started up with her thing about the book, and he hardly noticed me.

Mom comes up too fast on the car in front of us and slams on the brakes. She flings her arm out to keep Mikey from lurching forward, then pounds the steering wheel.

"You girls don't know your father! He slept with his cousin, Deirdre. They had an affair. Right under my nose."

"When?" I say in a small voice.

"When you were babies. But it started at Grinnell."

A recent memory flashes into my mind of Peter and me arriving at Dad's when he wasn't expecting us. His bed was unmade, and next to it sat an ashtray full of butts stained with lipstick. Bright red lipstick. I knew they weren't Hilary's.

"Was this Deirdre?" I ask now.

"Yes," Mom says, calmer now.

In the back seat, my sister and I trade anguished looks. More ugliness to swallow. A new, darker test of love and loyalty. I believe what Mom says. Dad is a sensual person, a seeker of pleasure.

We pull up in front of Grandma's white house.

"I thought she was going to drive off the road and kill us all," Megan whispers. We lie in the twin beds in Grandma's guest room.

"She's jealous because Dad and Hilary look happy. They are happy!"

Silence falls between us, and I feel the motion of the car again. There was such a depth of despair in Mom's sobbing; it was so absolute. An admission of failure? Unhappiness? Regret?

Megan pipes up. "Who's Deirdre?"

"Dad's cousin, on his father's side, from Grinnell. I remember her."

"That's your middle name."

"Yeah, pretty awful. I remember going to Berkeley to see her and her family. You were too little, or you stayed with Grandma. We took a ride on a ferryboat, and I thought I'd see fairies."

"Poor Mom," Megan says.

Chapter 25

On the day before Thanksgiving, at the Greyhound station in Oakland, Polly and Caroline take turns hugging me goodbye. "We're going to miss you *so* much," Polly says.

"Remember, you have to tell us *everything*," Caroline adds.

I find a seat in the third row, still smiling, still feeling the warmth of my new friends' goodbyes. We share the top floor of a nice old brown shingle boarding house near campus. University approved. A sundeck outside my window looks out on the Bay and the Golden Gate Bridge. We read and talk there. Music plays from Polly's portable stereo—the Beatles and the Stones.

The first time I saw Caroline, I was coming up the narrow stairway as she washed her face at the bathroom sink, wearing a bra and leopard-print half-slip, dark blond hair cascading over her shoulders and back. She said hello without any self-consciousness. She is small and more reserved than Polly, with an acid wit. Polly is tall and slightly knock-kneed, with long, thick brown hair, and she wears bright Marimekko-patterned dresses. She and I attend the entire series of New Wave films at Wheeler Hall. Afterward, Polly imitates Jeanne Moreau in *The Lovers*, frantically brushing her hair at the mirror and running to the window to see if her lover is there.

My new friends are smart and well brought up; they went to a boarding school in New England. Yet they like me! They haven't had much experience with boys, so they look up to me there.

I look out the tinted window as the Greyhound bus makes its way through the tangle of freeways, houses and factories south of the Bay. After San Jose, the countryside opens up. Gilroy with its water towers and broccoli fields, then a descent through boulders to Prunedale, and the plain of Salinas. The landscape looks dry after the acacia and eucalyptus of Berkeley.

I sit on the right side of the bus, the ocean side, as my sister and I did when we were young. It will be hours before I reach the coast. Earth dominates—dark furrows stretching in parallel lines to the coastal mountains. To the east, the dry, bleached bed of the Salinas River; no rains yet. I'm happy to be going home for Thanksgiving, the triumphant freshman, doing well in my classes. Peter will come home for the holiday, and Grandma will drive up from Santa Barbara, too. Little Mikey will be in heaven seeing all of us. Megan won't say much but I know she'll be happy and relieved to have us back.

The bus passes the mission at San Miguel, with its crumbling adobe walls and cluster of palm trees. I try to imagine these people—the family I love. I leave out the intruder, the interloper, the mistake. I have long practice ruling him out.

Will I see Larry? He didn't say anything about getting together when we talked by the pool in August.

The bus crosses the Santa Maria River, whitened and dry like the Salinas, and slows as it enters town. I know every building and street sign. On the right, the palm trees of Rick's Rancho, where a friend's mother took us and we spied on couples by the pool we imagined to be newlyweds. The Oriental Gift Shop, where we bought each other birthday presents. Miller's Drugs, where Celia and I got candy bars on our way home from El Molino. Celia won't be home this weekend; she and her mother moved to San Diego. *Will I see Larry?* I wonder again. Maybe my brother will tell him I'm home.

After dinner on the day after Thanksgiving, I'm at the dining table, ripping out the seam of a dress, when the front door opens and Peter enters. Close behind is Linda, his high school girlfriend. "Hello, sister! Look who I brought over for you!"

Larry huddles behind the other two, smiling sheepishly, looking handsome in a worn, brown leather jacket. *Oh shit,* I think, *I didn't wash my hair.*

"Hi, everyone!" I say. "Hi, Larry."

"Do you want to come with us to the drive-in movies?" Peter asks.

I look over at Larry, my eyebrows raised. He nods. "It's *Guns of Navarone.* Just your thing."

"Can I change?" I'm wearing stretched-out orange knit pants and my sister's old white sweater. It's not exactly clean.

"No," Peter says. "Show time is in fifteen minutes. Grab your coat."

He goes down the hall to my mother's room and tells her we're leaving.

Larry's white Comet is pulled up in the driveway. Peter and Linda get in the back, and I sit next to Larry in the front.

"How's Berkeley?" he asks, and I rattle on about my boarding house and my new friends. "They're really neat," I say. I tell him about the film series that Polly and I went to and how we dress up as hippies on Sunday night to have dinner on Telegraph.

"Cool," he says.

"Did you get the job at the radio station?"

"Yeah. It's crazy, cueing up three turntables at a time and pressing the right button for the news feed."

"What about school?"

He tells me they're putting on *John Brown's Body,* a play in poetry.

The night is cold and foggy, the drive-in south of town, off the old highway. We turn into a gravel drive and get waved past the ticket booth. Larry's father is the manager of the downtown theater, and the family has a pass. We pull up next to a speaker, front wheels on a rise, the better to view the screen. Larry attaches the speaker to his window and settles back against his seat. I inch closer. "Can you see, you in the back?" I ask.

"Sure, don't worry, honey." Peter's voice is muffled, and I realize he and Linda are kissing. The movie starts, the gigantic screen flashing with images of sea, boats, and rugged cliffs, the speaker booming out the soundtrack. In the back, the rustle of clothes and the unzipping of zippers. Larry and I sneak looks at each other.

"I can't follow it," I say. "Except for Gregory Peck's problem. He's the hero, right?"

"Right."

"This story is just like *The Iliad*!" I exclaim. "Achilles is so mad about Agamemnon stealing his woman, Briseis, that he mopes and won't join the battle. Just like Peck. *Hubris*."

"Hubris," Larry says, laughing and fingering my hair. The back of my neck tingles.

"I like Hector better than Achilles," I say.

When the movie is over, we drive to Linda's, and Peter and Linda get out. "Want to come to my house?" Larry asks.

I know about Larry's cottage—behind his parents' house in the older, southeast part of town. He's lived in the cottage since his brother left home.

"Okay," I whisper.

We turn from Miller Street to Camino Collegio, passing the houses of the rich kids who gave parties.

"Do you hear from Celia?" Larry asks.

"No. She went to San Jose, I think."

"Yeah, business administration," he says and shakes his head.

Larry turns into his street, a court, lined with palm trees and small, Spanish style houses. He parks in front of one where the lights are out, and I breathe a sigh of relief. He leads me up the driveway and unlocks the door. We enter a small kitchen, and he turns on a light.

Beyond the kitchen is a larger room, carpeted, with a long, high window on the far wall. Two daybeds occupy the corner, each with bolsters, covered in wide-wale maroon corduroy. A poster of Hayley Mills over one, and James Dean over the other. Larry turns on the wall heater and puts an album on the portable stereo, *The Freewheelin' Bob Dylan*.

"I love this," I say, as the familiar guitar chords and dancing rhythm come on. *Don't think twice, it's all right.* I sit at the end of the daybed under the window, take off my shoes and sit cross-legged. He lights a cigarette, then takes a pillow and sits against the wall in the corner.

"I'm not sure I need to tell you this," I say, "but I got worried after our last talk."

"At Mr. C's party."

"Yeah, by the pool." I sigh. "When you brought up Ray. I didn't know you knew."

"Right," he says encouragingly.

"I don't want you to think I'm hung up or anything. About sex."

"I never thought you were."

"I don't want you to be afraid of me."

"Come here," he gestures.

The only way to comply is to lie beside him, one leg over his. He tosses the bolster onto the floor and turns onto his side. Now we're facing each other. He puts his arms around me. The skin on his neck and arms is smooth and cool, smelling slightly of milk, and he holds me with just enough pressure. He's being leisurely, allowing me to feel safe, though it seems understood that we're going to have sex. That I have said yes. I want to tell him that I wouldn't do this for just anyone, that he is special to me, that he was the first boy I ever really liked. But I can't say those things; they'd sound dumb.

Instead, I take his left hand and open it. "Have I ever read your palm?"

"You're a fortune teller? a soothsayer?"

"Oh, yes." All I know is from a book I found at my dad's, a pamphlet with a black and red cover.

"In the fifth grade! You don't remember this? At Robert Bruce School, I read your palm. At our school carnival. You came to see Debbie and your old friends."

He kisses me, his soft mouth unafraid this time. "I hated leaving my friends at Robert Bruce."

"I like your fingers," I say. "They're spatulate."

"Let's do this later, okay?" He kisses me again, and I feel his erection against my pelvis. I sit up and pull my sister's sweater over my head. He unhooks my bra and skillfully takes my breasts in his hands, then makes a sound a bit like a gasp. He puts his head between them. I take my knitted pants off, glad now for the stretched-out elastic waist and kick them off the bed. He does the same with his jeans.

Now we're naked together, two white bodies, confused but taking care with each other. He strokes my hair, and it doesn't matter that I didn't wash it. Nothing matters but this.

He slips his sex inside me, and it goes in smoothly, easily. My body knows what to do and I don't fight it. The movements of our hips create ripples of pleasure—not the storm and release of my own efforts, alone, but the beginnings of that. After he comes and separates from me, I put my head against his chest and giggle. "That's done now."

"Was that okay?"

"Oh, yes," I say giggling. "Do I look different?"

"Beautiful," he says.

I feel a sticky wetness between my legs that feels like a prize. A reward. A badge of maturity.

I get home after two, and my mother grounds me for the rest of the weekend.

"At Berkeley our lockout time on the weekends is two-thirty," I tell her.

"Here it isn't."

Really, I think she's angry that I've been with Larry. She was his Latin teacher, and she's never liked him since. Larry comes to see me on Saturday night—that's allowed—and we sit in the den and talk.

"Do I look different?" I ask again.

"Oh, yes," he teases back. "Beautiful."

Back in Berkeley, on a Saturday morning in December, a series of bells ring on my floor, signaling that I have a visitor. I come downstairs in my robe—a nice one at least—to find Larry in the entry hall. He hitchhiked north and spent the night in a dorm with his old friend, Greg.

"Greg has tickets for the Bob Dylan concert tonight. Here, in Berkeley."

We sit and talk, and I play the spinet piano for him. I suggest lunch and change into a new orange embroidered dress bought at the Peruvian store on Telegraph. It's a brilliant fall day outside and we walk happily along Piedmont Avenue, under huge sycamore trees that are losing their leaves, passing International House, the stadium, and the Greek Theater.

"Always wanted to see Berkeley," he says. I feel proud. I take him to a favorite spot—the Café Espresso on Northside—and pay for lunch because he doesn't have much money.

"What happened to your job at the radio station?" I ask.

He shrugs. "It seems you need experience."

The words of Rilke, Pound and Neruda are written on the white walls around us. We're sipping sodas made with Torani syrups, mine tamarind, Larry's blood orange. We talk easily.

Before the concert, my friends help me get ready. A stylish senior, Maureen, does my hair up in a French twist and helps me with my makeup. "This guy is important to you, I can tell," she says. Molly and Caroline approve my choice of dress and shoes—heels.

At the Berkeley Community Theater, Dylan opens playing, as

usual, with an acoustic guitar. But after intermission, he comes back with an electric guitar and lets loose with the driving rock beat of "Maggie's Farm." Afterwards, on the steps of the Berkeley Community Theater, Larry and I stand close together under the star-filled night sky, grinning, feeling like we've witnessed history. That we're part of a great change.

When I come back home for Christmas break, I call Larry and right away he sounds different, as if he's in a bad mood. "I'd like to see you, but I can't pick you up," he says. His brother, at college in Arizona, took the Comet, even though he'd given it to Larry two years earlier. After a few awkward exchanges in which he doesn't offer a solution, I say, "I can walk over." I still don't have my driver's license.

It's a cold, overcast day, and I walk over in my new blue poncho, fringed and hooded, another purchase at Ship of the Andes. I'm dazzled by all the different styles I see on campus and drawn to what I think Joan Baez would choose.

Larry lets me into his cottage, looking tired and pale, wearing a faded gray sweatshirt. Our eyes meet for just a second, and he gives me a curt nod.

"Am I too early?" I ask, though it's 1:30. The blinds are still down, and his bed is unmade.

"No. It's all right."

"Seems like you're in a bad mood. What's the matter? Your car?"

He lights a cigarette at the stove. "No. The casting went up for our next play."

"*John Brown's Body?*"

He nods. "I didn't get a part."

"Gee!"

"It's not about my acting. It's because of my other grades. I'm being punished."

"Who by?"

He gives a little shake, and I wonder if he's hungover. "Mr. C. gave me the bad news, but I think my battleax of a mother had something to do with it."

"Shit," I say. Larry wants to be a professional actor, so this cuts deep. He doesn't like his mother. She spanked him in front of his entire third grade class, he once told me. She works at Larry's college, so she and Mr. Charlesworth would be chummy.

Larry puts his cigarette out in a used cereal bowl and, without saying anything, goes into the other room. He stands facing the wall heater, hunched over, warming himself.

I take off my poncho, wishing Larry had said something about it, and drape it over one of the two kitchen chairs. I walk over to him and thread my arms under his arms and around his chest. I'm wearing a pretty sweater, and I know he can feel my breasts against his back. I want to coax him out of his bad mood. After a minute or two, he turns around and holds me. Leads me to his unmade bed. This time, unlike the last times we've been together, we don't talk or laugh as we unzip our jeans and pull off our tops. There's no stream of banter or teasing; our movements seem forced, *pro forma*. We're taking off our clothes because we've done this before, lying down beside each other because our bodies have done this, He's touching my breasts and entering me because he's done this before. Is it because it's the daytime? Because he's depressed? I don't tell him what my grades were—two *A*s and a *B*.

Afterward, an empty, gray silence occupies the cottage. The heater clicks, and a lone jay squawks outside the window. I feel lost and stupid, thinking I shouldn't have come over. I stand up and put my clothes on. He doesn't get up to say goodbye.

I walk fast on the way home, disappointed and confused. I can't reconcile this Larry with the Larry of summer and fall, the boy-man who cared about how I felt, who saw deeply into my thoughts and feelings. *He'll be back,* I tell myself.

At home, I get busy. I pull two skirts out of my closet and set up the ironing board and sewing machine. Maureen, the senior on my floor, sews her own skirts, too, and they fall well *above* the knee. I cut off three inches.

Chapter 26

The acacia trees behind our boarding house have started to bloom, turning the hillside a fragrant yellow. New classes start—French Lit, Shakespeare, and an honors history seminar where everyone knows more than I do. My first semester confidence vanishes.

My eighteenth birthday comes and goes. I take walks under the acacias, up the switchbacks of Panoramic Way. I arrange branches in a vase downstairs, and we all get headaches. One evening we're gathered in Maureen and Helen's room, next door to mine. I idolize them: Maureen because she's stylish and sure of herself; Helen because she's kind and speaks with a slight, patrician lisp.

"In my sociology class," Helen says quietly, "we just learned that women who live together get their periods at the same time." She gathers up her long, wheat-colored hair in her hands.

"Our hormones float around and mingle?" Caroline asks.

"Like the dirt cloud around Pigpen," Polly adds, laughing, referring to *Peanuts*.

"Do *you* have yours now, Helen?" Maureen asks.

"Yes."

"Me too! Anyone else?"

My heart skips a beat, and my face reddens.

I shake my head. "I've always been irregular," I say, though it's not relevant. My periods were erratic in junior high but normal later. I get up off Maureen's bed. "I've got to read *Hamlet*," I say.

In my room, I take the calendar down from the wall and turn the page back to January. I pour over the notes, desperate for a reminder. I don't remember having my period during finals, or on the bus going home to Santa Maria. Not, of course, when I was with Larry. It had to have been before, during dead week. Six weeks ago. My heart seizes.

But maybe my periods are going back to being irregular. I sit at my desk to read *Hamlet*, but my mind goes its own way. Larry and I never talked about contraception—not the first, happy night, not after. I knew about rubbers, but the subject never came up. It would have been embarrassing, intruding on what seemed so natural.

Except the last time in Larry's bed wasn't nice.

The possibility of pregnancy is awful. Horrible. A deep chill goes through me.

"Oh no, 'tis an unweeded garden," I read. "Things rank and gross in nature / possess it merely."

I get up, change into my nightgown and huddle inside my blankets.

Over the next few days, I carry a tampon in my purse, sure my period will start while I'm walking down Bancroft, or in French Lit class, or at lunch on the terrace. But it doesn't. My body feels heavy, lumpy, ugly, and I start wearing loose clothes. I don't look at boys, and when I pass some frat boys holding up numbered signs in front of their house, they give me a *3*.

That afternoon, alone, I walk up Panoramic Way again. I pass cottages and gardens where I used to imagine myself living, years from now, a professor at Berkeley. Not any longer. I'll have to drop out of school. I'll have to support myself.

Magnolias are blooming in some yards, bare branches supporting waxy pink and white flowers. They're new to me, but I can't enjoy them; they make my heart ache. I climb an old stone stairway, flanked by pillars, one mossy step after another. *"It can't be true. You'll get your period,"* a voice says. But it's been more than three weeks, and my breasts are tender.

If Peter were here, I'd tell him. I can't phone him. Impossible to enter the shared booth next to the dining room, dial his dorm, and speak those words. And besides, he'd only tell me to get an abortion in Mexico or something, and that would cost money he and I don't have. It is the same with Larry.

I'm ashamed to tell Polly and Caroline. This is my cross to bear. They ask me to go to the movies on Saturday night, but I tell them I have a paper to work on. I go to bed early, and soon, a feeling creeps over me that I can only describe as bad. A crushing kind of annihilation, the same feeling I had at age eleven after Ray assaulted me, when I sobbed on the green couch. Then as now, no one to help me.

Hours later, woken by light and noise, I go into the hall. Maureen tells me Helen is too drunk to come up to bed. I take a blanket from my bed and run downstairs, where I find her on the couch. "I think I'm going to be sick," she moans, and I fetch a basin from the kitchen. I hold her beautiful hair while she throws up. "I'm sorry," she mumbles, and then falls back asleep against a pillow. I don't mind the smell or the sight; I feel like a nun, sacrificing my comfort, my rest. I sit on the floor next to her, keeping watch.

The following Friday, I walk south on College Avenue into a neighborhood I've never been to, looking for an address Maureen gave me. I have an appointment with a local doctor named Pritchard. Yesterday I went into Maureen's room when I knew Helen would be gone, closed the door, and told her my problem. "Maybe you know what I can do?"

The doctor's office is on the first floor of a respectable-looking, square stucco house, a magnolia tree blooming outside. In the waiting room, young women sit on straight-backed chairs against the wall. An older woman, with black hair severely coiled on her head, looks up from her desk. "What can I do for you?" she says coldly.

I whisper my name and the time of my appointment. She begins writing on a clipboard.

"Age?"

"Eighteen," I say, and she frowns. She is the doctor's wife, Mrs. Pritchard, I see from the pin on her white uniform. She seems to disapprove of us all.

"Date of last period?"

The office is warm and smells like the brewer's yeast my mother used to take, or beer, or urine. After I've waited for a half hour, Mrs. Pritchard calls me in, still with no smile. Dr. Pritchard is a small, white-haired man, dry looking, paternal. "You're fortunate that it's this early," he says.

"But we don't know I'm pregnant," I say.

"A test will take too long. And you'd have the extra expense." He'll give me a shot today, he explains, another one the following Monday, and a final one on Wednesday. "Martha," he calls, and his wife comes in. How many women has he given shots to? Is this all he does?

I'm told to get up on the table, to raise my skirt and lower my underpants. The shot will be in my left buttock.

I feel the needle go into my flesh and think for a second of being in Larry's bed, on his rumpled sheets; then a flash of heat, and my muscle relaxes as the needle comes out. Hurriedly I pull my underwear back in place and sit up.

Dr. Pritchard looks me in the eye. "Most importantly, young lady, you're on the shelf for the time being. Do you understand?"

"Yes." I climb down from the table feeling chastened.

"Make appointments for Monday and Wednesday," he tells his wife.

March 3
Dear Larry,

My period was late last month, and I was really scared. But a senior in my boarding house gave me the name of a legitimate doctor, right here in Berkeley, and I went to see him. He gave me some shots to "hasten" my period, he said, and I did get my period. So I'm all right. I just wanted you to know. I didn't want to worry you earlier. I hope things are going better for you in school.

Always,
Kate

Larry writes back right away. I open the letter in the vestibule, next to our little wooden mailboxes. The envelope is addressed in his large, almost scrawling hand.

March 8
Dear Kate,

I'm sorry you had to go through this, and I really wish I'd been there with you. I wish you'd told me sooner. I'd like to see you as soon as you can come down. Please let me know when you're coming.

Love,
Larry

The best part of the letter is the word *love* at the end, which *I* wasn't brave enough to use. In the foyer, I cry with happiness.

I don't go home. I'm afraid of testing our relationship, of finding out that he doesn't really love me. I stay at Berkeley until spring break, and when I do come home, it's with Polly and Caroline driving Polly's old Peugeot.

I have qualms as we enter my neighborhood, and I see it as

Polly and Caroline must—a boring, suburban tract, with kitschy decorative touches and ugly driveways. No way for them to know that ours is a better subdivision than others in Santa Maria—newer, cleaner, better maintained, a middle-class neighborhood. Caroline's family lives on Park Avenue and Polly in New Canaan, Connecticut. What was I thinking?

"We'll go out to see the wildflowers tomorrow," I say as we get out of the car. "You won't believe the lupine."

Our house, tan stucco with white trim and diamond-paned windows, looks smaller, the front porch dark, but at least the yellow rose on the trellis is blooming. The first person to greet us is Ray, springing out of his den, the TV blaring behind him. He grins and comes close to shake hands with Polly and Caroline. "Welcome, young ladies!" He's wearing denim overalls, and his hair is cut short, as usual.

"Hi, hi," I say, and push past him, avoiding eye contact. "Let us put our things away."

Mom will make a better impression, I think, and she does. She serves the girls tea in the living room and makes her best dish, chicken with mushrooms, for dinner. Polly and Caroline are at ease and make friendly conversation.

An hour after dinner, the three of us are sitting on the floor in Larry's studio, smoking pot. I wrote to him a few days before our trip, asking if we could we come over. He's cleaned up his place, I notice, and wears an ironed shirt. "I brought my grades up," he tells me. "I can do summer theater."

Polly starts looking through his records. "Not many, but high quality," she says and pulls out *Help!* by the Beatles. "Ah!" she says. "May I?"

"Of course." He's rolling a joint. "This is from your dope peddler of a brother, Kate." Peter is near Larry, at UC Santa Barbara.

He and I hugged, awkwardly, at the door, but no kiss; there won't be one tonight. No chance to talk, either. I feel stupid, bringing my friends here, forcing them to meet like this. They're the three most important people in my life, but how can they know each other? Polly and Caroline know how much I care about Larry, but not about my pregnancy scare. That's what I call it now. *A scare.*

We sit on the floor, and Larry passes the joint.

"I'm skipping the first song," Polly says, lowering the needle. "It's not by the Beatles." She tilts her head back and sings, "*It's only love . . .*" and Larry beats out the rhythm on the floor. I take the fragrant smoke into my throat and lungs. My breathing slows, and I feel pressure in my head.

"Who else do you like?" Larry asks Polly.

"The Lovin' Spoonful and the Beach Boys."

"The Beach Boys!" Larry shouts, laughing. "Those fops!"

"Great singing, great harmonies," Polly says.

"And you?" He turns to Caroline.

"I'm more a Beatles girl," she says, without looking up, not letting him see her beautiful, deep-set eyes. She's not going to let him see her humor. Other than a crush with a wrangler at a dude ranch, she hasn't had a love interest.

I'm wearing the same dress I wore last June when Larry took me out for ice cream. A slow song comes on, and instantly I feel sad, forgotten, ignored. I get up and drift into the kitchen. I begin dancing, modern-dance style. A minor chord is strummed on a single guitar. I hold still, then the voice sings or almost speaks: "*Yesterday . . .*" and I dance again, bending my torso to one side then the other, swooping my arms down and overhead, turning, lost.

"What's the matter with Kate?" I hear Larry ask the others.

"I don't know," Caroline says. "It must be the grass."

The next day, after taking them to see the lupines, I say goodbye to Polly and Caroline at the curb. "Don't go to Baja without me!" I tell them. "I'll be down on Wednesday."

When I come back in, Mom looks up from the magazine she's reading. "You seem rather immature when you're with those girls."

"What do you mean, immature?"

"I don't know . . . silly."

"We were having fun!" I cry. "That's what fun looks like!"

I want to say so much more, that Polly and Caroline are the first close friends I've had since junior high. That I was too ashamed in high school to be close to anyone—all because of Ray.

Chapter 27

"When you thought you were pregnant, you said you had that *bad feeling*," Frances says. "You used the same words when you told me about your fight with Richard. The fight that brought you into couple's therapy." She levels her gaze at me.

I think back to our first visit to Greta's office. The plants in the window behind the couch Richard and I sat on. Her warm, vivid presence. Yes, I told them then.

Frances asks, "Can you describe that bad feeling for me now?"

My throat tightens and my mind stops. Beyond the French doors, the wind stirs the dark, shaggy branches of the redwood tree. "It's hard."

"Try."

I close my eyes and force myself to see within. "The bad thoughts are like flashes. Richard doesn't love me. I've lost everything. I'm dizzy or falling." Another gust shakes the branches. I can't look at Frances, can't let her see this part of me. "I'm stuck in misery—no past, no future. A feeling like death."

"Yes." Frances absorbs my words, taking some of their weight.

"The worst is that I've done this to myself. I've failed at the only thing that really mattered to me. Family life. Love. Before Richard, I didn't have that fear."

"Yes, you did."

"When?"

"In the sewing room when you were eleven."

A feeling of cold comes me. "But when Richard was mad at me, the pain was so much worse . . . because I'd trusted him."

Frances shrugs. "And you didn't feel that with your mother?"

Our fight took place two years ago in New York City. Given a choice between a single room overlooking Central Park or a two-room suite in back, we choose the suite because Richard likes to be comfortable. I've just moved Mom into Brookvale and feel torn leaving her. "Go," my sister Megan insisted. "It's your anniversary and you need a break. They'll call me if anything comes up."

For our anniversary dinner, we choose a small, Italian restaurant on 54th Street. Walking there on Fifth Avenue, we swing hands. It's mid-December and cold. I wear a black silk dress and my favorite coral necklace, Richard, a jacket and tie.

"Now let's not have another fight!" he says.

I laugh. "No, no. Promise." Fifteen years ago, at another high-priced Manhattan restaurant, we had one.

"I forget. What was it about?" Richard asks.

"I interrupted you when you were talking to the wine steward. You took offense."

"Ah!"

"And then at the end of the meal, you made a quiet but nasty remark." Richard hates any sign of arguing in public.

The restaurant entrance is several steps down from the street, leading us into a small foyer where the maître d' helps us off with our coats and scarves. A small Christmas tree twinkles. The interior is quiet and softly lit, the tables covered in snowy linen. We order *parmigiana* of zucchini, *agnolotti*, bigeye tuna, and a bottle from a Tuscan winery we know. I relax. Away from home, I can enjoy luxury without feeling guilty about having more than our family and friends. The dishes arrive and are placed just so, and we talk about the play we saw that afternoon, about the exhibit we'll go to tomorrow. We always talk over dinner. The play excited me deeply—an adaptation of *War and Peace*. I feel one with Pierre, Natasha, and Andre. After we finish our *panna cotta*, I put my hand on Richard's.

"Lately, I've had this insight into my life," I say. "It helps me understand why my early life was so difficult. What I went through with Ray and Mom."

He nods, looking wary. I can see his mind working, fearing what I'm about to say. He's usually sympathetic when I talk like this. But I've been irritable lately, what he would call unstable. I feel shy, even scared, but the play and the wine have caused me to drop my guard.

"Maybe suffering is the purpose of my life. It's my fate. I'm meant to *bear* suffering."

"Your fate," he repeats, with obvious distaste.

I wait for more, for encouragement or understanding. He looks around for the waiter, then pulls his hand from mine. "What I don't understand," he says, not looking at me, "is why your sister, Megan, is so much less affected by your past than you are. She went through what you did but she seems fine."

I gasp. It's as if he's struck me. "I can't *believe* you said that!"

He throws down his napkin, gets up, and walks out of the restaurant.

I remain in my chair, an older woman wearing her best black dress and coral necklace, stunned. After a minute or two, the waiter asks if I want anything else and leaves the check, with two chocolate truffles. Luckily, I have my wallet—did Richard know that? I don't often when we go out. I take out a credit card. Tears stinging my eyes, I make a stab at the tip. Get up and walk back past the other diners, trying to act as if nothing unusual has happened. In the foyer, the maître d' helps me on with my coat and scarf, and I go out into the night. Alone, forever.

It's cold and windy. I hurry down the long cross city block in my narrow skirt and heels, hoping to see Richard waiting at Fifth

Avenue. He isn't there. No, he's striding rapidly two blocks ahead, anger propelling him. Why does he have the right to be angry and I don't? He's always been understanding about my past. He's always blamed my mother for staying married to Ray. "Any mother—even a welfare mom—would protect her children!" Now he sees me as a neurotic, a crazy person, wallowing in self-pity. Worst, he prefers my sister. Let him marry *her*!

I try to walk purposefully, suppressing my tears because they will make me easy prey to muggers. How dare he compare me to Megan? What does he know about her pain? She's an introvert, she's hardly talked to *me* about our past. All Richard knows is the cheerful, unassuming woman he sees when we're together. Pretty, too—and so much less trouble than her sister!

I'm on Fifth Avenue now, crossing near the Plaza Hotel. Richard is not going to meet me, he's abandoned me. He'll be mad for days. Yes, I chose the wrong moment. He was in his old-fashioned restaurant mode. And maybe I phrased it badly. I'll tell him that when I see him.

I push through the crowd of holidaymakers around the Plaza Fountain. At our lobby, I cross an acre of red carpet to reach the elevator bank. After another mile of the same carpet on the twentieth floor, I let myself in. The sitting room is dark, and I tiptoe through the glass doors to where Richard lies in bed, with the lights out.

I sit down next to him, still in my coat. "I'm sorry," I say and reach across the sheet for his shoulder. "That wasn't the right time or place."

He shakes my hand away.

"Please turn over. Please talk to me."

"I have nothing to say to you."

I turn on the bedside light. "Please, Richard. I'm miserable."

His hand goes up to shield his eyes. "Turn that off."

I turn it off. "Do you know how badly you hurt my feelings?"

"Do you *realize* what you did? After we talked on the way to the restaurant about not getting into a fight? I can't *believe* you!"

"But *you* said something extremely hurtful to me!"

"You always have a reason. You always justify yourself. Leave me alone."

It's no use talking. He's gone into his fortress, raised the drawbridge. I'm the enemy, I'm evil.

I turn off the light, take off my dress, my shoes, panty hose and necklace, and throw them down on a chair. In the marble bathroom, I wrap my naked self in one of the heavy, white robes that hang there. I turn out the light and tiptoe past the bed and into the sitting room, closing the glass doors behind me. One small lamp burns next to the sofa, covered in stiff brocade. I sit on it, tucking my legs under, making myself small. I pull the robe over my feet. The seat is hard.

Outside, the glare and noise of 51st Street press in through two long windows. A siren wails coming down the Avenue of the Americas. Taxis honk. Drunken shouts ring out; homeless people outside the subway entrance. I want to leave New York, to go home. Why have we come here?

In the bedroom, Richard snores. How can he sleep? This is another, greater abandonment. Doesn't he know I'm in agony? He has no idea how I feel, he doesn't care. I begin crying harder. Every harsh word he's ever spoken comes at me in a nightmarish chorus. *I always do wrong. I never learn. I'm unworthy of his love.* If I get angry, he stops loving me. *I'm a bad, worthless girl.*

The terrible feeling rips through me. I stand up, dizzy, a flimsy thing like a thistle being blown about. I can't trust the floor or the walls to hold me. How can the hotel put windows that open in rooms so dangerously high? They fall outward, shatter and break. Leading to empty, black space, a magnet pulling me. I go to the window and sit on the sill. I raise it.

A blast of cold air sweeps into the room, rattling the glass doors. I hear Richard stirring, awoken by the noise. "What's happening?" he shouts. "Where are you?"

I close the window and stand. "I'm here. I'm okay."

Chapter 28

I fling my arms around my mother who's waiting outside the bus station dressed in her school clothes, shoulders thrown back. She pecks me on the cheek. I take my two suitcases from the driver—a big red one and the small plaid Grasshopper that Grandma Stuart gave me when I was eleven. She leads the way to the car.

"What's this?" I ask. Mom opens a Volvo sedan, slate blue.

"My new car. Isn't it nice?"

I slide into the bucket seat, taking in the smooth leather. What a difference from the worn bench of her last car—a ten-year-old green Buick. What's gotten into her?

"Polly has a foreign car, too," I say. "She drove me to the station in her parents' old Peugeot."

"Who?" Mom shifts and pulls out into the street.

"Polly, my housemate. You met her at spring break."

"Oh, yes."

We turn from North Broadway onto El Molino. "I needed a better car for long trips," Mom says. "To drive up and see you in Berkeley for one thing."

I haven't told Mom that I plan to share an apartment with Polly and Caroline next year. I can hear her objecting already. *"Those girls are a bad influence. They smoke!"*

"You'll need to learn to drive this summer," Mom says.

"I won't have time. We're going to be really busy at the theater."

"I can't drive you all the time."

"I can walk."

"Not at night." We're on our street now, with kids on the sidewalks and lawns.

"Speaking of long drives," she says. "Tomorrow I'm taking Megan and Michael to Sequoia for a few days."

I gasp.

"We're going away for a few days."

"You, Megan and Mikey?"

"I start teaching summer school on Wednesday. And you start theater on Monday, so you can't go."

"Some welcome home," I mutter. My chest tightens, my breathing stops. "Ray's not going?"

"No."

Mom turns into our driveway, and I see the curtain of our window move; it's Megan.

I pull my suitcases out of the trunk. A small blond head comes around the car, and I feel Mikey, nine now, hurtle into me, arms around my waist. I am his second mommy. Megan waits her turn behind him.

Ray gets out of his chair in the den and steps into the doorway, pipe in his mouth. "Welcome home, honey."

I pick up my suitcase and nod, mouthing a hello. If I say nothing I'll be accused of rudeness. He shakes his head, puts his pipe back in his mouth. I lug the red suitcase past the bookcase and into the room I share with Megan. She carries the small one.

"Where'd you get this?" Megan asks. I'm unpacking, throwing dirty clothes on the floor. Megan holds up a raspberry nightie and looks at herself in the mirror.

"Polly my roommate gave it to me. She said it was too frilly for her."

The afternoon sun streaks into the bedroom, lighting Megan's copper hair. She's grown up this year, her seventeenth, and become pretty. Her bangs hang over eyes, made up to look like Barbra Streisand's. The notebook where she writes poetry and song lyrics is open on the desk. She sits on one of the twin beds now, covered in green madras. We've always shared a room.

"Can I wear that dress to auditions on Monday?" I ask.

Megan nods. "Are you nervous?"

I sit beside her. "Maybe I won't do summer theater. Maybe I'll go with you to Sequoia."

"What do you mean?" she says sharply. "You've got to do summer theater. I wish I could."

I'm thinking of the forest smell, the squawk of blue jays, and the wildflowers. A grove of redwood trees so immense that they make their own light. A cathedral. The General Sherman Grove.

"Remember the cherry phosphates?" I ask.

Megan nods. "They better still have them. I told Mikey."

I find my sister's eyes in the mirror. "Do *you* have to go?" I plead.

She looks away. She knows what I mean. Has Ray bothered her now that I'm gone?

"I have to go," Megan said. "She wants me to help drive. Sorry." She gets up and leaves the room. A minute later, the piano starts up, the theme from *Lawrence of Arabia*.

I carry my laundry back through the house. Ray's in the den still, and the news is on.. Mom's in the kitchen talking on the phone, probably to Harriet. She's taken a bath and put on an orange caftan sewn out of bath towels. She leans back in the chair, laughing. Here are other changes to go along with the Volvo. Harriet is a mannish, brilliant English teacher at the college. Always kind to me.

On my way back, I check the kitchen calendar where Ray enters his schedule. He's off today, on evening shift for the next two days.

He calls out on my way back. "Do you need some help with that suitcase? I can stow it in the garage."

"Okay. Just the big one." Maybe *he's* changed, too. "Thanks."

I close the door to my room—the knob feels flimsy—and feel my stomach clench. He thinks nothing of a closed door.

We sit down to dinner at six, the kitchen filled with summer light and smelling of hamburger and hot cast iron.

"I'm looking forward to seeing Bearpaw Meadow," Mom says.

"Maybe we'll see a bear, Mikey," Megan teases.

"I wish, I wish, I wish!" Mikey says.

Mom squirts ketchup on Mikey's bun. "What a thrill to see the giant sequoias again."

"We're going to see giants?" Mikey shouts.

"Don't talk with your mouth full," Ray says.

"No, no. The *trees* are giants," Mom says. "They're the oldest living things on earth."

"That park was full of mosquitoes." Ray puts down his hamburger and shakes his head. "Never forget that. Don't know why you like it so much."

Ray went to Sequoia with us just once, when I was fourteen, Mom's last try at a family vacation. That was the time he made a scene, accusing Peter and me of drinking.

"I thought I'd pull out the sweet peas tomorrow," Ray says. "Put in something else."

"So soon?" Mom says.

"They're finished. You didn't notice?"

"I guess not. That's fine then."

After dinner, I clear the plates, and Mom runs water in the sink. "Exactly *when* will you be back?" I ask.

Megan, catching the sharpness in my voice, looks up from the glasses she's gathering.

"Monday evening. In time for dinner."

How nice, how considerate, I think, and snatch up the napkins and napkin rings. Red for Mom, white for Megan, green for Mikey, blue for me, and black for Ray.

"Show Mikey the tree rings," I say.

"What?"

"The cross section of the tree with all the dates."

"Of course." Mom nods toward the refrigerator. "There's food there for you and Ray."

"The happy pair," I mutter.

Mom's head turns. "What?"

"Nothing."

I slide the napkins back into their rings. She doesn't ask about my grades or my hopes for the summer. She hasn't wished me luck in the auditions. She thinks I'm already lucky. If only she knew about my visits to the doctor this winter. My agonies over Larry.

Mom dries her hands and takes off her apron. "We'll get up early. I may not see you in the morning."

Chapter 29

The next morning, I lie on a lounge chair in the backyard, holding *Best American Plays of the 1950s*. I wiggle around, trying to avoid the torn patch in the webbing. My laundry is on the line. I'm wearing a pair of shorts belonging to my sister and a sleeveless blouse.

I'm halfway through the first act of *The Crucible* when the shade snaps up in the back bedroom—Ray getting up. I try to focus again on Abigail's speech to John Proctor. A few minutes later, I hear him in the kitchen, making coffee.

Bozo, our spaniel, licks my bare feet and puts his paws on my stomach. I push him away, read faster, holding the book high to block the sun. Finally, too hot, I roll out of the lounge chair. I cross the patio and open the sliding window, letting my eyes adjust to the dim interior. Across the room, Ray's form fills the doorway to the den. A tense energy is coiled inside him.

"How're you doing, Kate? Not too hot?"

Maybe I can afford to be a little nice. "It's a little hot. And Bozo was bothering me." I've said too much, admitted we belong to the same family.

"That fool dog! I'll feed him in a minute. Get yourself a cool drink of water."

Feeling light-headed, I fill a glass from the kitchen tap. *He'll go to work soon, at two-thirty,* I tell myself, but for now, I have to think. *You can manage him.* I swallow the last of the water. *He hasn't been that bad lately. You're smarter than he is.*

As I come back through the living room, he catches me by the shoulders.

"You're looking awfully cute, girlie." He pulls me closer and puts his mouth on mine—loose, sloppy, tasting of tobacco. An old man's mouth. I allow him to for a second, then pull away. I stare hard at him, willing my eyes to speak. *Do you see how I hate you, how you disgust me!* I back into my room.

I sit on my bed, shaking. My feet are clammy against the linoleum. I grab a corner of the green bedspread and wipe my mouth with it, trying to take comfort from the familiar—the seashells and sea fans that decorate my dresser and my sister's, the books in the small case next to my bed.

That wasn't much, I tell myself. *Not so bad. He didn't touch my breasts or unbutton my skirt or press his pelvis against me.* Still, a stew of bad feeling churns inside me. Rage at Ray, anger at my mother, shame, and self-loathing—because I let him.

Next time I won't be silent. I'll scream.

Walking, walking fast, away from home, wearing my sister's clean, lavender sundress, I'm on my way downtown to the fabric store. I'll shut myself in my bedroom, where the Singer is now, and sew.

If only I had a car, if only I could drive! In the winter I walked to Larry's. Today I'm not sure of his welcome.

Dottie's Fabrics is on West Main. I wait for the light to change at Broadway and Main. Across the street is Ruth's Fountain where Debbie, Celia, and I spent our allowance on cherry Cokes, Colliers Apparel, and the Santa Maria Theater. Sometimes Larry works there. I saw him on a ladder once putting up letters on the marquee. Today boys jostle in line to see *Batman*.

The light changes and I cross. Without thinking, I turn toward the theater, stride across the tiled entry and enter the lobby. "Is Larry here?" I ask the boy working the popcorn machine.

A deeper voice speaks up, Larry's father, Mr. Hohlman, a small man with sandy hair and gold-rimmed glasses. "He's not here. But I'll tell him you stopped by. Kate, right?"

I redden. "It doesn't matter," I say. "I'll see him at the theater Monday."

"No, no, I'll tell him this evening."

I rush out, sure Mr. Hohlman and the boy are laughing at me. How many other girls came asking for Larry? I'm acting like an eighth grader.

The wind blasts me as I turn the corner, tearing at the opening in my skirt. I fight to keep it closed. *Did Ray guess that I've had sex? Can he smell it on me? Is that what his look meant?*

At the fabric store, Dottie greets me, brimming with ideas. "What's your fancy today, Miss College Coed?"

"I was thinking a dress to usher in. I'm in summer theater again."

"How about your basic black?"

We find a Vogue pattern for a fitted sheath, princess lines, with a scooped neck and short narrow sleeves. Dottie zeros in on a bolt of rayon that looks like raw silk. "Smashing on you. Make it really fit. Your mother will say it's too tight but ignore her."

"She's not home this weekend."

"Good."

In the kitchen, a note is scrawled on the blackboard. "I fed Bozo. Salisbury steak in frig." Instead of a signature, he draws a caricature of his face—square jaw, crewcut, pipe. I eat the Salisbury steak out of its aluminum container then set up the ironing board. I forget everything. Eyes and hands take over, pressing, pinning, cutting. I iron next to the wall phone in the kitchen, and the iron cord keeps tangling with the phone cord. *Maybe Larry will call. Stop thinking.*

Cutting is my favorite part. I love the weight of the sheers in my hands, the click of their blades and slicing into the thin paper. I cut slowly, perfectly around the U-shaped neckline. I'll have to get a black bra. "Low enough to show some décolleté," Dottie said.

Décolleté, bosom, white flesh. I remember how Celia always bought her bras a size too small. Now I'm doing the same thing.

After eight it's too dark to sew. I go out on the front porch and then into the driveway where the sky opens up. A wash of pink settles over the gray roofs to the west, deep blue rising over it. From the end of the street, a rooster crows. The fields smell of cauliflower or broccoli. A pair of headlights flashes at the end of the block, a Buick, not Larry's Comet. The car turns into a neighbor's driveway, an engineer coming home from working late at Vandenberg.

"Come, Larry," I whisper to the darkening street. "Come now." I'm thinking of Rochester, calling over the moors. Larry will have to come before Ray gets home. He has to know I'm home—even if his father hasn't told him.

I go back in with a wild thought. I could go to my room, pull out my little Grasshopper suitcase from under the bed, and pack it. My clothes are clean, some even ironed. I could pack and walk to Larry's.

I sit down on the edge of my bed. Larry could be with another girl. At work. Out drinking beer with Claude or Richie, his theater buddies. What do I know about his life?

At 11:15, headlights flash across the window shade. Ray's car pulls into the driveway, then the garage; the engine clicks off. He lets himself in by the front door, stops for a second, and then goes into the kitchen and puts down his metal lunchbox. A few minutes later, the television starts up in the den, *The Tonight Show*.

Waves of raucous laughter drift out his window and into mine, alternating with the smarmy baritone of Johnny Carson. Ray barks out a laugh and knocks his pipe against an ashtray. I try to finish reading *The Crucible.*

The TV goes silent; lights are switched turned off. I turn the bedside light off and curl up deep into my bedding. My chest tightens, my breathing pauses. Footsteps come down the hall. I want to disappear, like Odysseus hiding from the Cyclops, on the underside of a sheep. I want to be atomized.

He stops outside my door, then opens it.

I continue to hold my breath, to make no sound.

He shuffles in, still in his work boots, and sits down on the edge of the bed. "Fast asleep kiddo?"

"I'm not your kiddo."

My back is to him. He touches my shoulder, shakes it gently. I won't be tricked this time. I jerk away, get ready to leap out of bed. *He'll stop soon,* I tell myself.

"Just saying goodnight. Nothing wrong with that."

I wriggle farther away.

"Okay, I can take a hint." He gets up and goes to the door. "Just stop flirting with me! Stop dressing like a whore." He slams the door shut.

I sit up and slam my arms into my thighs. Why didn't I scream at him when he called me a whore? My body is trembling, and I realize I'm scared. Scared of the violence I know is inside him. For eight years I've been afraid.

I throw myself onto my stomach and press my face into the pillow, sobbing. I wish I was in the mountains, in the General Sherman Grove, with Mom, Megan, and Mikey. The ground is dense and spongey underfoot, the tree trunks plant their giant feet firmly. Their bark glows, reddish and hairy. The bark is the secret to their long lives, protecting them from lightning strikes. I remember the blackened scar high up on one tree.

Chapter 30

Larry doesn't call or come by my first weekend home. At the auditions on Monday, he slouches in with Claude, a friend, both wearing sunglasses. They keep to themselves, and he barely nods at me. A new girl, Sheila, still in high school, reads the part of Abigail that I want. She has long, thick hair, nearly black, dark flashing eyes, and a wide mouth. When she reads opposite this year's actor-in-residence, Jack Gilbert, the rest of us are hushed, spellbound. She'll get the part.

"Sheila Graham," Mom says that night at dinner. "I taught her two years ago." She, Megan, and Mikey are back from Sequoia. She doesn't ask me about my weekend, and I don't say anything. We stick to the pact of eight years. Silence.

On Tuesday, the cast lists are posted in the entry hall at the theater. I sidle up close to Larry. "Jesus!" he says under his breath. Then, "You're still the golden girl."

We're both in *Of Mice and Men*, Larry as Candy, the old ranch hand, and me as Curley's Wife, the only female in the cast. I'm stunned.

Larry storms out of the building. Later, I catch sight of Mr. Charlesworth in the hall talking to Larry. "Character roles are much tougher than leads," he's saying. Larry remains sullen.

The next day we sit on the stage in a circle, a larger circle than last year when the cast was just four. Why did Mr. Charlesworth cast me as Curley's Wife? She speaks like an Okey, she's a floozy, a flirt, begging for attention! Last year I bound my breasts. For Curley's Wife, I have to flaunt my body.

Some of us have jobs that come with small stipends. I'm assistant to the publicity director, and Larry is assistant to the lighting director, Corinne, a teacher but young, the only adult we call by her first name. Larry hangs around with her night and day. *Are they lovers?* I wonder. She's stocky and dresses in jeans, loose shirts, and work boots; she wears her hair piled carelessly on her head. *Still, who knows?*

I study the men in the cast. I'm drawn to Mr. Gilbert who plays George, the lead, but I try not to show it. He's older—I don't know how old—self-contained and confident, aware of everyone and everything around him as if he has eyes in the back of his head. Mr. Charlesworth hardly has to direct him. He pulls the rest of us into his orbit and makes us better.

A man named Billy plays Lenny. He wasn't here last summer, but he's a company favorite. Tall and muscular, with hair as pale as straw. His blue eyes look startled, always. My favorite scene is the one I play alone with him, in the hayloft.

We rehearse for four weeks, from nine to twelve, in the darkened theater. Mr. Charlesworth sits halfway up the seating area, whispering notes to his assistant.

Day by day, I grow into my role, hanging around the men in the bunkhouse, begging for attention. I'm lonely—which I understand—and I don't love my husband, who's a brute, whose eyes look mean, always. The bunkhouse offers an escape. "I'm jus' lookin' for somebody to talk to. Don't you never jus' want to talk to someone?"

A note comes back from Mr. Charlesworth. *Be careful not to whine.*

I'm not interested in Larry's character, the old man missing a hand, slumped on his bunk, feeling sorry for himself. I want George, the handsome, smart man, who stands up to Curley.

"Show more anger," Mr. Charlesworth calls out one day. "You're a woman, not a child!"

"And I don't even have a name!" I shout.

"Good. Go with that."

On his bunk, Candy nurses his stump. In Act III, he calls me a tramp, and I yell back at him, full of spite. "You old goat. Bindlestiff!"

For the hayloft scene between me and Billy, Mr. Charlesworth sends everyone else out. It's quiet and dreamlike, just the two of us sitting in the hay. I don't have to try hard to be Curley's Wife. I am her—a child-woman with a dream. I come in carrying a suitcase, a beaten-up cardboard affair, about the same size as my Grasshopper, the one I imagined packing the night I was alone with Ray.

"I ain't gonna stay here no more," I say. "I'm going to hitch a ride to Hollywood." My chest opens; my heart sings.

Lenny talks about the place he and George are going to have some day, with chickens and rabbits. The beginnings and ends of our speeches overlap; we're not really listening to each other. The effect is nice, a layering of voices and colors.

I let Lenny stroke my hair. How good that feels! His hands are big and strong. He strokes me gently at first, then harder, pulling and hurting. I cry out, struggle, thrash. He pulls me to my feet, towering over me, choking me, and I fall back.

I die every day. I sort of like it. I like being sacrificed. *We must look dramatic,* I think, my dancer's spine arcing over, my long hair falling, his massive form over me.

By dying I can finally show the world my secret. Dying is a vindication. It says, *I tried to tell you! You weren't paying attention!* Larry will weep over me. He'll feel sorry he ignored me. I gave plenty of cues, didn't I?

Mrs. Charlesworth is the costume designer. She and I go to a thrift store where we find a tight, pink flowered dress with a plunging neckline for my bunkhouse scenes. A nicer dress for the hayloft—soft and silky, a deep green blue with a full skirt. "You have a nice figure," Mrs. Charlesworth says. "But for Curley's Wife we need more on top. Find the best padded bra you can."

At Colliers Apparel, the same shop where Ray took me, the saleswoman pulls out a wired and padded contraption and trusses me up like a chicken. My pale flesh spills out over the black lace edging.

Close to opening, we have costume parade. I take my turn in the pink dress, strutting across the stage in straw platform mules, a red flower on each toe. One of the men whistles, and others join in. Afterward, some of us, Larry included, lounge on the carpeted stairs, still in costume. Larry has come out of his funk and regularly entertains. I'm wearing my blue green dress with the tight waist. He gives me a sideways look. "One year they flatten you out and the next they build you up." The others laugh.

Stung, I scramble to my feet. One of my mules comes off, and I struggle to put it back on, feeling exposed.

I get back at Larry a few nights after we open in front of an audience. In the scene where he calls me a tramp, we lock eyes, as he faces downstage and I, upstage. After the line, I shoot him a private look, a mocking smile. He smirks, breaking character.

Offstage, he grabs me by the shoulder. "Don't you ever do that to me again!"

I don't apologize. He wants to be an actor; I hit him where it hurt. He can't use me that way.

Our play is a success. Usually during the hayloft scene, the audience is hushed, mesmerized by the quiet intimacy between Billy and me. One night they laugh when Lenny talks over my line; something is off in our timing. I know what to do to get them back. I let an extra beat go by before I begin my next speech. They hush immediately.

"Good girl," Mr. Charlesworth tells me afterward. "You had them." He watches every performance, standing near the exit. For an hour I'm elated; *I can do anything,* I think, *major in drama, go to New York!* Then I fall back to earth. I'm a beginner. I have an ordinary talent, not like Sheila's.

The night the show closes, Corinne throws a party in her cottage in the country. Everyone comes but Mr. Charlesworth and Jack Gilbert. I sit next to Billy on the carpet around a spool table, wearing the black sheath dress I made. "You made that scene so easy," he tells me. "You should take acting classes at Berkeley." A Woody Guthrie record plays, and Sheila asks who he is.

Larry comes out of the kitchen, carrying a tray of glasses filled with rum punch. Nearing the spool table, he trips on the rug and falls into my lap, still holding the tray upright.

His elbow sticks into my right breast. I feel a jolt of our intimacy.

"And I want a fire truck and a pop gun," he quips, pretending he's a kid and I'm Santa Claus.

"Sure you do," someone calls out.

Later, very late, I come out of the bathroom to find Corinne flopped down on her bed, a glass of bourbon balanced on her stomach. "Take a load off." She pats the spot next to her and I lie down. "What's up with you and Larry?"

"What's he told you?"

"Not much. Something's going on, though." She sips her drink.

"We started seeing each other, last fall."

"Umm," she says encouragingly.

"Then something happened. I don't know what."

"But you still like him?"

I mumble a yes.

"Then why are you flirting with Billy?"

"Larry's ignoring me. He's been mean."

"Yeah, sure." She takes a drag of her cigarette. "He can't figure you out. You don't show your feelings much, you know."

She reaches over me and stubs out her cigarette on the bedside table. Our chests touch. "And something else. He's afraid of your mother."

I groan.

"You should call her, by the way. She's probably worried."

Chapter 31

A week later, outside a dressing room upstairs, I sit on the floor stitching a hem in my *Crucible* costume. I play one of the bewitched girls. From the theater, sounds of rehearsal drift in; John Proctor and the judge.

Larry comes down the hall, walking in his indolent, toes-out way, and carrying a stack of lighting gels. He stops near me.

Billy, as John Proctor, shouts, "'You are pulling Heaven down and raising up a whore!'"

Larry and I stifle a laugh.

"Billy loves that line," Larry says. "He gets a kick out of using bad words. He was raised a Seventh Day Adventist." He puts the filters down on a chair next to me.

"That makes sense. He has this nice innocence. See my collar?" I hold it up—white lace.

"Yes?" he asks ironically.

"It's fancier than the other girls. Susanna is rich."

"Do you like Billy?"

A girl from the box office calls up the stairs. "Kate, your mother is here!"

"My *mother?*"

"She's outside waiting," the girl says.

The blood has left my face. Mothers don't come to the theater. I look beseechingly at Larry.

He chuckles and picks up his filters. "Better see what she wants." He moves toward the lighting booth.

I put my Susanna costume down and go to the landing at the top of the outside stairs, used to go from our dressing rooms to the stage door. Below me on the sidewalk Mom waits, wearing shorts and a plaid shirt.

"Mom," I say quietly.

She looks up. "Oh, there you are. I brought lunch." She holds up a brown paper bag.

I come halfway down the stairs. "I'm supposed to be working."

"Surely you have a lunch hour. I looked at your schedule, you don't have rehearsal." She looks around at the strip of grass between the sidewalk and the parking lot.

I groan. No one eats lunch there. And besides, Sheila and I are supposed to go to the A&W. I take two more steps down, my sandals inching over each tread, hand on the wooden railing.

"I thought we might talk," she says. "I so rarely see you." I catch a note of intentional mildness, as if to say, *I won't lose my temper like I did when you came home so late. I won't criticize.*

"Ssh." I point to the backstage door. "They're rehearsing."

"*The Crucible?*" she whispers loudly. "Is Jack Gilbert in there?"

I nod and come down. Rehearsal will be over in five minutes, and everyone will come out. They'll see me sitting where no one sits, eating from a paper bag . . . with my mother! Isn't there somewhere else we can go? Mom is sitting down already under a spindly tree. She opens the brown bag.

A male voice soars from the theater. "You are pulling Heaven down and raising up a whore!"

Mom smiles. "Mr. Gilbert?"

"No, Billy. He's John Proctor."

"It sounds as if they're coming along splendidly." Her face opens, her eyes shine with pleasure. Suddenly I know why she's here; *she* wants to be in the company; *she* wants to act opposite Jack Gilbert and be directed by Mr. Charlesworth; she wants to make new friends. She wants to be me! I should feel sorry for her.

She hands me a sandwich, wrapped in wax paper, and clears her throat. "I'm sorry for losing my temper the other night. You've been on your own for a year. I realize you've gotten used to not having rules and to coming home later. Nevertheless, it would have been considerate to call me."

"Sorry," I mutter and unwrap my sandwich cheddar cheese on rye.

"I was put out with Corinne for letting you stay so late. She probably served you alcohol."

I concentrate on chewing.

"I worry you'll get involved in drugs, like Peter."

"Drugs don't interest me."

"I've been trying awfully hard to get along with you this summer."

I feel a flash of surprise and anger. "Really?" Her words are like sandpaper on my skin. If she really cared, she wouldn't have left me alone with Ray! I haven't told her what he did and I'm beginning to feel uneasy about that. At the theater, Jack Gilbert, Billy, and Sheila—especially Sheila—pour their hearts out. Even I do on the stage! At home, I'm a mute or worse, false.

The backstage door opens and the company spills out, feet stamping on the wooden ramp, voices and laughter ringing out. Sheila looks at me and raises her arms as if to say, *"What?"*

"What's the matter with her?" Mom asks.

"We're supposed to go out for lunch."

"Oh."

Mr. Charlesworth emerges, tall, striking, speaking animatedly with Jack Gilbert. He spots us and comes over. "Good day, Elizabeth," he smiles. "I hope we're not monopolizing your daughter."

She jumps to her feet and smiles, girlishly. "Hello, John! The hours are long, yes, but you're doing fine work." She turns to Jack. "Mr. Gilbert, I don't think I've had a chance to tell you what a fine performance you gave us in *Of Mice and Men*."

"Thank you, ma'am." He nods, touching his hat. Then reaches into his pocket for his sunglasses.

She continues to gaze. I look away. "The whole production was so faithful to the novel. I've taught it a great deal, of course. The novel, not the play."

After an excruciating two minutes, the two men say goodbye.

"John looks tired," Mom says and sits down. "Where was I? Yes, money. I didn't insist at the beginning of the summer that you get a paying job."

"But I have a paying job. I'm earning a stipend." It isn't much—two hundred dollars.

"Your brother Peter is earning a thousand dollars from the Forest Service. Enough for his living expenses next year. Megan is babysitting. The whole family is sacrificing this summer. So that you can do summer theater."

"Sacrificing?" My voice rises.

"I'm making the meals and doing the laundry. Megan is helping with the housework and taking care of Mikey. I haven't asked you to do anything. You've been allowed to spend all your time at the theater."

My sandwich is dry, no mayonnaise. Sheila will be ordering a Teen Burger soon at the A&W, with bacon, tomatoes, dressing, and lettuce. I sigh.

"I know you've had to concentrate on your role. I didn't want to interfere. But maybe now—"

"I still have a role in *The Crucible*. I'm working on costumes and publicity. I have a press release to write this afternoon." I fold my wax paper once, twice, three times. "Now, would you please excuse me?" I want to say, *Mother, may I?*

The door opens and Larry and Corinne, wearing sunglasses, come out into the noon glare. I send them a pleading look.

Corinne calls out, "Hello, Elizabeth! Nice of you to bring lunch."

Larry nods at me and hurries to Corinne's truck.

Mom frowns, and I know why; Larry didn't say said hello and

Corinne shouldn't be driving off with a student in her car. That's fraternizing.

She pulls two apples out of her bag. "In a few weeks the program will be over and you'll be home more. I'm looking forward to that."

I feel a sharp stab in my chest. "But as soon as theater is over, I have to go to Berkeley and find an apartment!"

At first, Mom said no to the apartment, on moral grounds. She was afraid I'd let men spend the night. I told her I'd be sharing a room so that couldn't happen. Living off campus would save money.

"Go and come right back. I need you to look after Mikey. "

My heart pounds. The wind shakes the little branches above us. "I don't plan to come back. If the apartment isn't ready, I'll stay with a friend until September 1."

Mom doesn't look at me. She brushes her hands together to shake off the bits of grass. "I have to start school early this year. I'm department chair. I don't want to have to hire a babysitter. There's no need."

I try again. "Polly and Caroline are counting on me. I have to get our apartment ready." Polly is coming from Germany, where her family has moved. Caroline's sister is getting married in early September. I need to wash sheets, mop floors, buy sponges, shop at India Imports.

"Really Kate, this is the least you can do to help the family."

I get to my knees and stare down at the crown of her head, where her pretty brown hair divides into waves. I feel none of the loyalty or pity she wants me to feel. Those feelings have been scoured out of me. *Look at me*, I want to shout. *I don't want to live at home anymore!*

"Why can't Ray take care of Mikey?" I ask. "He's there all day, when he works evenings, or nights."

Mom shakes her head. She never mentions Ray.

The wind gusts again, catching the squares of waxed paper. I run to pick them up, crumple them, and come back. She holds the brown bag up. "Put them in."

It's no use fighting her. She's too strong. "The semester starts September 15. I need to be there at least a week before."

"Mikey and Megan start school September 8. You'll have plenty of time."

"Okay." I get to my feet. "I have to go now."

She remains on the ground. "You're being so unpleasant about this. It seems like you don't *want* to be at home anymore."

"I don't. I don't want to be at home." I feel a pang of sorrow—then relief.

Mom's face crumples, her head falls forward, and she begins to sob. "That's a terrible thing to say. I don't think I ask very much of you."

I kneel again on the grass and lean toward her. "Stop it. I said I would stay." She keeps crying. I touch her shoulder and feel a throb of the old affection. "I'll help with Mikey."

Mom takes off her glasses, wipes her eyes, and looks around, as if she's worried someone has seen us. "Couldn't we take a walk? I don't want us to part on a sour note."

"No. I have to write a press release before rehearsal at two."

Mom stands and picks up her purse from the grass. "All right then. I'll see you at dinner."

Chapter 32

Mom and I cross the Missouri River in our rental car, traveling east over a long, low bridge. Slow-moving, green-brown water swirls and eddies underneath. On the Iowa side, trees cover the squat bluffs. Everything is low.

"Across the wide Missouri!" I sing.

Mom starts the song: *"Oh Shenandoah, I long to see you!"*

"I hope the Elm House serves coffee before eight," she says. "Breakfast is at eight, but I often wake up earlier."

I tell her they probably do. I haven't mentioned my phone call with Julia yesterday, from the Old Market District. Later, I phoned Richard from my room. He insisted I didn't need to come home, that it was better for her if I didn't. "I think she can pull through this. She's eating and playing the guitar. Playing with Zorro."

"Talking?"

"Yes." She'd told him, too, about the conference with her supervisor. "It's her classroom management skills, the supervisor said."

"I figured." I got up from the bed and paced. "I never thought she should go into teaching! Why didn't I tell her?"

Richard sighed, and I knew what he was thinking, that my guilt and regret were useless. I sat again. "Do you think you can convince her to go back tomorrow?"

"I'll try."

In the car now, Mom turns toward me. "I hope Julia will stick with her teaching."

I take a quick inbreath. Mom does this sometimes, seeming to guess my thoughts. "She might be happier at a private school."

"She'll do more good in a public school."

Mom has no idea how adolescents behave now, especially in summer school. Nor of how sensitive Julia is. I force my attention back to the highway; a flat gray plane bordered by shimmering fields. The corn is as high as an elephant's eye, yes! The stalks are a damp green that shocks the eye. *Juicy*, I think, recalling the word Tolstoy or his translators used to describe the leaves as Andrei rides through the forest. I thought it a weird choice, but now I get it. The earth is black and moist.

"When was the last time you visited Grinnell?" I ask.

"I went back for my fiftieth reunion. That was a good while ago."

"Did you see some old friends?"

"Yes, Georgia. It was especially nice to see her."

On the highway, I approach a slow truck loaded with hay. I signal and move into the left lane.

"I wish you wouldn't drive so fast," my mother says, lips pursed, brow furrowed.

"That truck was going forty!"

"*We* drive more slowly." *We* is Karl.

We drive in silence, and I try to shrug off my irritation. Puffy clouds rise up in the north, white on top, dark gray on their undersides. The possibility of rain excites me. Mom closes her eyes and nods off.

When she and Dad were in their sixties, they rekindled their relationship, mostly by letter. After she and Karl got engaged, Karl put a stop to the correspondence. When my stepmother called to tell me my dad had died, I cried out like an animal, anguish pouring from my body. Later, still in that early stage of grief, I phoned my mother. "I loved him so much!" I said, crying.

Megan and I went through his desk, the same one he'd had when we were children. We found copies of *The Grinnell Review*, the college's literary magazine, edited by Mom, with his essays and poems. Mimeographed copies of the *Laidlaw Gazette and Intelligencer*, a newsletter put out by his cousins. Black and white photos of boys in flannel slacks and girls in plaid skirts; one of Mom, smiling at a picnic, her hair elaborately set. The best photos—developed by Dad—were of a dark-haired young woman, buxom, with a knowing look. "Deirdre," I told Megan.

Before leaving for Omaha, I burrowed into a family history, aided by the internet, and learned that Deirdre's daughter, Carla, now owns the Laidlaw house. Dad corresponded with her in the last decade of his life, a way of staying connected to Deirdre, I think. My mother was close to the cousins, too, and she and Dad gave me *Deirdre* as middle name. That was before the fiery end.

Now rain begins to fall on our windshield. The cars coming toward me have their lights on, and their wipers are going furiously. I struggle to find the lever on the steering wheel for mine, then to turn them to the fastest speed. Mom wakes up.

The July rain pelts down, harder and harder; I slow, from sixty to forty, to twenty. So do the other cars. The lane lines are hidden by the upward splash of water, I can hardly see. I slow even more. "We've got to stop," I say. Mom looks terrified.

"That would be wise."

An exit sign appears for Harlan and I take it, joining a two-lane road, heading north. Harlan is five miles away. Lightning strikes the corn fields to our east, then comes the thunder. "My, my, a regular summer storm," Mom says.

The rain continues, but I can see the white line. We relax a little, and soon reach a café and gas station with an open sign in the window. A man exiting motions me to pull in under the overhang. I turn off the engine. "You won't be in anyone's way," he shouts.

"What an adventure!" Mom laughs after we're out of the car. I'm laughing too.

Inside, two men sit at the counter, talking to a jovial, middle-aged waitress. "Sit anywhere you like!" she calls out, and we take a table next to the window. The café suits my idea of the Midwest—small, well-lit, clean, with tables covered in red-and-white checked vinyl. A tiered, circular case, displaying slices of cake and pie. The waitress serves us coffee and when we mention rain, she glances for the briefest second out the window. "Just the usual," she says. She recommends their homemade kolaches. When they arrive, we devour them.

"Better than your waffle at Americas Best, don't you think?" I can tease Mom now.

"*Much* better," she says, laughing. "That wasn't a very nice place. The women in *My Antonia* were always making these," she says of the kolaches.

"I loved that book. You gave it to me when I was young."

"It *is* one of my favorite books." Her voice warms; her eyes grow dreamy. "Tony is so changed when Jim comes back to see her. That grieved me. And her teeth are so bad."

We take the Grinnell exit from Highway 80 and drive ten miles north through flat farmland. Where are the apple orchards where my parents read *A Shropshire Lad*? No trace, just farm supply stores, a liquor mart, and a palm reader's storefront.

Mom directs us past the campus onto Elm Street where we park in front of an imposing Edwardian. It's freshly painted, with a wide front porch and pink and white petunias hanging from baskets.

At 2 pm, the air is warm and still; the grass and leaves breathe out moisture. On the front path, I crouch to examine the border, thickly planted with hostas, their whorled green and white leaves enclosing delicate flower spikes.

Mom urges me to get up. "I told the manager we'd be here earlier."

An hour later, Mom leads the way around campus. "That's Gates Hall." We stop in front of a red brick building with a high tower in the middle. "It was my dorm for two years."

"The tower looks like a battlement," I say. "Do you want to climb it?"

"It'll be closed now for the summer."

The paths are empty, the lawns grown back smooth and green after the students' departure. Mom shows me the chapel where she sang in the choir and the old refectory where they put on dances. Men were plentiful during her first year. After Pearl Harbor, most of them enlisted, and the girls had to dance with each other. Mom was hurt because her boyfriend, Gerald, Dad's friend, enlisted without first proposing to her. Dad was 4-F because of his vision and allergies.

We enter a grove of trees. "Remember the story you told me about coming home to your dorm and showing off your engagement ring?"

She shakes her head, draws her mouth into a line. "No. I don't remember." She gazes into the canopy.

"Dad had just given you an engagement ring, and you were in your dorm showing it to your hallmates. When they asked whose it was, you blurted out the wrong name. You said Gerald."

"If you say so. I just don't remember."

I push on. "You told me when I asked you why you divorced Dad. Your point was that you were on the rebound."

She stops suddenly, holds up a finger to shush me. "That could be a vireo."

We listen for a minute, but he doesn't call again.

"That's the new library," she says when we emerge from the grove, "where we'll go tomorrow morning. Isn't it fine?"

Mom wants to research the land grant college her father attended in the 1880s, and I plan to look at the Laidlaw archives for Dad's uncle and his family. Dad told me they were here.

We reach the edge of campus. "Can we go look at the house where Dad lived?"

Mom looks surprised. Then brightens and peers around, reconnoitering. "We can try. It's not far from here as I remember."

We walk into a neighborhood of modest houses, still old, all frame. "Here," she says. "Mimi and the boys had the upstairs flat."

We face a gray clapboard house with a tiny sloping lawn and a front stoop—103 Center Street.

"Lily liked keeping house for them. She liked entertaining, too."

I loved hearing Mom say my grandmother's name. A snapshot shows the two women at my fifth birthday party in the park along the cliffs in Santa Monica. My mother, my sister, two other little girls, and I play ring around the rosie. Grandma looks on, smiling, hands on hips, in her good navy knit.

We retrace our steps across campus where the shadows are lengthening. "What about the Laidlaw house? Where Dad's cousins lived?" I ask.

"My alumni newsletters announced that the college wanted to buy it and tear it down. I doubt it's there anymore."

"I think it is."

She gives me a skeptical look.

"I looked it up on the internet. Can we see it?"

She sighs and looks at her watch. "It's late."

"I can go by myself."

"No, no. I'll take you." We cross a wide athletic field that marks the edge of campus. Across the street is an imposing, two-storied house rising above a tall hedge. "That's it. I don't remember the hedge, but I do remember the porch and the gables."

The hedge is scraggly, and an entrance gate hangs on one hinge. The lawn is weedy and unmown, the paint on the house faded to a dull beige. Ads and circulars spill from the mailbox onto the porch.

"What a shame," she says and sighs.

"You were friends with the cousins, too, weren't you?"

"They were a lot of fun. Francine was musical, and Margaret was a great reader." Mom stares into the front window, a stained glass panel running across it. This must be the parlor, where Francine played, and Mom and the others sang.

"And Deirdre?" I say quietly, my eyes on her face.

"We were friends, yes." She looks away, eyes on the sidewalk. Then up again. "I saw her at my fiftieth reunion."

"Oh." I picture the two seventy-year-olds, in their best dresses, under a chandelier. "Was that the first time—"

"Yes. Since I discovered them."

My young mother awakens in the middle of the night, hears noise coming from the living room where her houseguest, her husband's cousin, is sleeping on a couch. I can't bear to see the rest.

"Oh God, Mom. I'm sorry." I put my arm around her shoulders. The heat has softened, and the air is lighter, less humid.

"When I saw her at the reunion, we both burst into tears."

Chapter 33

During dinner, Mom is quiet, and I wish she would talk, if only to put me at ease. The restaurant is good, near the town square and run by a young couple who serve fresh local food. I enthuse—the green beans are so fresh, the chicken so delicately braised! Without saying much, she slowly, methodically, addresses her plate.

The waiter clears our plates.

"Are you all right, Mom?"

"I'm a little tired. We had a full day."

"We did at that." I'm using her language. "I'm looking forward to the library tomorrow."

"Uncle Harry wrote some musical compositions, and papers, of course. You'll find them."

The waiter returns with the dessert menu. "Cherry pie?" I say encouragingly.

She pushes the card across the table. "I had that kolache this morning. And I promised I'd call Karl, promptly at nine."

"We have time."

"I don't want dessert. Or coffee." She looks at her watch again, adjusts it on her wrist.

Not another silence, I think, and open my mouth to stop it. "Dad told me I'd find copies of the *Laidlaw Gazette and Intelligencer*? Do you remember it?"

My mother's hands twitch on the white cloth. She spreads her napkin flat on the table. "All day you've been chattering about Philip and his Laidlaw relations. You never speak a harsh word about him. None of you children do."

My cheeks flush. She's right. Memories rush to the surface of the time when I was six and he called in sick to work, and I knew from my grandma's frown that he was hungover. The months I went as a college student without a letter. The much longer stretch of time that I stayed away from him because I couldn't bear to see him so far gone.

"You have a point," I say. "He was immature. Always going to the beach, you told us."

"Among other things!"

I feel a stab. "The affair with Deirdre was pretty bad."

"*Pretty* bad!"

"Horrifying, especially for you. Bad for us." I lean toward her and speak softly, my eyes on her face. "But he admitted his failings."

She frowns.

"He had humility," I finish.

Walking back to the Elm House, I feel the tension in Mom's body. The harsh, bluish streetlights shine through the leaves and branches, making sharp outlines on the sidewalk. The roots of the elms have buckled the sidewalk in places, and I grab Mom's arm to steer her away from them. When we get to our room, I'm momentarily cheered by the pink flowered wallpaper and the four-poster beds, covered with white candlewick spreads.

After Mom says goodbye to Karl, she goes into the bathroom and turns the bathwater on. I call Richard. He tells me Julia went back to school this morning.

"Thank God," I say. I hear the water in the bathroom being turned off. Then the squeaking of the metal tub as Mom steps in. I lower my voice.

"Do you think she'll call her therapist?"

"Don't know."

Mom gets into bed, in her own four-poster, and we say goodnight.

Her head rests on the pillow she brought from home, its case printed with small, blue flowers. Soon she's breathing evenly and deeply.

I try to read *War and Peace*, but it's battle scenes over rough terrain, and my mind keeps reverting to Julia and my father, both with their infuriating passivity. I wish I could slip into her body and inject her with my will. I put the book down and turn out my light.

Images of my father and Deirdre, naked on the couch in the living room, come to me, his beautiful, tanned limbs, her pale fleshy ones I can only guess at and see as my mother saw them. Copulation, fornication. I squirm and pull my nightgown down over my knees. The images expand—Mom in the doorway, lit by the hall light. Mom screaming. Did we children wake up? The house was small. Decades later, I caught my father in the pantry at nine in the morning raising a bottle of vodka to his mouth. Caught, he shrugged and gave me a sheepish, little boy look.

―

The next morning, as we get ready for breakfast, I try to smooth the back of my mother's hair, a place hard for her to reach. Her hair is her best feature—thick, wavy, brown, with only a little gray. I want her to look nice for breakfast.

Mom squirms and pushes my hand away, like a child. "Leave me alone."

"I just wanted to smooth it. You've slept on it."

"Not now. You're making us late for breakfast."

An hour later, as we load our bags into the car, the sky darkens and lowers, heavy clouds, purple with rain. Single drops fall as we get out of the car, then more as we make our way to the library. A pedestrian bridge leads over a grassy downslope to the entrance.

In the foyer, Mom turns around. "I need a new notebook. I'll just run over to college bookstore now."

"Okay," I say. I'm finished trying to help her. She sets out, without an umbrella, in her red windbreaker. She recrosses the bridge and goes over a rise, head down, arms swinging vigorously.

The deluge comes. Beyond the bookcases and the wide windows, the water sluices down. No point in going out looking for her. It won't bring her back any faster and I'll be wet, too. I ask the librarian for the Laidlaw archives.

Fifteen minutes later, Mom staggers back inside, hair sticking to her head, windbreaker dripping, pants soaked from knee to ankle. A paper bag holds her notebook, also wet. In the women's room, I help her dry off. I hold her pants under the hand dryer, press paper towels against her arms and shoulders. She rubs her head with more paper toweling. No rueful, "I guess that wasn't such a good idea, was it?"

Chapter 34

"Want to go to Point Sal with us?" my brother Peter asks. He gets out of his car, an old blue Plymouth, and hugs me in the driveway, looking thinner after his summer in the mountains, his hair and beard longer, the beard three shades darker than his hair, which is a pale red. Erica, his girlfriend, follows. She's short like him and stocky, with an amazing head of hair—true black—that hangs to her waist. She brushes it every morning out on her lawn, listening to the *Carmina Burana*.

It's early September. I've been to Berkeley to rent an apartment and taken care of Mikey while Mom started teaching. In three days, I leave for Berkeley for good. Peter knows that Point Sal is my favorite place, a wild promontory on the Pacific, with a long, sweeping beach and miles of cliff and rock. It's a beautiful day, warm, no fog, the best time of the year to be at the ocean.

I hesitate. I'm on a sewing jag. In the last week, I sewed a Twiggy style summer dress, and now I'm halfway through a maroon challis.

"Shame to waste this day," Peter says. The three of us look up at the sky, a hard blue over our heads. A dry wind stirs the small trees along the street, tossing the branches and leaves. The air feels electric.

"Larry's coming," Peter adds.

"Oh." My heart grabs. "Okay. Just let me get ready."

In my room, I pull out the Twiggy dress—a halter dress in a soft blue, green and violet fabric that requires I go braless. I study my image in the mirror. My legs and shoulders are tanned.

Doubt strikes as I hunt for my sandals on the closet floor. Larry hasn't called. Once again, Peter is the go-between, as he was last Thanksgiving. I sit on my bed to buckle my sandals. I take heart. By the end of summer, Larry was giving me encouraging signals. Maybe he asked Peter to ask me.

I grab a tote bag and a towel and go back outside.

Larry waits at the foot of his driveway, wearing chinos, a blue work shirt, and a pork pie hat.

"Good. You came." He slides into the back seat next to me. "I thought maybe you were in Berkeley already."

"That was just to look for an apartment."

"Did you find something?" He listens closely, his full mouth holding an incipient smile.

"On my last day, on College Avenue, near Bay View Terrace where you visited me—"

I look to see if he remembers. He does.

"A sign appeared miraculously! It hadn't been there the day before!"

I'm about to ask if he'll come and see me again in Berkeley. I've imagined lying in bed with him in my new room while the rain—the plentiful, romantic rain of Northern California—falls against the long sash windows. While in Berkeley, I went to the health services and got fitted for diaphragm.

My brother speaks up from the front seat. "Children, I have a surprise for you"

"Does it involve smoking or, I don't know, quaffing?" Larry asks.

"Not smoking. Not quaffing in the usual sense."

"Dropping then."

"Rats. Well, yes." Peter pretends to be mad. "I've saved two perfect tabs of acid, for the occasion."

"It's good," Erica puts in. "I had a really mellow trip from this batch last week."

Unsure, I look at Larry. I've never tried LSD.

"Two tabs isn't much for the four of us," Peter adds.

"None for me, thanks," Larry says. "I'll be your guide."

Did he have a bad trip? I wonder. *Or does he actually want to be our guide?*

"Your dress is perfect for tripping," Erica tells me.

Larry strokes the fabric, and then raises his eyes to my shoulders and face. "Fairy flowers," he says.

In the tiny settlement of Casmalia, we stop for provisions—a six pack of beer, ice, a quart of orange juice, to mix the acid in, and a Styrofoam cooler. The store regulars, farmworkers mostly, eye us, especially Peter with his long red hair and beard, and Erica, in her flowing white pajama pants. They give us a wide berth.

After another three or four miles, we turn off Highway 1 onto a narrow, bumpy road that winds up and around steep hills. The sky is the same hard blue as in town. Rabbits dart from bush to bush, and ravens and hawks circle overhead. Suddenly, through a *V* in the hills, the ocean appears. Peter pulls into a rough, graveled parking area on a bluff, and we get out.

"My God!" Erica cries, staring open-mouthed at the mile-long beach and, beyond it, the sheet of silver blue. I shiver, too. There's something about the day—the clarity of air, the fixity of sky and ocean.

"The ocean is flat," Erica says.

"Santa Ana conditions," Peter says.

Erica carries a blanket, Larry, the cooler, and I the towels and tote bag, and we make our way down a rough path to the sand. At the bottom, Peter takes off his boots and stumbles, whooping, across the sand and into the water. Erica lays out our blanket near the high tide line and wades in after him, her pants ballooning around her knees. I slip off my sandals.

"Want to get your feet wet?" I ask Larry.

"I'll just watch you frolic." He sits and opens the cooler.

I slide down a steep drop to the water, wrapping my skirt around my thighs, letting the cold surge knock me about. Even in September, the water is frigid, too cold to swim in. The currents are treacherous, too.

After a few minutes, the three of us dry our feet and legs and Peter gathers us into a circle on the blanket. Larry reclines, his head propped on an elbow.

With broad gestures and nonsense syllables, Peter opens the orange juice carton. He takes the acid tabs from his shirt pocket and drops them in.

"I hereby consecrate this holy mixture in the name of Timothy O'Leary," he chants and makes the sign of the cross. He turns to Erica. "Do this in memory of me."

We have no glasses, so we drink from the common cup. Erica lifts the carton to her lips, tilting her head back, then passes it to me. I take the liquid into my mouth, not too much, and swallow, still afraid of what the drug might do. Larry drinks from his Coors can.

Seagulls scream and circle high above us.

"What do we look like to them?" I ask.

"Interlopers," Peter says.

"Food!" Larry says.

The surf pounds, drowning out our voices.

I imagine myself up there, looking down on us tiny, earthbound creatures, specks on a rugged coast likely to crumble into the sea at any moment. Not now, not today, I pray.

The orange juice carton is empty. I wait to feel something.

Larry points to the south. "'That land belongs to Vandenberg. They have guard towers with binoculars trained on us."

"Righto," says Peter. "We're the missile capital of the free world."

"Let's storm the guard towers," Larry says. "Take down the missiles."

I touch Larry's arm. "Remember seventh grade when we went to the playground to watch the missiles go up?"

Larry chuckles. "I do." He hands Peter a beer. "What weapons have we at hand?"

"Missiles. Weapons. I'm getting a bad vibe," Erica said. "Let's move on."

We gather our things and walk north. I dart in and out of the incoming waves, staring at my footprints, shrinking and glowing in the wet sand. I begin leaping, doing the *grands jetés* I learned in ballet. My skirt gets wet and clings to my thighs.

Larry puts the cooler down and runs to me. "You're going to fall."

"So what?"

"You're wet."

"It's not a bit cold. Feel it!" I cry.

He grabs my hand, and we walk together. "Why were you so weird this summer?"

"You were weird, too. I didn't think you liked me anymore."

"I was getting negative vibes."

Giddy, I take the edges of my skirt and display it for Larry. "This is my magic garment! Like the one Ino gave Odysseus to save him from drowning. It confers immortality."

"I think you're high, Kate." He bats at my hand.

We've come to the end of the beach. On our right, the cliff has risen to form a towering landform.

"Is this Point Sal?" Erica asks.

"No," I say. "Just a little point. A minor point."

"Let's round the horn," Peter shouts.

"The horn of good hope," Larry says.

We enter the cove, bounded by dark rocks that rise up out of the water, gleaming in the sun. On the other side, rugged cliff rises, towers of ochre, rose and serpentine. I've been to this cove many times, but it's as if I'm seeing it for the first time.

Erica falls to her knees and begins sorting pebbles. "Wow," she keeps saying.

"With the beard, you remind me of a satyr," Larry says. He and

Peter open another beer.

"My true nature, yes." Peter unbuttons his shirt and takes it off; then his belt and jeans.

Erica looks up from her pebbles and laughs.

"You too," he urges. "We're children of nature."

She lifts her tunic over her head—she isn't wearing a bra either—then stands and steps out of her pajama pants. Her breasts are pendulous and her skin the same nut brown all over. Peter throws an arm around her shoulder and grins. They look like Cezanne nudes.

Larry gives me a suggestive look.

"You too," I say.

"You first."

I undo the tie at my neck and lift my dress over my head. "I'm giving up my immortality."

"Time you did," he says.

I slide my underpants off and Larry undresses, too. Why is this so easy? I feel as if I've been naked with Larry a hundred times before. Is this what happens after you have sex with someone? Erica and I put our folded clothes on a ledge.

Larry and I stand back-to-back to measure ourselves—height, legs, arms, and shoulders. "We fit together," I say. "Just the right size."

"You're browner. When did you get tan?" he asks.

We hold each other and kiss, then break apart. There's no place to be alone here. I lead him down to the water. The shore slopes sharply, so we have to plant our heels into the wet sand. We laugh and grab each other as the waves beat against our shins. The foam churns white on the pale green water. Our feet look bony and pale against the dark sand. A bigger wave smacks us. His arm tightens around me.

"Are you leading me to my doom?" he asks.

"No, we're in the middle of the story," I giggle.

"Good." Larry shivers so we go back to the blanket and Peter and Erica. They're naming animals. "We're deciding which animals we want to be," Peter says.

"No, which animal we *are*!" Erica says.

"There is a fish in me," I chant.

"A goat," Peter says. He clambers up onto the lowest ledge. And jumps.

"I'm a goat too," I call out, and get to my feet.

"I'm not sure I should let you," Larry said.

"We're safe, we're safe." Peter and I jump again and again.

We explore beyond the cove, jumping barefoot from boulder to boulder, balancing along ledges, running quickly across a shifting funnel of sand. Finally, we return to the cove. I have no idea what time it is. Our shadows are long across the beach, the sun has dropped, and the air cooled. The cove has shrunk, too, and the dark rocks that stood up so tall earlier are half covered by water. The tide has come in.

"Maybe we'd better think about leaving," I say.

"We had, we had," Peter says. "But where are my jeans?" He looks around frantically.

Erica, Larry, and I are putting our clothes on. Peter's are nowhere.

"Washed out to sea," he says.

"Triton's revenge," Larry says, and we laugh.

"It's not funny," Peter says, frowning. "My car keys were in the pocket."

"Shit," Larry says.

The two men start planning. "One of us will have to walk to the nearest farm," Peter says.

"You go."

"I don't have any pants!"

You can wear mine."

"Figure it out later!" I yell. "We're going to have trouble getting around the point!"

The way we came has vanished. We're going to get wet, plenty wet. I lead, holding the tote bag and blanket over my head, Erica behind me. I count the seconds between incoming waves. "Go!" I shout, as one wave begins to recede. Halfway around, she and I are hit by the next wave and struggle to stand. Huddled and wet on the other side, in the long shadow of the cliff, we wait for Peter and Larry.

"We ditched the cooler," Peter says.

When we reach the car, the sun is dropping into the ocean. Peter puts on Larry's chinos, but they're too small, so Erica hands over her white balloon pants and helps him tie them. Looking like a Cossack, Peter moves off toward the road in the twilight. He's going to the nearest house to call our mother. Erica, Larry and I get into the Plymouth to wait.

Erica hums and sings in the front seat, combing her wind-blown hair with her fingers. Our blanket covers her bare legs. In the back, Larry stretches out and puts his head on my lap. I stroke his hair, and slowly, our bodies begin to warm. Night gathers and the ocean roars below. The interior of the car feels safe and still. I keep my hand on Larry's head, and as he falls asleep, his hand stays on my thigh. I don't want to know if he feels the same way about me as I do about him. I'm just happy now.

Chapter 35

I'm lying in the lounge chair in the backyard, the Berkeley course catalog in my hands. In two days, I'll be gone. Polly, Caroline, and I will reunite in our nice old house on College Avenue.

I put a check mark next to *Dramatic Art 10A, 10B, 10C, Fundamentals of Acting I*. The sliding door scrapes open, and Mom steps onto the patio in her towel caftan, her face and rosy from the bath. It's four o'clock and she's just home from school. Ray is at work. The house casts a shadow over the yard.

Here comes the lecture, I think, *about Larry or smoking or, worse, dropping acid at Point Sal. Did Peter tell?* When she drove out to rescue us, she brought fried chicken, which was nice. We were starving.

She sits at the foot of my lounge chair, looking awkward rather than mad. "I need to talk to you about something before you leave."

I know all the registers of her voice—critical, angry, cheerful. She's nervous. She needs something.

I pull my legs to one side to make room.

"I'm thinking of divorcing Ray. Not immediately, but at the end of the school year."

I gape at her and sit up, surprised, yet not surprised. All summer she's seemed different—restless and irritable. Here it is: she wants a new life.

Not immediately, but at the end of the school year. I fall back against my chair. Too late to do me any good. A hard, bitter knot forms in my chest. "Congrats," I say drily.

She ignores my remark, continuing with what sounds like a prepared speech. "The only grounds I can think of are cruelty to you children." She looks down at her hands. "You told me once that he molested you and your sister."

My heart seizes. How long have I been waiting for this? How many years since Peter asked her to come into the living room on Pony Street? We had to summon all our courage.

"Is that true?" she asks now.

I look away, tears gathering in my eyes. I hate her for asking and hate myself for answering. "Do you think we made it up?"

Her head is lowered, eyes down still. "Did he ever do it again?"

"He never stopped."

"What?"

"*He never stopped!*" I scream.

She stares, mouth open, face slack.

"What did you think?" I scream again. "You never asked! You didn't want to know!"

She lurches out of the chair, almost tipping me over, and crosses the patio in two strides, as if she's scared of me. She should be. Seconds later, from the bedroom come sounds of drawers being opened and closed, closet door opening, hangers pushed.

Where am I? The air has cooled, the light receded, the shadow cast by the house, longer. The Berkeley catalog has fallen to the grass. Who am I? I'm the eleven-year-old again, crying on the green sofa, afraid she's pregnant, wanting her mother's help.

I get out of the chair and pick up the catalog. There are others to think of—Megan and Mikey. In a family crisis, I know my role.

I meet Megan in the living room. "What's going on?" she asks.

"Mom told me she wants to divorce Ray. She asked me about what he'd done to us."

Megan sinks down on the couch. "Oh," she says quietly. "Good."

Mom rushes in, dressed in the suit she wears to church. "Keep an eye on Mikey. I'm going to the lawyer."

She slams the front door, leaving us rooted in our places, Megan sitting, me standing. Megan has washed her hair and put it up in rollers. Her face without makeup looks young and frightened.

"I heard you scream," Megan says.

"I screamed, yeah." I know not to look at her. To witness each other's shame would be unbearable.

I go into the den where Mikey sits on the floor watching *The Flintstones*. I sit on the red ottoman and stroke his back. He doesn't seem to have noticed anything. Fred Flintstone is pretending he's SuperStone, performing feats of strength in front of an audience, leveling three bad guys with one blow. Mikey laughs, and I put my arm around him, pulling him close.

This is Ray's room, the red leather chair and ottoman, his. His pipe holder and tobacco sit on the bookcase above his Westerns and mysteries. I feel his sloppy wet mouth on mine, his stubble on my face. I hear him call me a whore.

From the living room comes the sound of the piano, Megan playing Schumann, "A Serious Moment." On the television, Fred Flintstone signs autographs—carving *X*s on stone tablets.

"Why's he doing that?" Mikey asks.

"He can't write so he has to make an *X*," I say.

At nine the next morning, Peter strolls into the house. Mom called him last night, and he drove up early from Santa Barbara. Ray comes out of the kitchen, coffee cup in hand.

"What are *you* doing here?"

"Left a book behind." Peter picks up the *Santa Maria Times* from the dining table.

Ray snorts. "More likely your dope. You forgot your dope."

Peter keeps his eyes on the paper, his voice level. "Not dope, Ray."

Something is going to happen, but I'm not sure what. Megan and Mikey are at school.

Now that he's here, Mom's lieutenant, I lose my place as the important child. I decide to clean the living room and begin dusting, restacking magazines on the coffee table and music books on the piano. I dust and polish every flat surface. Plump up the couch cushions and straighten the rug; take a vase of faded red dahlias to the kitchen and throw them out.

Mom is folding laundry in the utility room. I pull the upright vacuum cleaner out of the coat closet and turn it on. I ply it back and forth over the area rug, an orange and gold Scandinavian design, part of Mom's liberation. It's fun to rake patterns in it, like mowing a field of wheat. I think of *The Catcher in the Rye* and wonder what rye looks like and why rye instead of wheat. I begin to sing, *"What the world needs now . . . "*

An arm, Peter's, waves frantically above my head. "Turn that thing off."

I turn it off. The event Mom and Peter expect is happening. Ray stands before the open front door, head bent, looking at a piece of paper. I didn't hear a knock or see anyone arrive; the porch is empty. Mom stands a few feet from Ray, hands clenched at her sides, eyes on him.

He looks up from the page. "What's the meaning of this?"

"It's a court order," she says. "It says you have to leave the house immediately."

His face darkens. "What the hell for?"

"What you did to the girls."

"God damn son of a bitch!" he explodes. His face reddens, the tendons in his neck bulge. He crumples the paper and throws it on the floor. "I'm not going anywhere."

Peter picks up the order, steps forward and forces it back into Ray's hands. "Go, Ray. You've got to go."

"This is my *house!*" Ray shouts.

For a second I feel sorry for him. Couldn't Mom have warned him? Had a quiet chat in their room? Persuaded him to leave on his own?

Ray looks at the paper again.

"Go on now, Ray," Peter urges and moves forward, edging Ray back over the threshold.

Ray shoves him and bellows, "Everyone always believes the *woman*! Dirty, lying little bitches!"

Peter keeps backing him out of the house, and Ray steps off the porch and onto the driveway, still yelling and cursing. He yanks the door of his car open, climbs in, slams it shut. Backs the car out of the driveway and screeches off down the street.

Mom lets out a huge exhalation. She staggers back into the living room and sinks onto the couch. Peter closes the front door. He walks past me, still holding the handle of the vacuum cleaner, and sits down next to Mom. "It's over," he says, putting his arm around her.

Ray's words ring in my head. *"Everyone always believes the woman. Dirty little bitches."* For a terrifying instant, I believe him.

Mom is slumped on the couch and has taken her glasses off. As she half weeps, half laughs, Peter comforts her. He jokes. He's proud to be back in her good graces, no longer the son who takes drugs and lies. Neither of them notices me.

I unplug the upright and wind the cord around the handle, my eyes on them. Carry it back to the closet and shove it into place. *"Everyone always believes the woman."* Other women, other girls even, have accused him.

I turn to Peter and Mom. "Did you hear what he said? 'People always believe the woman.' Doesn't that mean—"

"Forget it," Peter says.

"I didn't hear a word he said." Mom laughs again.

"Poor Mom," Peter says. "You've been through a lot."

"And I *haven't*?" I say.

"Oh, sweetie!" Peter says. He pats the place next to him. *"Ding-dong, the witch is dead!"* he sings.

I sit. "Now you leave him?" I sputter. "Now?"

She makes no response. Her face is backlit by the morning sun, and she looks happy, triumphant even.

Chapter 36

"Well, there we have it!" Frances says. "The incriminating evidence. The nail in the coffin."

I look at her blankly.

"For your tribunal."

"Oh, right. The three-judge panel. The International Court of the Hague."

"She's guilty." Frances adds, dryly.

Her words give me no satisfaction. What I mainly feel is the confusion, the shock of the nineteen-year-old holding the vacuum cleaner. "I couldn't process it. One day, Ray lived with us, the next day he was gone, and I was supposed to be happy."

Frances nods. "Cognitive and emotional dissonance. You didn't know what to feel."

Today she wears a black jacket over a gray sweater, dressed for San Francisco. Around her neck hang the fine, gold chains she often wears, with two rings hanging from them. Rings she's inherited, I decide, too small for her tennis-playing hands.

Frances lives with others, I know, or think I know. When she had a cold once, she explained, saying, "You know, someone brings home a cold." She told me about her daughter, adopting a lop-eared bunny she found in a field. There are chickens, too.

"We don't know what your mother was thinking all the years she didn't act on the information you gave her about Ray. Or if she was thinking at all. She grew stronger, she had success in her career, she made a close friend, she grew out of any attachment, sexual or other, to him. She reached a point where *she* wanted to leave him. And to make absolutely sure that she would succeed, she grabbed at the nearest means. You. She *used* you. She didn't have to."

I squirm in my armchair like a kid. "She didn't *see* me!"

"Classic narcissism. The term is overused now. I wish there were another. No, she didn't see *you*. She saw, felt, and reacted to her own needs. Maybe she saw you as an extension of herself. She was in survival mode." Frances looks into her lap, clasps her hands. "That doesn't excuse her, of course."

"She never thought of hugging me that day."

"It's the same as in the sewing room."

I nod, remembering myself at eleven, seated at the sewing machine, her figure in the doorway. "Once, I met her at the train station in Boston. I'd been living there for a year, and she, Megan, and Mikey took the train cross country to see me. It was hot, July, and muggy. I ran down the platform and threw my arms around Mom. She didn't put down her suitcase to hug me back. This incident went down in my little black book."

"Of resentments."

"Here's another from the same year. Coming home from work on Christmas Eve, I found an attempt-to-deliver notice. I hadn't received anything from home, but I thought, *Here it is!* I rushed back to the post office in Central Square. It was cold and dark, the sidewalks were icy, and I was afraid I wouldn't make it by five. At the window they handed me a large envelope, a calendar from my aunt. I was crushed. I cried all the way home. *I* had sent presents home, to everyone in my family. *I* made sure they arrived on time."

"You expected her to act like a mother. Reasonable."

"I saw her as strong and capable! Even after I was a teenager and began to see cracks, I thought of her as a superior being. That day at the train station, she *should* have noticed me! She should have sent a package for Christmas!"

The next day, a little after nine, I'm buzzed into the memory care unit at Brookvale. I find my mother, as always, in the common room, one of seven women and one man sitting in a circle, in wheelchairs and recliners, blankets over their laps.

"The bus is late today," she says.

"Ah," I say, nodding. I get it. Hanne has not arrived to start the morning program. Usually, she greets the circle at nine on the dot, blond and friendly, next to her white board and calendar.

"Hanne will be here soon. Let me get a vase for these flowers. Dahlias," I say, pink and orange, grown in my garden.

"Oh yes, *dahlias*," she says, as if she remembers the word.

I go into the kitchen, which is open to the room, and say hello to Jesus, who's feeding Milly, the only resident still at breakfast. The others have had their bibs removed and their faces cleaned; they've been taken to the toilet and wheeled back into the circle. Milly is one hundred. Up until recently, she was one of the liveliest ones, always first to shout out an answer to Hanne's questions. "Who was the president before this one?"

"Obama!"

Since Milly's birthday, she's become quiet and now needs to be fed, as Jesus is doing. Mom doesn't like it when the staff feeds people. She reacts so strongly I feel she must have been forced as a child.

"Just one more spoon," Jesus croons, with genuine affection. Milly allows the tip of the spoon into her mouth.

From Milly, I'll learn how people die. First, their eating slows; they eat less; their food is puréed; soon a staffer, like Jesus, sits close to them, spoon-feeding. Next week Milly will keep her lips closed tightly; she'll push the hand away. Soon I'll realize that I haven't seen her for a week or two. She will be gone.

I find a vase on the top shelf of a cupboard and fill it with water. I hope I never have to see Jesus feed my mother.

A week later, I enter Frances' office wearing a flowered skirt with an asymmetric hem. "A tribute to youth," I say.

Right away, I tell Frances a dream. "In the dream, Caroline, my old friend from college, was complaining loudly that no one remembered her birthday. 'Let's go out, right now,' I tell her, and we go to the Rathskellar, our old haunt on Telegraph. There were four of us. First they seated us upstairs, then they invited us to go downstairs where the insiders met. Something special was going on there." Again, I see the stairs and the dark wood paneling of the cellar.

"Downstairs, the atmosphere was festive. We ordered and waited. The other guests asked us to sing with them. All we had to do was follow the lyrics on the wall. At first, I couldn't find the lyrics, but I tried to sing anyway, all four of us did. I finally noticed that at either end of the room were hospital beds, with dying patients in them. We were singing for them. On one end were the HIV patients. Then someone said, 'Let's go get Mexican food.'" I stop.

"What do you make of it?" says Frances.

"It's pretty obvious, isn't it? A birthday, a reminder of mortality. Caroline is a year older than I am. The Rathskeller is a cellar. We went down into it, as into the unconscious."

"Life and death so closely linked."

I hold myself still a minute, to recall the strange alloy of feeling—joy and sorrow; joy and fear.

"What does the dream mean for you personally?"

"I'm afraid of my own death. I'm afraid of my mother dying."

We sit in silence for a half minute, and then I lean forward, smiling. "You have to give me credit! Of all your patients, I have the best dreams, don't I?"

"Yes," she laughs. "You get an *A* for dreams."

Before the session is over, Frances asks, "Do you notice any changes in your daily life as a result of our work in here?"

I let my mind rove over the small incidents of my life—a dinner party with old friends, a visit from Julia, who is probably drawn as much to our dog, Zorro, as to us. She was in the valley for a bike ride. "Richard and I haven't had a fight in a long time," I say. "And the other day, after I'd done some gardening, I was raking up my cuttings. I got a wheelbarrow and loaded them. I remembered how, in the past, I'd go into the house and point out my effort to Richard, lording it over him because *he* doesn't clean up his stuff, just leaves it for the gardeners. This time, I didn't need to. I didn't even debate the issue. I just didn't need to." I turn my bracelet around my wrist. "It's a small thing."

Chapter 37

"It's a whole house!" Polly exclaims.

"Kind of," I say. Beneath us is a basement apartment. "But we get the big front porch and the funny old windows," Polly says, as she tugs at a crooked sash.

Caroline laughs when she steps into the kitchen where the red linoleum slopes down toward the back porch. The kitchen is big and the living room small, cozy with old, overstuffed furniture. "Kate should have the front bedroom," Polly says, "since she found the place." She and Caroline will share. We unpack our records and line them up against the baseboard, next to Polly's portable stereo. After dinner, we play the new Beatles' album *Revolver* and dance to "Yellow Submarine," waving dish towels like flags.

We play the record two more times, Caroline sitting cross-legged on the sofa, smoking, and Polly and I lying on the threadbare carpet. "Eleanor Rigby" is our favorite.

We tell about our summers, though we've written to each other often. Caroline met a boy at the publishing house where she interned, and they ate lunch together. She and her family spent weekends in Westhampton. When she talks about her family, her voice warms, and she uses special expressions like *boykins* for her brother. Polly tells about working as a counselor at a summer camp, about kids wetting the bed and getting homesick. I tell about summer theater and finish with my day at Point Sal.

"You dropped acid . . . with Larry!" Polly says.

"When Mom came to pick us up, I was in such a good mood I almost told her!"

"She would have freaked," Caroline says.

Late, silence falls among us. A long rectangle of light from the kitchen shines across the sofa arm and onto the patterned carpet. I make myself say it. "My mother is divorcing my stepfather. She got a court order kicking him out."

Molly sits up. "You're kidding."

"Why?" Caroline asks.

I try to sound offhand. "Because he molested my sister and me." It's the first time I've said the words outside my family. Behind the word is the more terrible one—*incest*.

"Shit, Kate," Caroline says. "That's horrible." She opens a pack of cigarettes, tearing at the cellophane.

Polly puts an arm around my shoulder. I feel the pressure of tears but hold them back. I mustn't be pathetic. Polly and Caroline like me the way I was last year—cheerful, confident, funny.

"To be perfectly honest," I say, "she's divorcing him because she's ready to. She wants to. The abuse started a long time ago."

"Jesus," Polly says. She lights a cigarette, too. "You must be relieved."

I nod, making an affirmative noise. Was that what I should feel? I feel raw and exposed.

"You never told us," Caroline says, her voice soft and low.

A silence and then Polly rushes to fill it, not wanting me to feel bad. "That's okay. We might have killed him. And then we'd be arrested and become a cause célèbre and you'd have to visit us in jail."

"Poison would do nicely." Caroline gathers her cigarettes and lighter, signs she wants the conversation to end.

"Or a net like Clytemnestra used," I say and begin to laugh. I see myself ambushing Ray in the front doorway.

Alone in my room, I wonder what Polly and Caroline are saying, whispering from bed to bed. They come from respectable, normal families. They spoke kindly, but they must be shocked and disgusted. I pull the blanket up around my shoulders. I've left home, yet the shame of home has followed me, to the house where I so hoped for a new life. Polly and Caroline will see me differently. They'll feel sorry for me.

The next day, Polly and I shop on Telegraph. I buy a bedspread at India Imports printed with the Tree of Life—decorated with fruit, monkeys, and birds. At Moe's Bookstore, we flip through the poster bins, trying to decide which art images best fit our identity. We could be so many different things! A man taps me on the shoulder; Hans Friedhof, my TA in music appreciation last year. "Nice to see you, Kate." He speaks with a slight German accent. We chat while I turn over the posters, Hans commenting. "Oh, yes, that's you," he says of the one I keep returning to, *Bières de la M*euse, an art nouveau poster showing a buxom redhead in a rose bower. The roses are full-blown, pink.

"I can call you, now, can't I?" he asks, eyes bright. I give him my phone number and later that day he calls, asking me to a concert Sunday afternoon at the Greek Theater. "That was fast," Polly says. "We've only been back two days."

I smile, feeling . . . what? Proud? Less miserable?

He arrives wearing a cravat and tweed jacket though it's warm for September. He's too old for me, I decide, as we walk to the amphitheater. He has a small paunch and sloping shoulders. I think of Larry's slim body next to mine as we stood in the waves.

In the amphitheater, an orchestra plays Debussy, "Afternoon of a Faun," and the breeze rattles the oak leaves over our heads. Hans listens intently. I know he hears everything, understands more than I do. Larry isn't here, and God knows what he's doing. I lift the hair off the back of my neck, knowing Hans will notice my shoulders and arms. I'm wearing the bare-shoulder purple dress that I wore to Point Sal.

At our house later, Hans charms Polly and Caroline, and they invite him to dinner. He puts Beethoven's Fifth Symphony on the record player and, smiling, cheeks glowing, waves his arms, conducting. "A simple F-major scale! That's all. But like no one has done it before!"

He's a little pedantic. But so confident and happy!

"What is your favorite music?" he asks me, after dinner.

Brahms' Fourth Symphony, the third movement, I tell him. "It makes me think of a deep and powerful river, flowing between rocks." When I lower the needle to the third band, he catches my arm. "No, no! You've got to eat your meat and potatoes first." He puts the needle to the start.

After Polly and Caroline go to bed, Hans and I sit with our backs against the sofa, shoes off. He's taken his cravat off, and he smells of lemony cologne. I relax and let him nuzzle my neck, feeling comforted. *He's not handsome,* I remind myself; he has those sloping shoulders, and he's too old. But he's so sure of himself. He wants me, and he likes me! Here, possibly, is a way out.

We lie down on my bed without undressing, on top of the Tree of Life.

He visits every night the first week of classes, taking possession of the faded mauve armchair in my bedroom. He pulls me onto his lap. I feel pressure, but also the easing of pain.

Hans is gentle and civilized, seducing me with words as well as caresses. I hardly notice I'm giving in.

"*Cool*," Miss Moore intones, putting quotes around the word. It's day one, Introduction to Acting. An imposing Black woman in a royal blue suit, Miss Moore sweeps our faces with her eyes.; all of us white but one. "That's the watchword of your generation. You want to look cool. You have been schooled to conceal your emotions. To let the head rule over the heart."

We sit in rows on folding chairs in the auditorium of a former girls' school. The floor is worn, the proscenium carved in arts and craft style. Clerestory windows bring in the morning light. I hang on to Miss Moore's every word.

"Think Humphrey Bogart, in *Casablanca*," she says. "In here, we're interested in feelings. In truth."

We do exercises in a circle, pretending we're Tantalus trying to reach an apple that keeps eluding our reach. We're Sisyphus, endlessly rolling a rock uphill.

I missed the deadline last year to apply for a scholarship, and I don't have enough to live on, just my child support check from Dad of ninety dollars a month. I get a job cleaning a professor's house once a week. No new clothes this year, a packaged tuna sandwich at the Terrace for lunch. Hans receives a loan of five hundred dollars, and we celebrate with a fancy dinner in San Francisco.

He lives in a cottage behind another house, a mile from our house. One Friday we have dinner there, smoke some grass and put on Mozart's *Cosi Fan Tutti*. I lie on his bed, which is like a bunk on a ship—high and wood paneled. He stands next to me, singing and waving his arms as a baritone and two sopranos sing, their voices weaving in and out of each other's. *Soave il vento*. Hans's features soften, and he turns into a woman! *Stop!* I think and pull him to me.

In mid-October, a letter arrives from my mother, in a business envelope, three neatly typed paragraphs. I sit on the Tree of Life bedspread to read it.

> *I write to tell you that a court date has been set for November 6. My attorney informs me that I need a witness to support the charge of cruelty to the minor children. I would like you to be that witness. I'll purchase a round-trip plane ticket for you, so that you don't have to miss more than a day of class.*

Her letter chills me. She doesn't ask how I am or how my classes are going. This is a business letter. My stomach turns over, and I'm again lying in the lounge chair in our backyard, under her command. It doesn't matter that I might not want to help her. It doesn't matter that going to court in Santa Maria might cost me a lot more than missing two classes.

"Refuse," Hans says. I've told him everything. "She can ask a friend, an adult for God's sake."

"You don't know my mother."

"She can use other grounds—mental cruelty. That's what everyone does these days; it's all *pro forma*. Say no."

But I can't say no. She's in my head and directs my will. *This will be the last time*, I tell myself.

The plane ticket arrives. I choose my outfit carefully—the plain, long-sleeved challis dress I sewed in summer, maroon with a navy yoke and cuffs. Hans drives me to the airport in Polly's Peugeot and kisses me goodbye. The closer the plane gets to Santa Maria, the more frightened I feel. The seatbelt is wrinkling my dress. The fabric is too thin; my legs and hips will show underneath. What will the judge think of me? What will he ask? I have the sensation of water rising around me.

The plane descends over the Oceano Dunes where Larry, Sheila, and I spent the day last summer. White dunes merge into agricultural fields, an oil derrick here and there, then light industry. Now the plane descends over the eucalyptus and oak trees of the county park where we had birthday parties.

At the tiny airport, Mom hurries me to her Volvo. She wears her best knit suit and heels. We drive north into town on Broadway and then make a right on Cook Street. We're near our first house in Santa Maria, the before Ray house—small and white with a brick wall and a pretty garden. Where a playground used to be, now squat city hall and the courthouse. The years tumble over in my mind, giving me a feeling of vertigo.

Dumbly, I follow Mom to the entrance. I have questions but don't dare ask them. Will Ray be there? Do I look all right? What will the judge ask me? I imagine opening my mouth to speak and vomit coming out.

Inside, we follow a corridor lit by windows on one side, courtrooms on the other. A man in pinstripes waits—Mom's attorney. We have ten minutes, he says. "I need to use the restroom," I say. My intestines are in turmoil. At the sink, I comb my hair, try to smooth the wrinkles in my skirt, and stare at my pale, stricken face. A far cry from the face I showed Santa Maria in the past. Kate Laidlaw was the model student! A proper young lady! Poised and confident. I feel naked.

The courtroom is not the dark, paneled chamber I imagined. Lit by fluorescent tubes, upholstered in beige, it's empty except for a stenographer, a clerk, and the judge, who's already seated in front. He looks younger than my mother, with dark hair and a receding chin, sitting hunched over a desk, eyes on his papers. "In the matter of *Elizabeth Carruthers vs. Raymond Carruthers*," the clerk reads. Where is Ray? We're starting without him!

When the judge calls my name, the clerk leads me through a low wooden gate to the witness stand. He asks me to put my hand on the Bible and to swear to tell the truth. I don't throw up, the right words come out.

"You are the daughter of Elizabeth Carruthers, is that correct?" the judge asks.

"Yes, Your Honor."

"You are one of four children."

"Yes."

"And you are nineteen years of age?"

Does that make me an adult? Does that make me responsible?

The judge hasn't looked at me. He's uncomfortable, I can tell. "Your mother claims that Mr. Carruthers has committed acts of cruelty toward you and the other minor children. Is that correct?" Now he lifts his eyes to mine.

I nod and look around. Where *is* Mr. Carruthers? Why not haul him in and make him answer for what he did? To two little girls, aged eleven and nine. Turning them upside down, groping under the white petticoats they were so proud of? Making them forget hopscotch and learn to fear men.

"Will you speak your answer, please?"

"Yes, Your Honor, that's correct."

"Thank you," he says and blinks.

I'm not a witness, I want to cry. Ray did these things *to* me! Does the judge know that? This whole proceeding is a sham.

He stares at the papers before him. "Thank you, Miss Laidlaw. You may step down."

This is all? I go back through the wooden gate, my underarms damp with sweat, my heart beating rapidly.

In less than fifteen minutes we're in the corridor again. Mom shakes hands with her lawyer, looking relieved, and he tells her when to expect the written decree.

I'm stunned, forgotten. What comes next?

Next is to follow Mom to the car. She doesn't look at me, doesn't notice the state I'm in. She looks at her watch. "Good. We have time for lunch before I take you back to the airport. I'll be able to make my department meeting at two-thirty."

I get into the passenger seat and slam the door shut. "I don't know why they call me a witness," I say. "I'm not."

She starts the car. "I don't know what you mean."

"He did those things *to* me!" I shout. "I believe that makes me a victim."

She shifts gears, missing first, and the car lurches forward.

Without saying more, we drive north to Brewer's on West Main, the best coffee shop in town.

The waitress sets a fancy tuna on rye in front of me, heavy with mayonnaise, pickles and tomatoes, a far cry from the sixty-cent sandwich that I buy on campus. I pick up one half. "This is my reward I guess."

Mom doesn't comment. "I'm applying for a teaching position in the Bay Area."

I gasp. "You want to leave Santa Maria? You love your job! You're making a good salary!" She's department chair with influence and even friends. Harriet, for one.

"I came to Santa Maria only because of work. I've always wanted to live in a city again."

"This would be for next year?"

"Yes."

I stare at my plate. She's following me and taking Megan and Mikey with her. "But Megan will be a *senior* next year!"

"She'll benefit by the change."

"No, she won't, Mom. It's not just school, but Dennis." Dennis is her boyfriend. "This is really mean."

"That's your opinion."

I don't mention Mikey leaving his father.

I bite into the bread and stare out the window, feeling her edging into my territory, pushing against my freedom. I can't wait to be at the airport, to be flying north, to be with Hans. Then dinner in the big red kitchen with Polly and Caroline. Polly will make something special. I'll feel normal again.

The waitress brings the check and Mom zips her purse open noisily.

"It's been hard for me to do this, Mom," I say.

"Do what?"

"Testify."

She pulls out a five-dollar bill and two ones, then opens her change purse. She looks back at the bill and then extracts another quarter and puts it down. "We can go now."

When I get home, I put the maroon dress in the back of my closet and don't wear it again. Now, when Hans and I have sex, I feel nothing.

Over the summer, the university changed to the quarter system—a frantic ten-week instead of the leisurely seventeen-week semester. The midterm in Survey of Dramatic Art takes me by surprise. I haven't done the reading, and I fail it. I dream that I'm walking down College Avenue dressed for class, with my diaphragm stuck to the back of my head. I feel stupid, heavy with torpor. For the first time in my life, I'm constipated. Sitting in the armchair with Hans after the exam, I cry for an hour. I've never failed an exam before. He's spending too much time here, I tell him. He agrees and we make a schedule.

In acting class, Miss Moore asks us to act out a symbol, without using words. I choose carefully and rehearse every day in my room for a week. The following Tuesday, the morning sun slants down from the high windows, laden with dust motes. Miss Moore calls my name, and I mount the three steps that lead to the stage. I take my place center stage, several feet above Miss Moore, who is poised and regal, notebook in her lap, surrounded by my classmates. I feel a surge of excitement, even joy.

I am a giant sequoia, the one I stood next to as a girl. At first, a seed, folded in a low crouch, then I uncurl and push through the soft, humous-rich earth. I rise, strong in my trunk, arms reaching for the sky. Then I'm struck by a bolt of lightning, a burning blow to the heart! I crumple and nearly fall. Then slowly, I right myself, my arms rise again, I hold my crown high, the tips of my branches touch the clouds.

"That was very moving," Miss Moore says. "But what were you?"

"A sequoia tree. When it's hit by lightning, it doesn't die."

"Ah! Survival." She gets up from her chair, approaches the stage, and raises her eyes to mine. She speaks slowly. "What is the lightning strike? The wound?" She clasps both hands to her side, and contracts her torso, as I did.

She walks back to her seat before I can bring myself to answer. Then speaks. "The wound is the place where the light enters you."

Chapter 38

"Your mother using you in this way, making you testify—that was another soul death," Frances says.

It's October, two years since I started seeing Frances. Julia and Dareh were married a week ago in our garden, next to the Japanese camellias I planted in spring. We toasted them at a long table in the early twilight, under lights the two had strung from tree to tree. It's a vertiginous drop from that celebration to the misery of my sophomore year.

"I was humiliated by the *D* in that exam." I close my eyes and shake my head rapidly. "I'd never failed an exam before."

"It shows how deeply you were retraumatized. You had a greater range of emotion than when you were a child. It was as if Ray attacked you again, in your more mature self. Your usual modes of coping were insufficient."

A charged silence fills the air. Julia waited until she was almost forty to marry. Did my history make it hard for her to trust men?

"Did you see a therapist?" Frances asks.

"I didn't know anything about therapy." I knew Cowell Hospital, the huge building at the top of campus where there must have been shrinks, but it never occurred to me to go there.

I let the images from that time pass through my mind, odd things like Hans's heavy trench coat, formerly his father's from World War II Germany; the first Christmas at home without Ray; a new lightness in the house; a late-night talk with Larry next to the Christmas tree;

entering the Fillmore Auditorium with Polly and Caroline dressed in our craziest outfits; ice on the front steps the morning of a final exam; Hans counting out the bills after selling his car.

I smile. "I had a showdown with my mother. She came to Berkeley for a job interview."

"She applied for a job in *Berkeley*?"

"Next door. Albany."

"Why does this not surprise me? Did she get it?"

"No, but she got one in Marin County. And moved to Berkeley the following year."

"Amazing. You confronted her?"

"She slept in my bed, and the next morning asked to borrow my bathrobe. When she found Hans' robe in my closet she lectured me. What do your roommates think of your behavior? You're setting a bad example for your younger siblings! Your behavior is immoral!

"I let her have it. 'What right do you have to judge me? After allowing Ray to stay in our house all those years!'"

"You were getting stronger."

I tell Frances about the next few months, how Hans left Berkeley to work in Germany with a famous composer. "I cried for a week, but I think I was relieved."

I run my fingers along the velvety cloth of my armrest, remembering. The weather grew warmer, the cherry trees bloomed on College Avenue, and Caroline, Polly, and I bought the same dress at Joseph Magnin but in different colors. We threw a party.

A wave of lightness—a reminder of youth—comes over me. "I took a contemporary music class, pass/not pass because it was upper division. When the professor handed back the midterms, he announced that I'd gotten the highest grade."

"That'll teach you."

"I took a French Lit class I loved, too. The texts were in Old French and deciphering them was like the music class. I just got it. I was smitten with the professor, too. Mr. Barry." I see him in his rumpled suit, young and smiling, speaking French with a Philadelphia accent.

"I took a modern dance class, too."

"Ah!" Frances says approvingly.

"The studio was so beautiful—high and light. As soon as I walked in, I felt happy. The teacher was a small plump woman. She played a drum or a tambourine while we danced."

I tell Frances about the Merce Cunningham back exercises, which we did at the beginning of class, a classic sequence where we moved through all the positions for the feet, opening our arms and flexing our spines until we swept our hands across the floor and came upright again. I loved the quiet symmetry of these exercises, their simple beauty. At the end of class, we ran and leaped across the floor. When I left the studio, joy coursed through my body.

"At the end of the term," I tell Frances, "I met my French teacher, Mr. Barry, at a concert, and he introduced me to his wife. I was wearing my purple halter dress and heels, and my hair was pulled up on top of my head, Brigitte Bardot style. I remember feeling proud and grown-up."

"You were finding yourself. Becoming."

Chapter 39

At noon, when Mom and I step out of the college library, the sun shines through dripping leaves, and the lawns steam. I breathe in deeply. "Mmm, smell the ozone?"

"No," she says. She doesn't smell anything.

I suggest lunch downtown on the square where I remember a café with a red awning and outdoor tables, somewhere we can talk without being overheard.

A young waitress greets us inside, dark haired, with short, straight bangs across her forehead and an array of earrings in one ear.

"Can we sit outside?" I ask.

"*Shurrre,*" she drawls, rolling her eyes. She wears a small post in her nostril, too. "As soon as I dry off the table and chairs! Can't have you sitting in the wet, can I? That wouldn't look good."

We wait outside while she mops off the nearest table and chairs. Mom studies the menu. I look out to the park. Just across from us children occupy a playground while their mothers sit on a bench, talking. A girl and boy play on the slide while two toddlers dig in the sandbox. One wears a pink tutu over her shorts. The scene—the women on the bench, holding take-out coffee, talking and laughing—warms me. I remember those outings. Are the women faculty wives—or professors themselves?

At the park entrance stand two stone pillars, each topped by a granite ball. They remind me of the ones in the park across from

Grandma's house in Santa Barbara. I tried to sit on one once and felt my pubic bone for the first time. In the park itself, great trees soar, forming layer upon layer of shades of green, like an old-fashioned stage set. I want to lose myself in them.

"Are your clothes dry?" I ask Mom.

"Quite," she says. "It was only a little rain."

And lightning, I want to add. Would it be so hard to laugh at yourself? To admit you should have listened to me? If she softened one inch, took off one layer of armor, we could breathe. The waitress has finished drying one chair and moves to the second.

If she softened. Why do I expect my mother to change? Tears burn in the back of my throat, and I look away.

"Look Mom, a bandshell!" I point to a metal roof jutting out over what looks like a stage. "They must have concerts."

"How nice," Mom says.

The waitress straightens and grins. "We sure *do* have concerts! Every Saturday in summer, really neat concerts. This week, there'll be traditional Scottish music and dancing. You should come!"

"We have to leave Grinnell today," I say. "Too bad. That sounds fun."

"I used to dance the Hornpipe when I was little. Where are you—"

Mom looks up at her for the first time. "Is there any cream in the clam chowder?"

The waitress ponders. "I think just milk. I know what you mean. Chowder can be so gloppy and rich. I'm lactose intolerant so even with just the milk I can't have it. But it's very popular. Chef adds a little bit of bacon." Mom makes a face. "I'm vegan so that double rules it out."

"Will you check, please?" Mom asks curtly.

"Sure!" She sweeps her hand toward the chairs, inviting us to sit.

"That waitress is too chatty!" Mom says once we're alone.

There she is again, the stern teacher, the arbiter of behavior. I think back to other moments: she scolds a driver who slammed on the brakes to avoid hitting a child; she scolds me, a crazed bride, for throwing the wedding bouquet too many times.

I take a sip of water. "I like the waitress," I say. "I like talking to her." How many more meals do Mom and I have to get through? My feelings are becoming dangerous. "Interesting to see a nose stud in Grinnell," I say.

"You always talk to the staff. You talk too much in general. You talked all the way across the state of Iowa yesterday."

"You were asleep half the time, so I doubt that. People converse when they're together. That's normal, Mom. You're married to a *very* quiet man, and you're not used to talking."

"That's not true. We do talk."

I look to make sure the waitress isn't coming out. "Just now, you were rude to the waitress. She's young. She was trying to be nice."

The waitress bursts out now, making the bell on the door ring. "Just milk, chef says. It's very healthy."

"Thank you," my mother says formally. "I'll have it then."

I order the market salad and smile at Straight Bangs, without inviting more talk. She glances from Mom's face to mine and backs away.

Across the street, a boy flies past the playground on a skateboard. The mothers look up in time to see him jump the entrance steps and land safely on the sidewalk.

Stiffly, Mom pulls one arm out of her red windbreaker. *Be gentle,* I tell myself, she's old. "You seem tense, or upset, Mom. Can we talk?"

"I don't know what you mean." She pulls the other arm out and turns to arrange the jacket on the back of her chair.

"Last night you said I held Dad to a different standard than you, that I didn't hold him responsible the way I do you. You're right. He was irresponsible. And I know he wasn't the best husband."

She looks at me warily, then unfolds her napkin and smooths it across her lap. "Don't you think this is rather a public place to be discussing such matters? At breakfast the other day, you made quite a scene."

I look around. No one but the mothers and children across the street. "I just said something conciliatory. I said you were right about us blaming you and not holding Dad responsible."

"If I recall, you also implied that I lack humility."

"I guess I did."

She twitches in her seat. "I was so pleased when you asked to come on this trip. I thought we could have a pleasant time together. Now it seems you've been planning to confront me all along."

"I didn't, really. I hoped the trip would bring us closer. But we keep getting on each other's nerves."

She takes a sip of coffee.

"I want to work things out with you," I say. "And time is running out."

"If you mean I'm going to die soon," she says sharply, "that seems an exaggeration."

"Grandma became senile—"

"She let herself get too heavy. She had arterial sclerosis. The doctor tells me I'm perfectly fine."

Her face wears the closed look that's become habitual, the I-know-everything-and-don't-want-your-opinion look. She has no idea of the tangled mess of feelings inside me. One of them is new; I feel like a coward for not speaking. False.

"Back to what I wanted to explain about Dad," I say softly.

"I told you I didn't want—"

The café door tinkles open, and the waitress emerges with our lunch. She must notice our grim faces again because she says little. In front of my mother, she carefully sets an old-fashioned white bowl with handles, steaming and full. My market salad comes next.

"Anything else?"

"Thank you, no," I say quietly.

She backs away.

Mom stirs her soup, then raises a spoonful and blows on it. Maybe the food will calm her.

I let her eat in silence and begin on my salad. After she has finished half her chowder, I say her name and search out her eyes. "I need to finish. When I was about fourteen, Dad asked us if our stepfather treated us all right."

Mom stiffens, her hand tightens into a fist. I'm dragging her back to a time and place she doesn't want to go to.

I tell her the rest of the story. "When we told him no, that our stepfather didn't treat us all right, he cried." A gust sweeps the trees, causing their greens to rustle against each other— gray green, green, gold green. *Help me!* I think.

Mom's breathing accelerates, her eyes dart around. She puts her spoon down and levels her eyes at me. "I do not understand why you keep after me like this, why you can't drop it. You are happily married, one marriage your whole life. You have a wonderful daughter. You're well off, you travel. You've had a much happier and more successful life than I have! What do you have to complain about?"

My throat tightens, and I fight the urge to back down.

"That's what you see of me, Mom," I say quietly. "What you don't see is that sometimes I'm very depressed. Yes, Richard and I have been married a long time, but we've had—we still have—really difficult times."

I keep my eyes on the trees. It is so hard to expose my own suffering. "When he and I fight, I get very down on myself," I say. "I feel I don't deserve him. When Julia got so depressed in college, I fell apart. You don't know these things."

"No, you haven't told me." She takes her napkin from her lap and folds it.

Shall I bring up Julia's present trouble? I take a long sip of my iced tea. No. The old trouble comes first. "I was affected by those years on Verbena Street."

Again, her breathing quickens, her eyes dart around. "I made sacrifices for you children. I left Mikey at home before he was two so that I could earn money to support you. Ray didn't make much.

I took classes to get a permanent credential. I fed you and clothed you. Four children in a small house, papers to grade, laundry to keep up with."

Across the street, the little girl in the tutu has moved toward the slide, where the older children climb. She bangs on the metal.

"I know you worked hard," I say.

The boy whoops on his way down the slide and knocks the little girl over. She bursts into screams, and her mother jumps up from the bench and rushes to her.

"That mother wasn't keeping close enough watch of her child," Mom says, frowning.

The mother cradles the child and speaks in her ear, brushes bark off her legs and kisses her head. My heart beats even faster. "She's doing exactly what you *didn't* do! You never told me you were sorry about Ray, you never asked if I was all right. You never held me." I stop for a second, take a breath. "Dad didn't *do* anything, no, but he asked! And when we told him, he cried. That meant something to me!"

She closes her eyes and begins breathing fast.

I don't care. Before I know it, I'm saying the words that may kill her. "I was eleven. He tried to put his penis in me! You never asked if I was all right. You never said, tell me if he does it again! You didn't want to know that he might be coming into my room at night, feeling me under the sheets, waylaying me in the hall. One morning, I came back home and found him with Megan on the couch. She was twelve, she'd been practicing. You never asked! For eight years!"

Mom is panting and crying, struggling to get out of her chair. She grabs her purse, forgetting her jacket, and runs across the street. "Mom, stop!"

I go inside to find our waitress.

She looks out the window and sees the empty chairs. "Oh dear!" she says.

"Can I just give you this?" I hand her two twenties.

"Of course, thank you."

In the park, Mom is a small figure moving fast. I think of Gates Tower nearby, with its battlement top. My heart seizes.

I pick up her red windbreaker, still a little damp, and run cross the street. The toddler who fell on the slide has stopped crying. The mothers are packing up buckets and shovels. Before I reach the bandshell, I spot an enclosure of pale green shrubbery. Inside, Mom sits on a stone bench. Her body is bent and heaving. Relieved, immensely relieved, I hurry to her side and put my arm around her. How I wish I could stop my ears from hearing her wailing! It enters straight into my heart.

"Please don't cry, Mom. I'm sorry." I'm crying now, too.

I hand her a tissue. She takes off her glasses and mops her face.

"What you've said is true," she says. "I know that."

"It's okay." The shrubs around us are lilacs, their blossoms spent. My mother is old, I think, eighty-five years old. She has come as far as she can.

The sun warms our backs. The smell of moist leaves and grass fills our throats and lungs. "I should have told you this earlier, but Julia has had a tough week. She took Tuesday off and came home to Napa."

"Oh, no!" Mom says. "Poor dear Julia!"

"She went back to school on Wednesday. I think she'll make it." We walk slowly back under the stirring branches. "I love these trees. Are they maples?" I ask.

"Silver maple," she replies. *"Acer Saccharinum."*

Chapter 40

It's Saturday, two days after Thanksgiving, a sunny day in Napa. My sister and I, followed by our husbands, come out to greet the arrivals. Zorro leaps and barks, tail going madly. Out of the car step Stephen and his wife, Carrie. Smiling, arms out, we meet, not knowing whether to hug or shake hands.

Stephen approaches first, fair-skinned, of medium height, round in the midsection, but light on his feet. Carrie, with pale skin and dark auburn hair, smiles even more broadly, bending over to pat Zorro as she nods and repeats names.

"I've found our brother! I've found him!" Four weeks ago, my brother, now called Michael instead of Mikey, called, talking so fast and loud, I had to ask him to start over.

"The best news was that you wanted to be found!" Megan says now, as we traipse in through the front door and hang up our coats. Stephen signed up for the DNA matching service ten years ago. He'd almost given up hope of finding us.

"Come, come," I say, and while Richard finishes preparing lunch, my sister and I lead Stephen and Carrie to the wall of family photos.

"That's our older brother, Peter," Megan says, her voice lively and quick, pointing to a grinning, middle-aged man in a tweed cap. She's still lithe and pretty, her once bright hair the color of cinnamon sugar.

"Our wedding," I say, of the black and white portrait of Richard's family and mine, under a spreading oak tree. It's late afternoon on a winter day. The women wear long, floral dresses, the men wide ties. I carry a homemade bouquet.

Stephen peers closely at the picture, then indicates our mother, who is smiling with her eyes half-closed. "How old was she here?"

"Fifty," I say.

"Funny," he says. "I don't see a resemblance in the other photos, but here I do. There's a school photo of me, taken in the eighth grade."

"Yes," Carrie says, "The mouth and the cheeks."

"It's partly the bangs. I had hair then," Stephen laughs.

"You know what my first words were when Michael called?" I say. "I said you'd better be able to spell."

We laugh. Stephen is a journalist and fiction writer who probably spells better than any of us. Over lunch, we discover we love the same American authors and places—the Western mountains and deserts, the Pacific coastline and cities. He grew up in Ventura, south of Santa Barbara, where he was born. We're all nostalgic for the California of the fifties and sixties.

We eat white beans and prawns at our long table, the afternoon sun streaming through yellowing wisteria. Orange persimmons with their branches attached decorate the table.

We piece together our story. "I remember a little about when you were born," I say. "I was six. We'd moved away from Los Angeles and back into Grandma's house. Peter and I went to school together. I broke my collarbone and had a brace on my back." Stephen listens closely. "I remember seeing Mom in the bathtub with a big belly."

He nods. "My parents didn't tell me I was adopted until I was in my fifties. It's the only thing I hold against them. They were terrific parents." His half-closed eyes look away, just a slight angle, from the person he's talking to. "My father's lawyer convinced him *finally* to tell me because he worried I'd find out after my father died."

That's what everyone did then, we agree. They thought it was better for the child. Stephen looked enough like his parents that he never suspected.

"This is what Dad told me he and my mom learned about my birth mother," Stephen says. "She was thirty years old, separated from her husband, with three children. And she was a teacher in Santa Barbara."

These words, passed down over the years, stop my breathing. Who else could be Peter's family but us?

"My birth certificate," Stephen goes on, "the real one, not the one I had for so long, says that I was adopted at the age of one day."

We're all silent for a moment. "Imagine," Carrie says simply.

"I remember Mom going away to the hospital." I falter and look down. "And I remember her coming home without you."

Stephen leans toward me. This is the only time he will press me. "Do you remember what you were told?"

I look down at the flickering candle. My eyes sting. Am I responsible, too? I've taken on my mother's guilt. "Grandma told me that the baby was lost. I think that's what she said."

"Peter was told the baby had died!" Stephen says, his voice rising. He and Peter have talked by phone. "He said he was sad because I was a boy."

"Oh, *Peter*!" Megan cries out. "He shouldn't have said that."

"But is it true?"

"I don't know," I say. Peter was eight and would have demanded more than I was given.

"But he exaggerates," Megan says. "You'll see when you meet him. He'll tell you wild stories."

I pass the salad. Peter's remark has stirred us up, as he always does. I want to protect Stephen from getting hurt, but I can't. He needs to know us.

"What I remember about that time is that Grandma was in charge. The mood was tense, as though Mom was in trouble, or they weren't getting along. When we were older, Mom told us the truth." I play with my bracelet. Even after Mom told me, I rarely thought of the boy she gave up, and when I did, I imagined a sad, neglected kid.

"*I* looked for you!" Megan says, taking the salad bowl. "A few years ago, I called all the adoption agencies in Santa Barbara."

In California, adoption records are still closed, Stephen says.

"I see so much of this in my work," Carrie says. She's a social worker. "Secrets held over time."

Society is more tolerant now, we all agree. Things are better.

"Except for the president we've managed to elect!" Richard says.

We groan. "Time for pie!" Megan says. She and I clear plates while the men fall into the inevitable question of which Democrat has the best chance of beating Trump.

"I love Bernie," Richard says. "He'll do fine in the primaries but in the general election, I don't know."

"We like him, too," Carrie says. She has pulled out her knitting, a soft, pale green baby blanket.

"Who's the blanket for?" Megan asks.

"Oh, I don't know, just some baby," Carrie jokes.

I'm dying to tell them about Julia's pregnancy but force myself to keep quiet. She's made us promise to wait until she's passed the three-month mark. Her baby is due in May.

"Julia's impressed by Buttigieg," I say.

"So is Ivan," Stephen says, of his son who's in his last year of college in the Midwest.

Megan cuts into her pie, and I serve. Stephen bakes pies, too, he says, but he's failed at making a lattice top, like Megan's.

"I'm curious, Stephen," Megan says, after a pause for eating. "Was a father listed on your birth certificate?"

Stephen shakes his head. "The line was left blank."

"Any ideas?" Megan's husband asks, glancing at Megan and me.

We look at each other and groan. "Must have been someone she met after she left Dad that September. She moved us into a house in Lawndale."

"I could search," Stephen says.

Carrie puts her hand on his arm. "Better to leave it alone. This has gone so well up to now."

We laugh. I look across the table at Stephen. "Do you want to meet Elizabeth?"

Megan breaks in. "There's no point, Kate. She's too far gone."

"I just thought we should ask," I say, in what I hope is a calming tone.

"I don't think I need to meet her," Stephen replies, somewhat formally.

After Stephen and Carrie leave, Megan and I clean up, and Richard puts away the leftovers. My back to the others, my hands in suds, I speak up. "I think we should tell Mom. It's too big a thing to keep from her."

Megan cries out, "There's no *need* to tell her, Kate! It could upset her or confuse her. It could be traumatic."

"Take it easy," I say, twisting around to look at her. "If you don't want to tell her, okay." I turn toward Richard. "What do you think?"

He shrugs. "I can't say."

—

The following Monday, in the lobby at Brookvale, Jerry, the custodian, is putting up the Christmas tree, a mighty symbol, artificial, reaching to the atrium ceiling. When all the decorations have been hung, he'll set up an electric train around its base, headlight glowing, horn tooting. Colorful packages will sit under it.

I find Mom in the common room, in her place in the circle, looking up at Hanne, the activities director. Gertie, a new arrival in Life's Neighborhood, smiles at me. *Medication,* I think. Last week she had a meltdown at the front entrance, screaming and flailing as Jean-Pierre and two aides tried to restrain her. "I want to go home! I want to go home!" she wailed.

Now Hanne asks the group to name the state they're from. Mom's is no longer the first hand up. Maxine, a tall woman in the back, pipes up. "Utah! But I've lived in three other states!"

I whisper in Mom's ear, "Would you like to go to the garden?"

"Oh, yes," she says, and Hanne waves goodbye.

I push her down the hall and enter the code to let us out. It's such a simple code I'm surprised the residents haven't escaped.

Through the lobby, past the piano, and I maneuver the wheelchair through the doors. It rained earlier but the garden looks dry enough. "Tell her!" my brother Peter said when I called to ask his advice. His wife, a psychiatric nurse, came on the line. "Be gentle. Don't ask any questions. No pressure. Just announce it as a happy thing."

I park her wheelchair near the bird feeder hanging from a liquid amber tree and sit beside her on a bench. "I have some good news for you!" I say, smiling brightly, almost chirping. *Sesame Street,* I tell myself.

"Oh," she says vaguely and looks up and around for birds.

I take her hand and repeat myself. Now she looks at me, recognition returning.

"We've found our half-brother!"

Her eyes focus and then wander, as if she's searching.

"The baby you had in Santa Barbara. In 1954."

She looks at me. A sparrow alights on the bird feeder. "Well, that's good. I've been looking for him for a long time."

This is the longest sentence I've heard from her in months. It's not true, of course, not literally true.

"His name is Stephen and he's very nice. Very intelligent." Does she care? "He grew up in Ventura."

Her head moves to the left. "I thought he was in Santa Barbara."

When we visited, after we moved to Santa Maria, did she search the crowds on the sidewalk and in the park, looking for a boy his age?

"He's a writer," I go on, still in my *Sesame Street* voice. "He loves the same authors that you do. Like Wallace Stegner!" I pull a magazine from my tote bag. "See? He wrote this article."

She looks away, her gaze moving to the bird feeder, swaying in the breeze.

"I gave him copies of your books. The ones you wrote."

Again, this fails to move her. She's unable to make the leap from baby to man. Her forehead gathers, her mouth opens. She can't get the words out. "How—?"

"How did we find him?" I explain about DNA matching services. "Michael did it—your son Michael. He and Peter share fifty percent of their genes. He's lived in San Francisco for many years. All this time and we didn't know."

Mom's torso has slipped to the left, and I stand up and adjust the pillow the aides put there. I want to ask one more question, though I know I'm pushing my luck. I need to know for sure that she has understood. "Do you remember if the baby had red hair? Peter said he did."

Her eyes moisten and she shakes her head. She picks at the blanket covering her lap. Time dissolves and I see her, an exhausted, young mother in a hospital bed, holding her newborn. "I had him for so little time."

Chapter 41

Barefoot, wearing worn jeans and a long-sleeved T-shirt, I settle into the green armchair in my bedroom. It's a small chair in a corner, hardly ever used. Next to it, a rattan stool, where I set a glass of water, along with my phone. Outside, the wisteria over the terrace is beginning to flower. I've canceled the party I like to throw in spring, the Ladies Wisteria Luncheon. No one but us will sit under this year's bloom. My phone ticks off the seconds leading to noon. I try to slow my breathing.

"Good morning, Kate!" Frances says warmly, and some of my anxiety melts.

"This is weird," I say. "I hear some people are using Facetime and Zoom."

"We can talk about that."

"Seeing might be weirder." I can tell she'd rather not. "I know your voice pretty well." I know all its registers. Better yet, I know her pauses.

"Are you comfortable? Where are you?"

"In my bedroom, in a nice chair." A lady's chair, just my size. I think of Goldilocks.

"How are you feeling?" she asks.

I say nothing at first. I take a deep breath in. I don't have to get this right; in fact, there is nothing to get right. "I'm in shock, like everyone else. I didn't expect this. It happened so fast. A week ago, a friend told me she and her husband were going to Costco to stock up ahead of the pandemic, and I thought she was crazy."

Frances says nothing, and I wish I could see her face. "Maybe you stocked up early, too."

"Never mind about me."

"But I *want* to know you," I say, and immediately wish I could take it back. Is she the mother I turn to in this crisis? "My habit is to think that people are overreacting. That nothing bad will happen that hasn't happened before in my lifetime." I stop, remembering the day the Bay Bridge broke. "Then came the Loma Prieta earthquake. And our fires. They'd never happened before."

"No. In our lifetime we haven't experienced a pandemic. This *is* a pandemic. Are you worried?"

"Not particularly. Not about my health. I've lived a long time."

"That sounds a little glib." I see her eyebrows rise.

Zorro is scratching at the door. I get up to let him in and return to my chair. He settles at my feet.

"What about the social isolation?"

"I don't mind. I have my writing. And a quilt to sew."

"Ah, for Julia's baby."

"It's made up of hexagons, which are really hard to join. Each one a print of gold, green, coral, and ruby. It's kind of Persian, for my son-in-law, and it reminds me of Dad's geometrical objects."

"Lucky baby."

"Except he or she will be born during a pandemic." I smooth the linen covering the arm of my chair, pulling, straightening, as if that will make the pandemic go away.

"Her baby shower was canceled. Along with everything else. Concerts, trips, dinners, haircuts, visits... poof! Gone." A new feeling creeps into my chest—uncertainty, dread. Zorro, all black wavy hair, is curled into a ball. Little Bug, I call him when he does this. I tuck a foot under his belly and run the other along his flank. My feet are getting cold. I'll have to remember to wear socks next time.

"I'm worried about my mother, too," I say. "I can't visit, of course, and neither can anyone else. No hairdresser or the religious ladies who read from the Bible and annoy her. No singers."

"All provide social stimulation, yes. The shutdown is going to be hard on that population."

"Last Monday, I asked if I could go in just to explain to her. Who knows what she's been told? Or if she's been told. 'We're having an epidemic,' I said. She wouldn't recognize the word pandemic. I told her it was like the flu epidemic of 1919, when Grandma took care of people on the prairie. I told her she and I had to help by not seeing each other. I think she got it."

"Good."

"She's always been a good citizen."

"Let's hope it won't be for long."

"It will be over by May, people say." The breeze brings a whiff of wisteria through the open window. I sip water. "New York seems like a nightmare. All those sirens, the hospitals full. Doctors and nurses wearing garbage bags because they're short of protective stuff." I dig my toes into Zorro's hair.

We let a few seconds go by. Then, in a more urgent tone, she asks, "Are *you* afraid?"

A greater unease stirs in my chest, near my breastbone, vague, nameless. What time is it? I can't see without taking the phone from my ear, so it's the same as in France's office where the clock is behind me. My chest tightens even more. "Maybe I'm a little scared. Other people are afraid, and it's catching. Time seems kind of stopped."

I allow the word *fear* to knock about in my brain for a few moments. "This will sound odd."

"Go ahead."

"Do you remember a game from the seventies called The Ungame?"

"No. Tell me."

"You drew cards with questions on them, personal questions, and you answered them. No one could interrupt you while you answered, and you could take as long as you wanted. They had to listen."

"Kind of like here."

"Richard and I were playing with our two closest friends, Jill and Morgan. Jill drew a card that said, 'Tell about a time when you were afraid.' She told about being alone in a town in France without Morgan. When my turn came next, I said I wanted to answer her question. That was allowed. 'I'm *never* afraid!' I announced. 'I can't remember a time when I was afraid!'" Now, I start laughing and pitch forward in my chair, giddy. "Isn't that funny?"

"It is funny."

"It's like I didn't recognize the word! It wasn't in my vocabulary. My mother *never* expressed fear. We were *never* allowed to be afraid. Fear didn't exist!" I'm gasping. Tears wet my cheeks.

Frances laughs, too. "Easy to be unafraid if fear doesn't exist!"

My laughter subsides, and I catch my breath. "I was afraid all the time! I was afraid of Ray coming into my room, afraid I was pregnant, afraid no one at school liked me, afraid of my mother. Once in high school a male teacher offered me a ride because it was raining hard, and I refused him. I was afraid all the time."

A silence falls.

"And now, what are you most afraid of?"

I close my eyes to allow all the feelings and thoughts of the last hour to come to rest, like snow in one of those paperweights that you turn upside down and then right side up.

"I'm afraid for Julia and her baby," I say quietly. "Terribly afraid. She's due in six weeks. Who knows what state the hospitals will be in? She won't be able to have Dareh or me with her!" I'm crying now. "I'm so afraid for them all!"

Chapter 42

Four weeks later, on the front porch at Brookvale, I tap on the window to let them know I'm here. A few minutes later, an aide, not Jesus or anyone I know, pushes Mom's wheelchair up to the window and turns the chair so she faces me. Mom points to me, looking surprised, and I hear her say, "That's my daughter."

Her face looks pale and thin, her skull painfully exposed. Someone has brushed her hair back from her forehead, severely, erasing her look. The hair stylist doesn't visit anymore. I wave and gesture madly.

"She can't hear you," says the aide.

"Is she wearing her hearing aids?" I point to my ears, but the aide misunderstands. Is anyone checking her batteries? In the past, I've had to remind them. Without her hearing aids, she's lost. I'll call when I get home.

I show Mom the roses I brought—dark red, Mr. Lincolns, from the bush she gave me twenty years ago. I gesture toward the front door, asking the aide to meet me there. Attached to the roses is a note, telling my mother that I love her, and that Julia is fine. She's two weeks away from her due date.

On the way home, I decide not to call about the hearing aids. Case numbers are rising, spreading from cities to rural areas. Nursing homes are hit hard. The staff have their hands full.

On May 8, Julia gives birth to a healthy, seven-pound boy at Alta Bates in Berkeley, Dareh at her side. Photos come instantly of a swaddled, dark-haired infant with red, scrunched up features, eyes closed, not yet ready to face the fluorescent world. Julia looks wrung out but elated. "I wish I could do it all over again," she says.

"Kian," she says, when we ask his name. "Farsi for *king*."

Richard and I decide not to go to the hospital, since we'd only be able to see them through a glass door.

A week later, we drive to Berkeley, though traveling from one county to another is against the new rules. In their small apartment, filled with flowers and cards, smelling of breast milk and baby, I hold Kian. His features are smoothly sculpted, his own. His eyes search the air, following his father's voice as Dareh moves toward me, coming back to me when I sing. *"Rockabye baby, in the treetop . . ."*

—

On Mom's birthday, the new activities director, Eric, organizes a Facetime call linking her to her children—Peter, Megan, Michael and me. All but Stephen.

She appears on the screen, wearing a red birthday hat, and surrounded by Jean-Pierre, Jesus, and others. Jean-Pierre holds a small cake, lit with pink candles.

"Happy birthday, Elizabeth!"

"Happy birthday, Mom!" She's ninety-six.

"Look at the screen, Elizabeth!" the staffers shout.

She looks back and forth at their faces, confused but happy.

"Look at the screen, Mom!" we call out on our phones. "We're here."

Chapter 43

I get used to talking to Frances on the phone, to coming into the bedroom a few minutes before noon and settling into the green armchair, where my body has left its mark. Our conversations mark time over a summer where my only other distraction is driving to Berkeley with Richard. We sit on a tiny lawn outside Julia and Dareh's apartment building and gaze at Kian. Lying on the hexagon quilt, he gazes and kicks, first on his stomach, then his back, and we croon to him. One week he lifts his head, two weeks later his shoulders, then his whole chest. We clap and laugh. He smiles.

"I was sewing on the patio," I tell Frances today. "I heard a noise—a rushing or whirring—it seemed too loud to be natural. A bird flew right over my head, a red-tailed hawk, I'm sure, and then it wheeled up into the sky. There were two up there, circling."

"Magnificent creatures. This moved you. How?"

"I felt awe. Gratitude. Something very deep. I took it as a sign. That Kian had a protector." I let out a huge sigh.

It's July, the fifth month of the shutdown. At the fairgrounds, people line up in their cars to be tested. Everyone I know has been tested. Brookvale has built a Plexiglass screen on the front porch, where residents sit on one side and visitors on the other. A staffer cleans the Plexiglass between visits. Julia and Dareh clean their grocery bags.

"I saw Mom yesterday," I continue, after telling Frances about the hawk. "I'm allowed to see her on the porch now."

"How did she seem?"

"At first, when Eric pushed her out, she seemed confused. Her face looked gaunter, with those terrible dents at her temples. Or maybe it's just the way they're combing her hair. She was playing with the fringe on her blanket."

"Did she know you?"

"Once she was settled, she looked through the glass, yes. She raised her hand just a little. She tried to say something, but I couldn't hear. I stuck my head around the edge of the screen—Eric was gone—but I still couldn't hear. The traffic noise was too much. I held up a photo of Kian and told her he was her great-grandchild. I don't know if she understood."

I'm quiet for a long moment.

"She may have lost the ability to know what a photo is."

I think about this, all it entails. "I stayed the whole twenty minutes. Without being able to hold her hand . . . it was hard. I showed her the dahlias I'd brought." Again, I'm silent.

"Yes. And again, you're alone. Your siblings have made no plans to visit?"

"No."

I'm comfortable now with silence during these sessions. I use them to cast my mind into other pools and eddies. Interactions with Richard or with a friend, issues in my writing. Dreams. There I catch one.

"I dreamed the other night that my old theater director, Mr. Charlesworth, cast me as Cherie, the sexy lead in *Bus Stop*. He said I should start dressing the part, and that felt like a come-on. He said we'd read some of our own writing at rehearsal, and I rushed away to look for my manuscript. I found pieces of it here and there, but nothing complete. When I came back, everyone was sitting in a circle, waiting for me, ready to read the play. I sat down, but I didn't have the script, and I had to read off someone else's."

"I wonder if the dream is about analysis," Frances says. "You're concerned about performing well for me. You don't have the script."

Her response is predictable, but I take the bait. "Yes! I wish there were achievement markers. Ways to measure how far I've come. Like my reading program in sixth grade, where we advanced by color—from brown to purple. I ripped through the colors."

"I bet you did."

"I want *you* to tell *me* I'm done. Ready to graduate."

Frances says nothing.

Outside the window, the wisteria is a sea of green, with a few purple blossoms here and there. "I'd like to at least be done with the mother stuff."

"What would it take to move on?"

"When I stop feeling the need to tell."

The following week again, I tell Frances about a visit with Mom.

"I guess there were a lot of complaints about the Plexiglass. About visitors not being able to hear, and Eric wanted to try something new. He brought out this little sound system that they use or used to use for Karaoke night—with a microphone. He would hold it for her. 'Would you like to say hello to your daughter, Elizabeth?' When he offered it, she opened her mouth."

"Oh, dear," Frances says.

"She thought they were feeding her! Maybe they are feeding her now."

"It sounds as if she's deteriorating further."

Frances doesn't have to ask. My distress pours out of me. "It was awful to see." I shudder and hug myself tightly. "It was so unlike her! Such a loss of dignity! What would she think if she knew?"

"Perhaps it's fortunate that she doesn't see herself. She doesn't know."

I rub my hand along the arm of my chair. "I'm a little mad that

I'm the only one having to watch her decline."

Frances waits a few seconds before speaking. "You could ask your siblings to come."

"No, they should want to come."

Chapter 44

Eric leads me past the Christmas tree in the lobby, decorated as usual even though residents are confined to their rooms. I follow him to the locked door of the memory care unit, and he buzzes us in. After nine months I'm allowed inside.

"I'm so sorry," he says, his eyes and brow contracted, his voice close to breaking. He's so young and untried that he hasn't learned what the others have—to act as if nothing terrible is moving through these corridors.

"It's all right, Eric. I know you've all done your best. I don't blame you."

He hands me a package containing full PPE—yellow plastic gown, nitrile gloves, face shield, paper booties, and paper shower cap. He coaches me on how to put it on. We're in the middle of a new surge, brought on by the Delta variant. Brookvale reported two cases in November, then more in December. Yesterday, Mom was diagnosed.

Jesus, also swathed in yellow, checks my garb and leads me past the sign on her door warning others not to enter. The blind has been lowered, and the room is in half light. Mom lies face up on her bed under an afghan made by women from her church. Her body makes only the slightest rise under the covers. She breathes slowly and lightly, but without strain. I'm not allowed to touch her.

"She doesn't seem to be in any pain, does she?" I ask Jesus. It is so hard to talk through the shield.

He shakes his head. "None at all," he says. He tells me he's sorry.

"It's okay, Jesus." I stop myself from saying more, from admitting that I'm glad the Delta variant found Mom, that she might have been waiting for it. Might have offered herself. I haven't seen her since the cold weather began and visits through Plexiglass were stopped.

"Has she woken?" I ask Jesus.

"Not since yesterday."

"The hospice nurse will be here soon," he says and leaves. I glance around, to see if anything needs tidying. Her lamp and tapestried footstool have been pushed out of place, and I straighten them. I refold the ruby lap blanket that Megan knitted and lay it again over the back of her armchair. Such a pretty chair, covered in a floral chintz—white, red, and blue. A lady's chair. The lampshade is crooked, and I straighten it. The bookshelf has been dusted, and the wastebasket emptied. Her possessions look forlorn. Provisional. They won't matter soon.

At 11:20, Barbara, the hospice nurse, bustles into the room, her garb swishing. "I'm sorry to be late. I had two other assessments this morning." She puts her backpack down and steps close to the foot of the bed. "Oh, my. She's very declined. More than I expected."

I try to absorb this new word—*declined*. Barbara takes Mom's temperature by mouth. She lifts her arm and puts a blood pressure cuff around it. "Even this doesn't wake her," she says. She pulls the covers off and gently slides one hand under Mom's shoulder and the other under her hip. With care, she turns her so she's on her stomach. Mom stirs and opens her eyes briefly. "I thought that would do it," the nurse says.

"Hello, Elizabeth. I'm your nurse, Barbara." Then to me, "They're taking good care of her here. No bed sores."

I move to the side of the bed where Mom can see me. "Hello, Mom, I'm here!" Then to Barbara, "I'm worried she won't recognize me with this shield."

"She'll know you. By your voice. The hearing is the last sense to go." Gently, she turns Mom onto her back, and she goes back to sleep.

"It can't be long," I tell Richard when I get home. "She was so weak before. The virus came along, and all it took was one little touch, light as a feather. Down she went. She didn't fight it."

"They'll put her on morphine."

"The nurse told me she ordered it."

I call my siblings, and we say versions of the same thing. "As long as she doesn't suffer."

"She isn't herself anymore."

"Her time has come."

"How long?" my sister asks.

"I don't know. She's very low. It shouldn't be long."

My brothers live in Colorado, my sister in San Diego. The country is in lockdown, all travel discouraged. Michael asks me to play a recording of a piano piece he composed for Mom.

———

Her dying is long. I bring my laptop and play Michael's recording. I play Handel's *Messiah*. I read Psalms from the Bible. A.E. Housman's *Loveliest of Trees*. On the third day, two aides hover next to Mom's bed, feeding her. "She woke up!" one says. "She's taken a little soup."

Oh, no! I think. This isn't what we want.

"I'll see you tomorrow," I tell Mom before leaving, and she smiles at me.

The next day, her eyes are closed again, and she's taken no more food. Jesus comes in every hour to check her pulse. "Thirty-two," he tells me. Her blood pressure is low, too. Before he leaves, he inserts into her mouth a tiny vial. "This keeps her peaceful," he says. He wears no gloves. "She isn't contagious anymore," he says.

I take mine off and stroke her hand.

———

"I talk to her about her children and her grandchildren," I tell Frances. "I name each one of them and tell her they love her."

"Good. Have you told her you forgive her?" Frances asks lightly, even slyly.

"No."

"Why not? What have you got to lose?" Again, the casual tone. Breezy. The question might have been about anything—giving someone a call, inviting her to lunch.

This is a change. "I guess I could. I guess it wouldn't cost me much."

The next day, I bend close to Mom's head, which rests on the pillowcase covered in blue flowers, the same one she took to Omaha. I take her right hand in both of mine. "Remember our troubles, Mom?" Her eyelids flutter. "There were things I held against you. I was angry." Her lips twitch, as if she's trying to smile, and her head moves an inch toward me. "I forgive you."

She squeezes my hand.

The next day I find the door to her room open and a gray-haired woman, a resident, in her armchair. The woman stares at me without speaking. I rush into the hall to find Jesus. "There's another patient in there!"

He hurries back to the room. "Dorothy, come on now. It's almost lunch time." He takes her by the arm and leads her out. What drew her to Mom's room? She knows something important is going on in here. She sees the aides going in and out.

On Christmas, I read Mom the story from Luke. Again, I talk about her children, grandchildren, and now great-grandchild. Two days later, my store of readings and music exhausted, I recite the opening lines of the twenty-third Psalm. "He restoreth my soul," I say and then stumble, unable to remember what comes next.

Her lips keep moving. "He leadeth me in the paths of righteousness..."

On the tenth day, Jesus finds me next to the bed, crying. "Don't you have any other family who could come?"

I feel worse now. To save face, I defend my siblings. "Yes, but they can't travel." Is this true? Megan could drive from San Diego, though it's a punishing distance.

Richard comes with me the next day and suits up. He talks to Mom, calling her by name, offering to her ears that beautiful male voice that she loved so.

"This is so hard!" I tell Frances later that day. "I don't know if I can do it anymore."

"Tell your siblings! Tell them how you feel!"

I write them an email. *"This is the hardest thing I've ever had to do..."* They respond, telling me how sorry they are they can't be with me. It's my sister I most want with me. I decide her husband is telling her not to come. I don't want to be angry at her.

On the eleventh day, Mom's feet are cold and blue. "It can't be long now," Jesus says. That night, she goes for two minutes without breathing, the aide tells me. The following day, her feet are warmer.

"Why are you taking so long at this, Mom?" I beg. "I give up! You win!"

In the middle of the night, the phone call comes. "At two I found Elizabeth unresponsive," the aide says. An hour later, the hospice nurse calls, confirming her death. I go back to bed and sleep.

Chapter 45

One by one, faces pop up on my computer screen, my brother Michael from Colorado, wide-eyed, already bursting with talk. "How are you, Kate? Did you play Mom my music?"

Richard and I sit close together at the dining room table, sharing my laptop. The camera angles up toward the pendant lights and wooden ceiling. Michael wears a thick sweater.

Megan, a soothing presence, appears from her kitchen, her husband by her side. Julia follows with Kian in her lap, seven and a half months old, grinning and wriggly in a leaf green onesie.

Megan exclaims and makes faces at him. "You're wearing your great-grandma's favorite color, sweetie!"

Now my nephew, Sam, from Brooklyn, is with us, his hazel eyes crinkling as he smiles. His sister, Lily, from San Francisco. We trade greetings until Peter signs in from Colorado, our *éminence grise*. His wife, Willie, sits beside him.

"I'm so glad to see you," I say, tears welling.

"Thank you for taking such good care of our mother," Michael says. Of the siblings, he's the most earnest.

"I'm just glad Mom's released from her suffering," Peter says. "That was awful."

"Amen!" Michael says. He still looks younger than us; his strong jaw and cheekbones make his face look different from our soft, English one. "Let me show you the altar I made for our mother." He carries his laptop to a shelf holding a photograph of him and Mom hiking in Austria, a rose, and a Navajo basket she gave him.

"I've been thinking about how strongly she believed in me as an artist," he says. "All the way back to high school, when she sent me away to the Cambridge School." She sent him because he wasn't getting along with Lach, her third husband.

"I could say the same," Peter adds. A blue baseball cap covers his sparse hair, the same color as Megan's. Wrinkles make his eyes smaller, but they have the same irreverent gleam as always. He and I recall Mom's trips to Denver for the openings of his art shows.

"If she said some unkind things about me near the end," he says, "I know she couldn't help it."

"She adored you as a boy," I tell him. "You were the man of the family."

Megan turns to the young people. "You should know how much your grandmother loved you when you were babies."

"She *loved* infants," I add. "After each of you was born, she came and stayed for two weeks. She loved rocking you. She insisted we breastfeed. Very big on doing things the natural way. Feed the baby as much as and often as the baby wants."

Lily says how grateful she is that her grandma helped her go to grad school. Megan remembers her love of nature and the outdoors. Richard remembers her traveling alone, at eighty-seven, to meet us in Europe. "At Heathrow she couldn't find the bus to Gatwick, so she asked a bobby for help. He lifted her up! 'There it is, lady!'"

Sam remembers her dancing at his wedding, her last big fling.

Peter speaks up again. "I remember how much fun Mom was when she was young."

Megan and I trade glances, and she murmurs, "Really?"

Lily brings up Mom's ninetieth birthday party, at Megan's house in San Diego.

"We were all sitting around the table," I say. "Do you remember? After the cake we asked her which decade of her life was the happiest.

She said—"

Megan breaks in. "'The time in Santa Maria when you kids were in high school!'"

"We smiled and nodded but we couldn't believe it," I say.

"Early dementia," Megan says.

"Blissful forgetfulness!" says Peter.

"Actually, it's not supposed to go that way," Michael puts in. "Her long-term memory would have been less affected than her short-term." He's serious, knowing we're thinking of his father. He knows the truth about Ray. After struggling for a long time, he's come to terms with it.

"Mom's body is at the local mortuary," I tell them. "Thistlewaite and Weggins. She'll be cremated, but not until a death certificate is issued. They said it will take some time. The coroner's office is swamped."

"Should we send the obit to the *Santa Maria Times*?" Megan asks.

"Absolutely," Peter says. "She was famous there."

Kian has been careening back and forth in Julia's lap, and she hands him to Dareh. "Once, I was riding in the car with Grandma. I think we were going to the library, and we passed that mortuary—the one you just mentioned—and Grandma said, 'What a Dickensian name!'"

We exclaim and laugh. For a minute, she's with us.

"Maybe it's not a coincidence!" Willie says.

"I gave the director her red plaid skirt and jacket, the outfit she always wore at Christmas. To be buried in," I say.

"You mean cremated," Megan says.

"Right. I keep forgetting."

We talk for an hour—lovingly, happily. As soon as the shutdown is over, we decide, we'll have a service at her church in Berkeley. We say goodbye.

Richard and I start dinner, cutting carrots, washing lettuce, putting the skillet on the stove. "That was really nice," he says. "I couldn't help comparing my family to yours. My brothers would never have been able to have a conversation like that. But they would have come."

"I thought she wanted to be buried in Omaha, but that's not what her will says," I tell Frances a few days later. "It says Mountain View Cemetery, in Oakland, next to her husband, Karl. They bought a double plot there, years ago."

"You sound disappointed."

"I am! I never liked him. He was so controlling of her. And a double plot without her own headstone?"

"Why do you wish it were Omaha?" Frances asks.

Why? Is it sentiment, my wish for her to lie next to her parents instead of her fourth husband? "When I was with her in Omaha, we visited the cemetery where her parents were buried. It had a singing tower. On Sundays when Mom was young, she and her parents would go there to listen to the music."

I take a sip of coffee, remembering the Gothic tower on a hill, my grandparents' gravesites below under an oak tree. "We went on the last day of our visit, the day after our big confrontation. I got the feeling I wanted to go more than she did. She was quiet and listless. I was the one to suggest we stop and buy flowers." The flowers were nothing special—daisies or mums from a nearby supermarket.

"She might have been tired," Frances says. "Emotionally spent."

Zorro scratches at the bedroom door and I get up to let him in.

"Looking at that trip now," Frances says, "what strikes me is that you went with her in the first place. You made the trip."

I stroke Zorro's head. This is one of those times I don't see where Frances is headed. "It wasn't so unusual. Megan and I took her to Sequoia, too, a few years later."

"Omaha was different. You went *alone* with her, into the lion's den."

"She was strong then. She was still bossing me around."

"Tell me what you remember of the trip now."

I take a deep breath. Images pass through my mind, some of

them from photos—Mom at sunset next to the river. In front of her elementary school. Ignoring the young woman next to us at the café.

"I'll say it again. She was strong, ambitious, purposeful. She walked all over, climbed up and down stairs. She was marshaling all these facts and dates in her head! Once when I invited her to my lit class as a guest, she spoke for thirty minutes without notes. I think she was in her seventies then."

Frances murmurs a vague assent, only mildly impressed.

"In the photos from Omaha, she looks pretty. At eighty-five, still pretty. That was at the beginning of the trip, before we argued."

"You're telling me about her but not about you."

I smooth the linen cover of my armrest. *Lettuce green? Pistachio green?* My mind drifts to the greens in the Crayola box I had as a child. *Fern green, middle green, forest green.* How long before I can give Kian his first Crayola box? "Remember the pie chart I told you about?"

Early in our sessions, as I agonized over whether I loved my mother or not, I drew a pie chart. On one half were the dark sectors. Brown, gray, black. Anger, bitterness, disappointment, judgment. On the other half, the light ones—red, orange, yellow. The things I liked about Mom and felt grateful for. Our love of words and music. Nature. Vegetables.

"Of course I remember," Frances says.

"I felt a kinship in our bodies, too. Our skin, our hair, our movements. Some of the time, in Omaha, we were, I don't know what the word is, in synch."

"Even though there was conflict?"

"The conflict has to be there, I know that now. The old feelings won't disappear."

"Acknowledging them makes it easier to see the good. What else do you remember?"

I remember breakfast in the atrium of the Marriott on our last day. I remember Fort Omaha, the elms and the stately houses. "By the last morning, there was a good feeling between us. When I left her at the historical library, she waved goodbye, a loose-wristed, floppy wave, which was how she always waved. It reminded me of the time I met her at the train station in Boston."

"When she didn't put her suitcase down to hug you," Frances says.

"Right."

"You recorded the incident in your book of resentments."

"My little black book." I feel calm talking about this now, no bitter knot in my chest, no feeling of need. "It was July, hot and muggy. Maybe she was hot, or tired. Maybe Mikey had been a handful on the train."

"At the time, you expected her to hug you. To show the same love for you that you felt for her."

"Yes." I shift my hips in my narrow seat. I realize I've been gripping the phone tightly.

After a long pause, Frances speaks again, slowly. "In other words, *she* should have felt the same as *you*. It's like the other incident you told me about, when you ran to the post office hoping for a Christmas present."

"Yes." I remember the icy sidewalk, the early dark.

"Again, you expected her to feel and act the same as you."

I let her words settle in my mind, like snow falling lightly onto the tiny chimneys and sloping roofs inside the paperweight.

"Do you see what I mean?" she asks.

I take a deep breath. The snow stops falling. The scene is still. "You mean, she and I are not the same. She's different from me."

"Exactly. Separate. Different." She lets a few seconds go by. "Something else you're missing. In both memories."

I rest my head against the back of the chair and look up, past the curtain rod where one drapery ring has let go of the pleat, up to the planks that rise to the roofbeam. I'm like a dog sniffing. Searching. "What? I'm drawing a blank."

"In the two scenes, you only see your mother and what she failed to do. You're missing yourself. What were you doing?"

"I was running. Toward her or the package."

"Exactly. You ran toward her. You opened your arms to *her*."

The back of my throat tightens.

"Even then," she continues, "at age twenty-two, you were capable of loving. You still are. Look at you now, visiting her on the porch, trying so hard to connect with her through the Plexiglass. I said earlier that what struck me most was that you traveled to Omaha with her. You stayed at the terrible motel. You wanted to reach her. You didn't give up."

Frances's words flow over me, like a blessing. Tears sting the back of my eyes.

"Love isn't a mathematical equation. A zero-sum game. You learn it everywhere. It's like yeast, in the air, ready and waiting for a hospitable environment."

"It's a little more personal than that," I say, wiping my eyes with the hem of my T-shirt. "I mean, *people* taught me."

"Okay."

"My grandma at my bedside raising and lowering my arm, asking if it hurt."

"Yes."

"Miss Jensen hugging me in the supply closet."

She makes the quiet murmur of assent I know so well.

"My brother Peter yelling after I told him about Ray. My sister whispering to me in bed." My voice breaks saying their names. "My father when he cried. Richard. All of Richard."

"And on and on."

Chapter 46

"Have I told you about my retirement?" Frances says brightly, one day in February. I grip the phone, cheek pressed against the screen.

"No!" I gasp. Shock and fear race through me.

"But not for a year."

"Oh." I let out a sigh. My grip on the phone relaxes. "That's probably all right. I should be ready to quit by then. Way before then, in fact."

"We'll see."

Within a few days, Frances appears in a dream. "You and I were having a session," I tell her the following Wednesday, "but not on the phone. We were together, face-to-face, sitting on the floor, tailor style, like modern dance class. First just our hands and then our feet were touching. Then you drew me close and held me. You told me that after you retired you were going to give classes on James Joyce."

I'm in my bedroom, as usual, but Kian is asleep near me in his porta-crib, arms flung out like an archer, head to one side, dark and lustrous. His blue and white onesie is printed with whales. Julia and Dareh are hiking in the hills, looking for the first wildflowers.

I go on telling Frances the dream. "You named some of the people who would be in the classes. Well-known artists and intellectuals. 'Are these your clients?' I asked. I wanted to be in the class! We talked about saying goodbye and about me changing. 'You're being born,' you said. It seemed that you didn't want to leave me as I was being born."

I let a moment go by. "That's it."

"Beautiful," Frances says. I hear water running. Is she rinsing a dish?

"The being born part is because of Kian, I suppose."

The water sound stops. "Your dream makes me think of the dance you performed in your acting class. About the tree."

My mind travels back, through the years of our sessions and the decades of my life. My acting teacher was Miss Moore who wore suits, one royal blue suit with brass buttons. Our class met in a creaky, old auditorium. The morning light came in through high windows, shafting across the worn, wooden floor. Miss Moore asked us to act out a symbol. I practiced in my room, concentrating hard on sensory impressions, the spongey soil, the hairy, red brown color of the bark, the immense height of the sequoia tree.

"I wouldn't call it a dance," I say.

"When you told me," Frances says, "you got up out of your chair. You showed me the tree being hit by lightning. It was wrenching and beautiful."

I get up out of my chair now and go to Kian's port-a-crib. He's still asleep. Lightly, I stroke his back.

"Your teacher quoted from a poet," Frances says. "Rumi, I think."

I keep stroking Kian's little turtle-like back. "She said, 'The wound is the place where the light enters.'"

Acknowledgments

MY DEEP THANKS and appreciation to my coach, Angela Pneuman, who shepherded this book from its tentative beginnings six years ago to the novel it is today. She was always able to see what the work could grow into. Over the last eighteen months, Christine Henneberg has been a most perceptive and supportive reader. Thanks, Chrissy. Michelle Huneven offered encouragement and important late suggestions. My pandemic-era writers' group—Rachelle Newman, Kirsten Michelwait, and Susan Carr—greatly assisted with mid-stage drafts. During the long years of composition, Marilynne Kanter offered continuous support and helpful prodding.

Thanks to my editor, Greg Fields, at Koehler Books, for encouragement and for understanding the book so well.

Deepest thanks and love, finally, to my family for their patience, support, and help. My sister, Katherine, read and encouraged. My son, Sam, served as ace copy editor, website designer, and technical right-hand. My son, Andy, provided a beautiful cover photograph. My husband, Greg, read and commented on every single draft I asked him to look at—too many to count.

www.ingramcontent.com/pod-product-compliance
Lightning Source LLC
LaVergne TN
LVHW041905070526
838199LV00051BA/2508